THE TROUBLE WITH PATIENCE

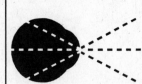

VIRTUES AND VICES OF THE OLD WEST,
BOOK 1

THE TROUBLE
WITH PATIENCE

MAGGIE BRENDAN

THORNDIKE PRESS
A part of Gale, Cengage Learning

GALE
CENGAGE Learning·

Farmington Hills, Mich • San Francisco • New York • Waterville, Maine
Meriden, Conn • Mason, Ohio • Chicago

GALE
CENGAGE Learning®

LIBRARY OF CONGRESS CATALOGING-IN-PUBLICATION DATA

Brendan, Maggie, 1949–
    The trouble with patience / by Maggie Brendan. — Large print edition.
        pages cm. — (Virtues and vices of the old west ; book 1) (Thorndike Press large print Christian historical fiction)
        ISBN 978-1-4104-7883-2 (hardcover) — ISBN 1-4104-7883-1 (hardcover)
        1. Frontier and pioneer life—Montana—Fiction. 2. Montana—Social life and customs—19th century—Fiction. 3. Large type books. I. Title.
PS3602.R4485T76 2015b
813'.6—dc23   2015004938

Published in 2015 by arrangement with Revell Books, a division of Baker Publishing Group

For my dear sisters,
Doris and *Dianne*

It has been my experience that folks that have no vices have very few virtues.

ABRAHAM LINCOLN

A gentle answer turns away wrath,
but a harsh word stirs up anger.

Proverbs 15:1 NIV

1

Nevada City, Montana Territory
Spring 1866

Trying to beat the rain, Patience Cavanaugh hurried up the single main street of raw Nevada City. But large droplets began to pelt her way ahead, leaving that distinctive smell when spring rain mingles with the thick dust of a dirt road. She wasn't sure why it mattered to her if she were wet or not. It wasn't likely anyone would be taking any second glances. She knew all too well her figure was a bit fuller than her younger and more slender counterparts in this frontier town.

She sighed and hurried on, clutching the basket of fruits and vegetables from the market. But her real worry was how she would survive here without a single tenant yet in her boardinghouse. Run-down though it might be, it was the only place of its kind in a small town busy with newcomers coming and going. Many of those were miners hoping for a gold strike at Alder Gulch, and when they did — strike gold, that is — everyone knew before you could holler "jackrabbit." A few folks stopped in for lunch now and then since she'd hung the new sign over the boardwalk — CREEKSIDE INN. She'd kept its original name in her beloved grandmother's memory. Wouldn't Granny be sad to see her once-beautiful boardinghouse fallen into neglect since her death? But Patience didn't have the where-withal to make the needed repairs, and most of the miners didn't have the wherewithal to pay her for room and board, even if they were so inclined.

Poor Granny . . . But poor me. What have I gotten myself into? Moving to a town where she didn't know a soul, only to realize how long it would take to return the boarding-house to a thriving business. One glance at the dilapidated clapboard building provided all the evidence she needed.

Reaching the front door just as the bottom fell out of the dark cloud above her, Patience hurried to the kitchen with her purchases, looped her cape within easy reach on a nail by the back door, and decided a good cup of coffee and a fire would take the chill away, maybe lift her

10

spirits a bit. Then another long afternoon . . . waiting, hoping, and praying.

Jedediah pushed the desk drawer shut and
stared out the window to the other side of
the street. Some movement had caught his
eye, and he stood up, his hand automatically going to his gun holster as he moved
closer to the window. Outside, a man, reins
for his horse in hand, cast furtive glances
around at his surroundings. He sidled up to
a chestnut horse tethered in front of a store
and quickly released the cinch underneath
the horse's belly, yanking the saddle right
off the horse's back. Just as the man slung
it onto his own horse, Jedediah snatched his
hat from its nail and ran out the door of his
office.

"Hey, you! Hold it right there!" Jedediah's
shout brought all street activity to a stop.
He waited, right hand loosely resting on the
holster.

"What? You got a problem, Marshal?
Can't a man saddle up his horse in the
middle of this here town?" The man paused,
his hands on the top of the saddle.

"Not when it's a stolen one," Jedediah
warned, his tone and gun-ready stance carrying more weight than the words. A small
audience was gathering.

He moved forward a few steps across the street, and the man pushed his cowboy hat back, then spit a long string of tobacco juice into the mud in front of Jedediah's boots. "You accusing me of somethin', Marshal?" He looked around at his silent audience with a sneer and reached for the saddle's straps.

"Don't have to." Jedediah narrowed his gaze at the young fellow. "That horse belongs to my friend Monty, and I'd advise you to put his saddle back just like you found it. But either way, you'll be getting acquainted with the jailhouse." He spoke deliberately, took another slow step, and started to pull out his gun. The man looked at the weapon, wavering with apparent indecision.

Two doors down, Jedediah heard the front door of the Creekside Inn slam back on its hinges, and a quick glance showed a young woman starting up the boardwalk toward them. Jedediah already had caught a glimpse of the new proprietor. He hadn't spoken directly with her yet, but he'd heard her name was Patience and that she was attempting to reopen the boardinghouse.

Jedediah held his hand up, palm out, as she drew closer. "Ma'am, stay back till I settle this." By now a few more passersby had stopped to watch the altercation, but he paid no mind to the growing crowd.

"Why, Marshal," the man said, "you act like I'm a hardened criminal!"

The marshal took another step forward. "In the past you'd have been strung up for stealing a saddle in these parts —"

"Marshal, you can't mean that!" Jedediah heard a female voice call out toward his right. He didn't take his eyes off the thief, but he groaned inwardly at the thought of an interfering woman.

Ignoring her, he continued to address the man in front of him. "Lucky for you I abide by the sworn office of the marshal," he said, keeping his voice low.

But she wasn't done yet. "There's no cause to hang a man for stealing."

Jedediah turned his head, his gun steady on his prisoner. "I don't need some woman mucking up the law," he said through clenched teeth, "so go on back to baking your biscuits." What was it about females? Did they always have to have the last word? Actually, this one *was* kind of pretty when her face flushed pink like that. He tipped his hat to her and returned to the task at hand.

"Well, I never!" she shot back. "I will not be talked to that way!"

"Suit yourself, lady," said another voice, male this time, "but Jedediah here is not known for his soft touch. Best you stay out of his way." He watched as his friend Monty strolled up.

The thief dropped his hands from the saddle, fingering the holster at his hip.

"I wouldn't even consider that if I was you," Monty drawled. "The marshal's right. That's my horse and saddle."

Jedediah looked between his friend and the saddle snatcher. "Don't worry, Monty. He'll put it back — won't you?"

In a flash, the thief drew his gun. But Jedediah already had his aimed, and like greased lightning he fired his handgun. The force knocked the weapon from the thief, who immediately howled, grabbing his hand in pain. Jedediah had heard the woman's scream from behind him and shook his head. "He'll live, lady," he said over his shoulder and turned back in disgust.

"I warned you, you no-account scoundrel," he went on. "Now, put that saddle back on Monty's horse and don't try anything foolish again. If you weren't going to jail before, you sure enough are headed there now."

The man glared at him. "Are you crazy? You near took my hand off! Can't you see I won't be able to lift that dumb saddle?" He removed the bandana from his neck and wound it around his hand, dripping with blood.

"Should've thought of that before committing a crime against a law-abiding citizen in our law-abiding town," Jedediah answered, motioning with his gun toward the saddle. "What's your name?"

The man's halfhearted attempts to remove the saddle merely dropped it on the ground. "Shorty," he muttered. He struggled to lift the saddle back onto Monty's horse.

"Now step away," Monty ordered him. "I'll tighten the cinch myself."

Shorty snorted his contempt as Monty picked up the thief's gun and handed it to Jedediah. "A word of warning," Monty added. "Stay away from me and my horse if you know what's good for you. I just might give our marshal here a little help." Monty cinched the straps and swung up into the saddle.

Jedediah poked his gun into Shorty's side, and they both shuffled across the street to the jailhouse.

Patience followed them and shut the door behind her. "And just what can I help you with, Miss . . . ?" the marshal barked over

15

his shoulder, glaring at her. He shoved Shorty into the cell and twisted the key in its lock.

"Cavanaugh. Miss Patience Cavanaugh. Perhaps the question is what I can help *you* with, Marshal Jones." She stood firmly in place, arms crossed above her waist. But she felt far less confident than her stance suggested.

He gave a short laugh. "I've never needed help from any woman and don't intend to start now."

Shorty snickered behind him. "Ya just might now."

"This is none of your concern, Shorty." Jedediah threw him a look of distaste and motioned Patience away from the small cell toward the other side of the room.

As soon as he sat down at his desk, she picked up the conversation again. "Perhaps we can start with your manners — for example, when a man insults a woman in front of half the town, it's customary to apologize!" Patience's hands gripped the sides of her dress to avoid their shaking. She wasn't sure what possessed her to barge into the marshal's office like this, but the man was rude, confirming things she'd heard about him. She had to admit — only to herself, of course — he was handsome in a rugged sort of way. Fairly tall, sturdy build, tanned leathery skin, light brown eyes with flecks of green and a mustache curving down around his lips. From the look of his furrowed brow and dark, bushy eyebrows, he didn't seem too pleased that she had entered his domain.

Shorty's voice intruded once more, his grinning face pressed against the bars. "That's right, ma'am. He sure's a rude —"

"Will you please shut up, Shorty! Or I'll do it for you."

Patience could see the muscles in the marshal's jaw working. He now looked her square in the eye. "Apologize? When you're intruding on the law? Is that the way a lady behaves? Hardly. Now, if you'll excuse me, I've got paperwork to fill out. Don't let the door slam on your backside as you leave." He jerked open the desk drawer and tossed his hat with precision to the hook on the wall, revealing a thick head of brown hair indented around his head from his hatband. He pulled out a sheaf of papers and began sifting through them, grumbling under his breath about "all this paperwork he left for me to do."

"Marshal Jones," she pressed on while a small voice inside wondered if she was going crazy, "I am offended when you tell me to go back to baking biscuits, like I am some empty-headed female. I assure you that I am not!" She'd gotten quite a head of steam up by the time she finished.

Shorty's voice joined in the argument. "Those biscuits you bake are beautiful, ma'am!" She saw him grinning again at her from across the room, but she ignored him.

The marshal leaned back in his chair, steepled his fingers in front of him, and stared at her. He finally shrugged. "That so? Look, I know very little about you except for the fact I can smell your biscuits baking — and they smell mighty good, I might add."

"It doesn't matter what you *know* about me, Marshal, it's how you *spoke* to me." She wasn't about to let him off with a little sweet talk. "It's likely you'll never get the opportunity to know me better. You were rude and demeaning, telling me to be quiet like I was some child." Patience tried to keep her voice steady, but she could feel that her face was warm. "And if you talk like that to other women — well, it's no wonder you haven't found any woman that will have you!" She heard the prisoner snort his delight at the exchange.

"She's right," the thief called. "I always treat a lady with respect, jes like my mama

18

taught me."

"Sure you do." Marshal Jones threw him a disgusted look. "Just like you honor other people's property." He stood and picked up an empty mug from his desk. "If you're finished jawing at me, I'm going to get myself a cup of coffee . . . unless you care to stay and get to know me better," he said, eyeing her with a sarcastic grin.

"And you, Marshal, are sorely lacking in any social graces. I don't know why I expected an apology from you." She took a deep breath and clasped her hands together. "But since you offered, I'll take that cup of coffee." She was very surprised at herself since she wasn't normally comfortable talking to men.

She took a seat in the chair in front of the desk, adjusted her skirts, and waited. He had an uncomfortable look on his face, momentarily staring at her with his mouth open as though to speak. Instead he took his mug over to the potbellied stove, poured it full from the coffeepot, and returned to plunk it down on the desk. He went back, grabbed another mug from the shelf above, slopped coffee into it, and stalked over to her with it. She nodded her thanks as she accepted it. He went around his desk and sat down.

How dare he look me over as if — as if I were stock to be evaluated for purchase! If she never had to set eyes on him again, it'd be too soon.

"Marshal," she began once more, "you are not aware of this, but I'm writing a collection of devotionals to help people. I have always faithfully read the Scripture and take its heeding to heart, and . . . and, well, I want to extend grace wherever it is needed." She stopped for a deep breath. "In fact, the one I wrote just this morning deals with regret, and remembering how the soldier felt after gambling for Jesus's robe, how he was looking for grace. Perhaps you have a few regrets . . ."

His eyes glazed over and she wasn't even sure he was listening. He drank coffee, shuffled papers, finally stood and went over to the stove, refilled his mug, and returned to the desk. "Well, *Miss Patience Cavanaugh,* I don't know about grace, but there's one virtue you clearly forget to extol — humility." As he set his down, the two mugs banged together, nearly spilling the coffee into her lap.

Shocked, she sat up straight, squaring her shoulders. She took a sip, and it made her cough and sputter. She put the cup down on the desk and pushed it away, then cov-

20

ered her mouth with her handkerchief to keep from choking. The coffee was the worst-tasting brew she'd ever drunk. *Who knows how long that's been sitting on the stove?* she thought with a grimace.

"I take it you don't want a coffee refill," he said with a grin. She shook her head and glared at him above her handkerchief.

Far worse than the coffee was the attitude of this man. She was not going to sit here and listen to his belittling comments.

She pushed her chair back, rose, and moved slowly toward the front door with her head held high.

Shorty's voice followed her. "You seem mighty humble to me, lady."

Patience went straight to her kitchen and began peeling and chopping potatoes and carrots with far more vigor than necessary. She was angry at that cocky marshal and his even cockier prisoner. They had no right to mock her, when all she was trying to do was . . . what? She truly did want to help people — that's why she was attempting to make this broken-down old boardinghouse into something thriving once more, why she put her best into cooking lunches for the town's residents, why she was diligently doing her devotional writing . . . Wasn't it?

Her granny had told her once that people should take the specks out of their own eyes before accusing others of faults. Patience put down her chopping knife with a sigh. Today she'd probably wound up only embarrassing herself, alienating the marshal, and providing some humor for that poor Shorty.

She picked up the knife with another sigh to finish the stew for lunch. She'd totally forgotten she'd been planning to go to the post office when she'd heard the confrontation. *But,* she reminded herself, *I only just opened the boardinghouse a short time ago.* Perhaps when word got out about it being available again, newcomers would inquire for a room. She prayed it would be so. *And, Lord, I do want to show grace and humility. Teach me, please.*

Jedediah propped his feet up on his desk, leaned back in the worn leather chair he'd inherited from his predecessor, and took another swallow of the thick black liquid the lady had ungraciously complained about. Well, she hadn't actually said anything, but she didn't have to, what with all her choking and sputtering. He couldn't help but grin as he put his mug down and looked over at his prisoner, finally quiet and asleep on the cell's cot. He'd hold Shorty till the end of the week when the circuit judge made his rounds and pronounced a sentence.

Jedediah shook his head with another grin. What a lame-brained thing to do in broad daylight — in the middle of town, no less — and right across from the marshal's office. But he knew folks like Shorty liked taking risks. In fact, he probably thrived on it. What amused him most was this Miss Patience trying to interfere. Maybe she was simply being impulsive, but somehow she didn't strike him as being that kind of woman. And he sure would like to know how she came to take him up on the offer of coffee. But he was one up on her since she'd nearly choked on it. He took another sip and grinned once more.

Actually, she had really pretty green eyes, though her expression had been accusing and dour looking. When she'd walked out, he couldn't help but notice, in spite of her simple calico dress and apron, her clothing did not hide her feminine curves.

He sighed. No need to even give her a second thought. She spelled trouble, and he wasn't looking for any. He was new in town, new on the job, and didn't need anything she had to offer. But he couldn't deny he had been hankering after one of those fresh, hot biscuits Monty bragged about. His own cooking left something to be desired, so he ate most of his meals at the Longhorn Café. Maybe he'd give Creekside Inn a try . . . maybe get her ire up again. Another grin.

But then he closed his eyes, and another face, this one smiling, floated behind his eyelids. Emily worked at the Longhorn. Now there's a woman he'd like to get to know better, but that would mean eventually opening up about some things he didn't care to reveal. He sighed and turned back to the stack of papers he'd probably never get through at this rate.

2

Not even a slight breeze had moved through the trees until a clap of thunder broke the heavy, eerie atmosphere. Jedediah remained motionless on his horse in the clearing, his shirt soaked with perspiration and stuck to his back. Two other men on horseback flanked him, staring up into the huge elm tree. He felt the bile creep up into his throat as he watched a man hanging above them in the hot air. The victim had been caught stealing cattle, and by law Jedediah and his vigilantes had every right to string him up. One of the men, Cash, chewed on his cigar, then turned to Jedediah with an unspoken question. On the other side, Ned moved uncomfortably in his saddle. Jedediah finally snapped open his pocket watch and nodded to Ned. "Cut him down and haul the body over to the two docs in town — they use 'em in their anatomy lessons."

Ned walked his horse forward, standing up in the stirrups to reach the rope, just as another bolt of lightning split the clouds and struck the elm tree with a loud crack, once more breaking the stillness of the hot summer —

The clatter of Shorty's metal water cup against the cell bars jerked Jedediah from his nap. "Cut that out!" he barked as his feet slammed down from the desk to the floor. *Blasted fool.* The dream had taken him by surprise, and reliving it brought up the scene he'd just as soon repress. While it was legal to string up a horse or cattle thief, those memories haunted him still. With each incident, he had tried to justify it to himself. Sometimes it worked, sometimes not.

"I wuz jes wantin' some cold water," Shorty whined. "When's dinner in this fancy hole-in-the-wall you put me up in? Hope it's fried chicken." He gave a snort that said far more than his words.

Irritated, Jedediah walked over to the cell, grabbed Shorty's cup, and filled it from a pitcher behind his desk. "Supper is when I say and what I say it is." He shoved the cup back to his prisoner through the bars.

Shorty gulped the water down. "How long you gonna keep me in here?" he grumbled, wiping an arm across his mouth.

"Until the circuit judge shows up. If you're lucky — and I am too — it could be Friday."

"Guess I'll have to make do watching you and that nice lady argue."

Jedediah did his own version of a snort. "Don't plan on that happening again."

Shorty grinned, exposing an unhealthy row of teeth. "Don't bet on it. A lady like her ain't givin' up, I wager. Could make ya a good partner. Sorta smooth the edges off."

Jedediah shook his head and growled, "And just how would you know the first thing about me and what I need?" He turned away before Shorty could reply and stalked out the front door.

By midweek, Patience was delighted to have two boarders. A man and his wife from back east were planning on moving to Montana. They were stopping here in Nevada City while they determined just where they would settle, Mrs. Burton explained.

Patience was so excited to have paying customers that she took extra care to make the room as appealing as possible. She even found some pretty grasses to display in a jar on the dresser. When the two came down for supper, they raved over her fried chicken and blueberry cobbler.

"How did you learn to make such a wonderful meal, Miss Cavanaugh?" Mr. Burton asked. He touched his moustache with his napkin and leaned back in his chair with a satisfied expression.

"Yes, I'd like to be able to cook like this," Mrs. Burton nodded, her diamond earrings catching the light from candles.

Patience felt her face flush, and she murmured, "Thank you. I had a lot of practice growing up. My mother had a weak heart but was very particular about everything, so I had to learn to do it right at an early age."

Mrs. Burton set her fork down. "That must've been very hard on you as a young girl. Do you have any siblings?"

"No, though I would have liked one. The doctor told my mother she should never have had me in the first place. After I was born, she never fully recovered."

"Very sorry to hear that, but we are the recipients of your culinary talents, thanks to your mother." Mr. Burton smiled his approval.

Patience took a deep breath to get her nerve up. "I hope you don't mind if I tell you I'd appreciate it if you could spread the word about my establishment when you can."

"We'd be happy to. Our room is nice and clean, and the whole place looks homey. That's more than I can say for some of the places we've stayed along the way."

"I still have painting that needs to be done and some repairs, but it will take time for me to get this place back to the way it was before my grandmother died."

"I'm sure with your natural instinct for perfection, Miss Cavanaugh, you'll get it done." Mr. Burton beamed and nodded at her. "Thank you for a delicious meal. Now, Liza, how about we take a nice evening stroll and check out the sights?"

Jedediah took his time with his dinner at the café, a surreptitious eye on the cheerful Emily. He was fully aware he had a prisoner to feed sooner or later, but the scoundrel could wait. Emily's flashing brown eyes seemed friendly enough, but he soon realized she wasn't flirting. It was just who she was — nice and friendly to all the Longhorn customers. He wasn't savvy on the ways to court a woman. In truth, it had never mattered that much to him before. But now that he was getting, as Monty would say, "a little long in the tooth," he needed to keep his eyes open for possibilities. He was in a new town with new options, so just maybe . . . *Oh, forget it.*

He watched as she lifted a tray of used dishes, then paused by his table.

"Is there anything else I can get for you,

29

Mr. Jones?" she asked, balancing the tray against her hip.

"Oh, I've had plenty, but maybe you could wrap up a couple pieces of chicken for my prisoner?"

"I can do that." One eyebrow cocked upward. "It'll be a few minutes, though."

"Take your time. There's no rush. That's what he gets for trying to steal a saddle in broad daylight."

"Yes, then I'll refill your coffee cup while you wait." She moved to the kitchen with the tray, shoulders stiff and back straight.

He found himself wanting to offer to carry the tray for her. Foolish notion, to be sure. Emily was used to the work, obvious by the way she carried herself with nary a complaint. She'd make a good wife — strong, industrious, and enduring. Not that it mattered to him. She was too young, and he wasn't looking . . . or was he?

The front door of the restaurant banged open against the wall, shaking the upper glass so hard Jedediah wondered that it didn't shatter.

"Marshal," a man yelled, "you're needed down at Criterion Saloon." Everyone in the café looked either at Jedediah or the shouting man. "Some dandy and a miner with a bag o' gold got to arguin' over a game of cards. Ya better hurry!" He held the door ajar and waved his arm in the direction of the saloon.

Jedediah saw that the man was his friend Joe and took a deep breath. "Right — I'll follow you." He shoved back his chair, glad that he'd at least finished his meal before the fracas started. "I'll be back for that chicken, Emily," he called over to her. He tossed some bills on the table as he quickly donned his hat. An evening brawl was a common event in Nevada City. Normally, he could keep the peace, especially if it was between miners, but when it came to professional gamblers, it didn't always end so well.

"All right, Jed," Emily said with another smile, tucking away the bills he'd left as she began clearing his table.

Jedediah followed Joe down the boardwalk. A miner that'd never had a big gold strike, Joe seemed to not let that get him down. He was a familiar face about town, with his shaggy beard and graying hair tucked underneath a floppy leather hat, guiding his donkey piled high with pickaxes and miners' supplies down Wallace Street, the main road through town. Any gold he did find at Alder Gulch was quickly squandered away on alcohol and women. Despite all Joe's laziness, he was decent enough, and

Jedediah couldn't help but like the old fella. Occasionally they would sit on the porch outside the jail, chewing the fat as they watched the folks of Nevada City coming and going.

Before they reached the Criterion, the swinging doors flew open and two men stumbled out, yelling at one another. It sounded like the miner was accusing the gambler dandy of cheating him.

"You liar! You know you did somethin' to that deck of cards 'fore you dealt the hand!" The miner held his fists up, but Jedediah knew the man was no match for the gambler and his slick ways. "I ain't no dummy," the miner added. He shot a wad of tobacco into the dirt, then wiped his mouth on his sleeve. Jedediah almost smiled at the futile attempt to look tough.

The gambler removed his jacket, threw it across a hitching post, rolled up his shirt-sleeves, and reached up to smooth his mustache. "You'd have to prove it, little man, and I don't hear any eyewitness verifying your story."

The red-faced miner swayed a bit on his feet — no doubt from a few rounds of liquor.

Jedediah strode up to the two men. He knew most gamblers carried a small derringer, and he figured the gambler would use it rather than lose the gold he'd just won. "Let's settle this peacefully, or I'll haul you both to jail. I've got plenty of room." Joe and others from the saloon stood about, watching the proceedings.

"Step aside, Marshal. I'm not lettin' this scoundrel get away with cheatin' me outta my gold!" The miner staggered toward his assailant.

The gambler smirked. "You shouldn't play cards with a professional then."

The miner fumbled in his pocket, and the gambler withdrew his derringer, firing once. As the miner crumpled to his knees and fell over, Jedediah drew his gun, shooting the gambler in the chest. The dandy fell on his face onto the dusty street, a pool of blood below his chest.

Gasps came from the crowd, and a voice muttered, "Somebody shoulda warned 'im about Marshal Jones."

"He's dead, all right," another man said, bending over the gambler.

Jedediah stuck his gun into the holster and walked over to examine the miner. Joe quickly joined him and helped roll the first dead man onto his back. There were more gasps as they saw what the miner had been reaching into his pocket for. "Well, I'll be

doggone! He didn't even have a gun, Jed."
Joe was holding up a chain with a gold cross.

Jedediah bent over and lifted an eyelid of
the dead miner as the crowd pressed closer.
"This didn't have ta happen," Joe murmured. "Wonder what he'd planned on
doin' with it?"

"Praying, most likely. Joe, see if you can
find any papers on him. We'll need to notify
his next of kin." Then turning to the crowd,
Jedediah said, "Someone go after the under-
taker. Tell him we have two dead."

He stood, hands on his hips, staring down
at the miner, feeling sorry for him, hoping
he didn't have a wife and kids. Jed didn't
usually feel this concerned about a gunfight.
Maybe he was getting soft. Time was when
settling a fight or overseeing a hanging
didn't bother him like this.

Later, after seeing the men's bodies taken
to the morgue, he remembered Shorty's
supper. It'd be cold now — like the two men
who'd just lost their lives. He didn't want to
dwell on it. He'd had no choice but to shoot
the gambler when he'd shot the miner. And
he wasn't feeling sorry about that since the
miner wasn't even carrying a gun. Just a
cross — a small gold cross. It brought to
mind the wooden cross in the little clapboard church back in Mount Joy, Pennsylva-

nia, when he'd first heard the gospel preached, first took it as his own. A lot of water under the bridge since that time. Plenty of drifting through Kansas, Texas, and Colorado before coming here. He wiped his brow and breathed a brief prayer for the miner's soul and his family. But there was weariness deep inside as he carried Shorty's supper to the cell.

He stood and watched his prisoner devour the chicken. "Keep your nose clean, you hear?" he said. "Don't want to see another body carried off to the cemetery anytime soon."

In the evening after each pan was cleaned, dishes washed, rinsed, and put away, Patience would retire to the parlor and sit in front of the carved cherry desk. Her grandmother's Bible was precious to her, and Patience kept a diary — just a simple notebook — to write down her thoughts as she read each evening. She reflected on how much she had grown in character, what she was learning from her reading, and how God was blessing her.

She finished reading the first chapter of Philippians and had just begun the next one when she came to words that seemed to leap off the page: "In lowliness of mind let each esteem other better than themselves." Patience put the book down on the desk and stared into the cold fireplace. She finally let herself wonder about the way she'd acted when she marched in high dudgeon into the middle of the marshal's arrest the other day. Was this what he'd meant?

She closed her eyes and the Bible with a sigh. Did she think she was better than he? Was what he had said about humility more or less true about her? About her lack of it? It was a bitter pill to swallow. That was not how she wanted others to see her — lacking in humility, boastful. But maybe even that thought was prideful — more worried about what people thought of her than God's view of her.

Well, anyway, she'd have to give this some more thought, prayer. And it was right to apologize somehow, even though she'd declared he'd never get the chance to know her better. By the time she'd tossed and turned more than half the night, she had an idea.

3

Patience smoothed the crisp, clean sheets across the bed and tucked them in, breathing in their fresh smell of the spring outdoors. Her new boarder, who called herself Emily, was a pretty young girl who worked at the café just down the street. "I've been living in the back of the café," she had explained, "but I sure would like someplace nicer . . . like here." The girl smiled, and Patience liked her immediately. It turned out that it would cost Emily only a little bit more than her current room.

Patience was tired and very tempted to crawl between the sheets herself after tidying everything up. She stood with her hands on her hips, surveying the spacious bedroom. It had taken her most of the morning to lug up a bucket of suds to wipe down the window and mop the floor. Now sunshine sparkled through that window, highlighting the fluffy pillows and rose-colored quilt adorning the bed. After numerous trips up the stairs today, her legs and back were sore. But she hummed to herself, trying to forget how weary she was.

She was truly happy to finally have a few more boarders. Not everyone ate in her dining room all the time. But she always provided a hot breakfast in the morning and a good meal at supper. She had changed her schedule so that instead of giving them lunch, her boarders were on their own — which freed her up to do her chores and find a little time to herself. Guests who had previously come for lunch now often joined her boarders for the evening meal.

She gathered up her cleaning supplies to take downstairs and paused, rubbing her back, at the bedroom window. Her mind drew her back to the town of Helena, her mother — and Russell. She and Russell had become friends, and she was pretty sure he was about to ask her to marry him. And then came his tragic death. She still agonized over it all, wishing she knew more details about his accusers and the awful hanging.

Setting the cleaning items down once again, she shook her head and turned away from the window, her stomach in a knot at the terrible memory and the appalling scene she'd imagined way too often. She was still sure it was all a terrible mistake. Russell had just begun a small ranching operation with his brother, Nathan. There was no way he would even think of stooping so low as to steal a neighbor's cattle. Never. Of *that* she was sure. Her heart ached at how unjust it all was.

They'd met at church where she played the piano, and together attended several dances and outings. He'd been charming and, in her mind, perfect for her. When she'd learned of his death, she thought her life was over too. She hadn't seen Nathan since and idly wondered if by now he'd moved away.

Back in Helena, she'd considered driving over to their place to see what she could learn, but she would've had to rent a buckboard and horse, and money was as tight in Helena as it was here. Besides, she reminded herself again, Russell had never invited her to his ranch, probably because he was so busy fencing it in. Either way, there wasn't anything she could do about it now, but it was hard convincing her heart of that.

Only a few months after that terrible loss, her grandmother had passed away, leaving the boardinghouse to Patience — much to her mother's dismay. Patience had been happy to leave home and start fresh. Especially away from her mother's eyes, both pitying and prying.

It was hard to believe the place needed so many repairs after being open only about two years. It looked like it had been hastily built, and with the constant flow of miners and travelers, it already had begun to show wear on the rugs and furniture. She'd just have to live with it until she could squirrel away some money to get things done the way she'd like them. At least she'd keep it clean and neat.

Patience shook her head and turned her attention to happier thoughts — her situation *was* beginning to look up. Tomorrow she would find out if she could buy paint for the front of the boardinghouse. It was in desperate need of a sprucing up, and she thought she could do it herself. She'd have to borrow a ladder, but she figured someone around here would loan her one. Emily would know of someone, she was sure.

As she turned to leave the room, satisfied now that it was as immaculate as she could make it, her eye caught her reflection in the mirror above the dresser. At twenty-five, she was considered an old maid. Right now she was a sight to behold — smudges on her face, unruly dark hair falling from its pins, buxom on top and hips flaring beneath her soiled apron and dress. But her green eyes were still clear and bright. She considered them her best feature. Now, if only she could look like the new boarder, Emily — a little taller and thinner — she just might see a bit of interest from some eligible bachelor.

Patience sighed, picked up the mop bucket and cleaning items, and made her way downstairs. No point in whining about her looks. She couldn't change what she was, but hopefully someone of God's choosing would look at her heart and not her outward appearance. *Stay focused on the tasks at hand and work as unto the Lord,* she repeated silently. She wanted her grandmother to be proud of her — maybe look down from heaven with a smile. It made her sad that her grandmother had a soft spot for her that her own mother did not. Especially after her father died. Without him there to intervene on her behalf when it came to her mother's demands, she felt her life had been totally controlled and stifled.

She decided to have just another tiny slice of her lemon cake. That would surely make her feel better, wouldn't it? Tomorrow she would pay the marshal a brief visit.

Patience placed sizzling sausage, scrambled

eggs, hot coffee, and fresh biscuits on the sideboard for her guests. Three biscuits she kept aside, wrapped in a blue-checked napkin. She paused, considering whether to add the sausage to her basket. It seemed that a man like Marshal Jones would enjoy meat with his biscuit, so she tucked two of the sausages in with them. She donned bonnet and shawl and picked up the basket. If she got to the marshal's office early enough, no doubt it would be breakfast she was delivering.

She stepped into spring's chill, pausing to watch the morning sun just beginning to spread its golden rays across the mountain ridge. She surveyed the small town, barely six blocks long, which was host to thousands of miners traipsing to and from Alder Gulch. With three general stores, two saloons, a butcher, livery stable, and blacksmith, even at sunup there was always steady activity. She lifted her skirts at the end of the boardwalk to avoid the disgusting road littered with horse droppings. So unlike Helena. *But I don't miss living with my mother,* she reminded herself. She rather liked her newfound independence. She would no longer be viewed simply as a spinster but instead as a businesswoman with her own boardinghouse.

Delicious fragrances drifted from The Star Bakery as she hurried along. She'd bought a cinnamon bun there once, and enjoyed chatting with Hannah, the middle-aged lady who owned the establishment. But it was an extravagance she really couldn't afford — at least not very often. She nodded to Hannah through the shop window and hurried on.

She was pleased to see light from the marshal's window and quietly swung open the wooden door. She found him leaning back, hat over his face and boots resting on his desk. She called out a cheery good morning as she placed her basket on his desk. Yanking off his hat, he quickly sat up, boots thumping on the floor, and blinked at her. He swept his hand through thick hair and ran his fingers over his mustache. It appeared he'd slept in his chair all night.

"What in the world are you doing here at this hour, Miss Patience?" he growled.

"You could be a bit nicer, Marshal — a little less grumpy," she admonished, tucking her arms beneath her shawl. "Actually," she said, moderating her lecturing tone, "I brought you some of my biscuits as a peace offering for my rude interfering last week. By the looks of you, I'd say you haven't already eaten — am I correct?"

He just stared back at her — *Disbelief or*

43

irritation? she wondered — and she was afraid he was going to throw her out. She stared back into his deep-set, dark eyes and at the dimple in his chin — which she bet could be disarming if he wasn't always scowling.

Jedediah pulled the basket over and lifted the napkin. He closed his eyes, sniffing the hot biscuits. "Oh my! Miss Patience, for this, you deserve an olive branch *and* a good morning!" He rubbed his hands together and licked his lips — apparently delighted by the addition of the sausage links. Standing up, he motioned toward a chair. "Uh, please have a seat while I boil some coffee to go with this mighty fine peace offering."

She complied and watched as he filled the pot, added coffee, and lit the wood stove. She noted his shirt pulled tight across his broad back and the shaggy, dark hair curled into his collar. When he turned around to retrieve two mugs from the shelf, she pretended to be gazing out the window.

4

Jedediah was not of a mind to wait for the coffee to brew. He reached into the basket and picked up the lightest biscuit he'd ever seen, then sat down and took a bite of pure pleasure. He swiped a hand across his mouth and grinned at her.

"You might like to try a bit of sausage with your next bite," she suggested. He nodded agreement and soon savored the flavors of the sausage and biscuit together in his mouth. This breakfast — and the one who'd brought it — was like the fresh air he enjoyed when he went into the mountains on a spring day. He looked at her over his biscuit, at her pretty green eyes and that sprinkle of freckles across her cheeks. She remained quiet as he finished the biscuit and picked up the other sausage link.

"Miss Patience," he said, shaking his head, "the truth is, I don't think I've ever had a more delicious breakfast. Monty was indeed correct," he added. "Why don't you share this last biscuit with me?"

"I — oh —" And then she sprang from her chair and rushed to the stove, where the coffee was boiling over. Grabbing a dishtowel, she lifted the coffeepot and placed it to the side, then partially closed the oven's damper to lower the heat from the fire.

Jedediah was at her side in two strides. "See what happens when a man gets distracted with good food and a pretty lady?"

She went perfectly still. "I've never been called pretty . . ." Her voice trailed away and her gaze remained toward the floor.

He shifted on his feet and took the towel, his hand brushing against her knuckles, and placed the coffeepot back on the heat to finish brewing. She seemed more reserved, maybe even bashful, than when they'd first met. Was she simply putting on a front to win his favor? "Well, you should've been. Didn't your ma ever tell you that?" he said from where he stood near the stove.

"I don't recall her saying much of anything complimentary," she said quietly as she moved back to her chair. "I'd rather be called intelligent though. Anyway, I only came here this morning because I wanted to apologize for the way I intruded in your duties the other day. I had no right."

"No. You didn't." He grinned. "Apology accepted." The air was thick with silence. He filled two mugs and brought one over to her.

"However, you're not completely off the hook," she said from behind him as he returned to his chair behind the desk.

Why do women always have to have the last word? He sighed. "Well, I'm sure —"

"You obviously think I'm empty-headed just because I'm a woman," she hurried on. "Why, I run a business that will soon be quite successful, just as it was before my grandmother died. Though I am struggling to make ends meet, with repairs and all, and needing supplies —"

"Woman, do you ever know when to quit talking? How can I get a word in edgewise with you nattering on?"

She pulled her shoulders back and lifted her chin as if to say something else, but she must have decided against it.

"I'm sorry if I hurt your feelings," he said into the silence. "That was not my intention, but if you'd let me finish, I have a proposition for you."

"Whatever do you mean?" She shot to her feet, set her mug on the desk with a bang, and crossed her arms over her ample chest. "I'm not in the least interested in your 'proposition.' I'm not that kind of woman!" She stared at him angrily, then marched across the room toward the door.

His laughter no doubt could be heard down the boardwalk. He recovered, but she looked back at him as if she'd just eaten a lemon. She grabbed the door handle, her lips in a tight, thin line. Miss Patience was a strong-willed woman.

"Are you quite through?" she shot at him, adjusting her shawl tightly about her shoulders.

"Hold on," he said, stretching his hand out toward her. "Don't go getting the wrong idea. Sit back down and drink your coffee. I'll explain." Her brows knitted together, but she moved back to the chair and picked up the mug.

What was that fragrance he'd gotten a whiff of as she passed? Pleasant, but not too strong. Some kind of flower — or *flour*? He almost laughed aloud at the thought that the flour she made her biscuits from might have an aroma, but she seemed in no mood to be trivial, so he didn't ask. "I'm listening," she said, though her expression didn't match her words.

"Here's how we can help each other," he said, watching her sip at her coffee. "I have a posse of five men riding out with me tomorrow at daybreak, looking for a man wanted for murder. Do you think you could make us up some of your box lunches? It'd sure beat hardtack and beef jerky."

"Well, I don't know if I'll have time, with running the boardinghouse an' all —"

"I'd be paying you, of course, but you'd need to throw in a piece of chicken or meat. Maybe you could do that occasionally for us, but it might often be on short notice. You know, like an arrangement. I could help you with your earnings, and you could help me with better-tasting lunches. What d' you say?" He watched as she seemed to consider it.

"Maybe . . ." She gazed across the room. "I have to fix large meals anyway — the extra money could help me." She paused, then said, "Are you handy with a hammer or paintbrush? I could surely use someone to do a little patching up on the roof and such. What about it? You know, when you're not in pursuit of criminals."

He crossed his arms while he thought it over. "I think I could manage to find some free time. If not, maybe one of my men can help out." He reached out a hand, and she stood to shake it. "I think we have an arrangement, Miss Patience, one that's good for both of us." As he shook her hand, he was surprised at her firm grip. And her calloused palm — another surprise. He didn't think he'd ever met anyone quite like her. Maybe all the more reason to keep his distance.

"Fine, then. I must be going," she was saying. "You can stop in for the boxed lunches tomorrow before you leave with your posse — I'll have them ready."

The front door flew open, and both of them turned as Hannah from the bakery entered, a basket on her arm. "Well, Jed," the older woman said with raised eyebrows, looking from one to the other, "I had no idea you had company this early in the morning. I've got your breakfast. Just like usual."

Jedediah cleared his throat. "Morning, Miz Hannah. Have you met Patience Cavanaugh?" The older lady had more or less taken him under her wing since he'd arrived. He didn't mind, even though he wasn't much used to anyone fussing over him. But it felt nice in a motherly sort of way. Occasionally, though, she could feel like an irritating thorn in his flesh.

Hannah beamed at Patience. "Why, yes, I have. It's nice to see you again, Patience." But then she caught sight of the biscuit nestled in the napkin on Jedediah's desk. "What's this?" She almost gasped. "A biscuit?"

"Yes, ma'am," Patience said. "I made them for my boarders this morning and brought a couple to — to the marshal." Patience seemed a bit intimidated. "I had no idea that you regularly supply him with biscuits."

Hannah didn't say a word, but reached over to pinch off a bit of the biscuit and put it in her mouth. Tilting her head, she looked at Patience. "These are better than mine, and I thought I made the best biscuits in these parts. Why, it's light and delicious!"

Quite an admission, he thought to himself, considering her obvious pride in her own baking. He watched Patience's face as a tinge of pink brightened her cheeks and her green eyes sparkled.

"Oh, I daresay they can't hold a candle to yours, Hannah," she murmured.

"Sooo . . ." Hannah turned to Jedediah with twinkling eyes. "You won't be needing my biscuits any longer?"

"Oh, no, Hannah!" Patience hurriedly interjected a response. "This was a peace offering for my . . . well, my ill-advised public lecture to the poor marshal."

Hannah laughed. "I can't see a young lady

like you having to apologize, but your offer seems as good as any to get to know a fella better. But that's all right." She gave Patience's arm a pat. "I've heard it said that the way to a man's heart is through his stomach. You'll make someone a good wife, Patience," she added with a sly glance at Jedediah.

Jedediah chuckled. "If that ol' wives' tale was the truth, you'd be the one courting me, now wouldn't you, Miz Hannah? In fact, Miss Cavanaugh and I just reached an arrangement of sorts where we can help each other out."

The older lady eyed the two of them, looking rather skeptical. "I see. Well, give these to your prisoner then, Jed." She held her basket out.

"I would, but he was released yesterday. Got only a firm warning from the circuit judge since Shorty didn't actually manage to steal anything."

"Oh, well, in that case, I'll ask what you can do about the potholes in front of my establishment. It's such a muddy mess, and isn't good for business. All those wagons getting stuck in front of my bakery, and . . ."

As she prattled on, Patience murmured, "I'll leave you two to discuss this." She retrieved her basket, the last biscuit and sausage remaining in the napkin on the desk. "Good day, Hannah. I'll see you later, Marshal." She gave them a wave and quietly left.

Hannah stared at Jedediah after Patience was gone, tapping her hand against her folded arms.

"What?" But Jedediah already knew what was foremost in her thoughts, wagering that it wasn't about whose biscuits were the best.

"Patience seems like a very nice woman, don't you think?" Her eyes held a mischievous gleam that made him uncomfortable. He was used to her scrutiny, but he wasn't about to play into her matchmaking scheme.

"Can't say I've really noticed." *Not true and you know it.* "I know very little about her."

"Well, I can tell you that she is a wonderful woman. I've gotten to know her when we've shared a livery buggy to get to church over in Virginia City. We've —"

"Look, Hannah, I've had very little sleep and have a lot to do before the day gets rolling. So if you'll excuse me, I'd like to finish eating, then get cleaned up."

Ignoring his grumbling, she continued, "A pretty lady like Patience? I'm not fooled, Jedediah Jones. I have a feeling the

53

'arrangement' you made with her is going to work out very well."

Jedediah stuck the sausage into the biscuit and took a bite. Hannah wasn't going to be easily put off, so he might as well settle in for a while.

"Perhaps you could ask her to the church picnic over in Virginia City. It'd be a nice little ride with her —"

He nearly choked on his mouthful. He swallowed hard and washed it down with a swig of coffee. "Picnic? I rarely get to either church or a picnic. You know all I've got to do around here."

"Then there's no time like the present to get started. Just promise me you'll give it some thought. You do believe in the Good Lord, don't you?" Hannah picked up her basket to leave.

"Of course I do — it's just that my duties . . ." He didn't try to explain further. *And I don't like pretending to be a nice churchgoer just so folks will think better of me.*

Hannah flicked a napkin against his forearm. "No work is more important than the Lord's work, I'm sure, so that's no excuse." The expression on her face told him there would be no arguing that point. "Well, I must get back and open up the bakery. Why don't you drop by later on this week, and I'll save you one of my cinnamon buns fresh from the oven?" She winked at him.

He took her elbow and walked her to the door. "I promise to take you up on that."

"And to consider church, or at least the picnic?"

He rolled his eyes and opened the door to the morning chill without answering.

She reached up and pinched his cheek. "I'll stop nagging now so you can get back to work."

He felt genuine care for the older lady in spite of her attempts to interfere in his life, and he leaned down to plant a kiss on her forehead. She gave him a warm smile. "Thank you, and 'bye now."

He just shook his head as he watched her bustle away to the bakery. Their conversation brought to mind his encounter with Miss Patience. There was something about her . . . and not just those enormous green eyes. His feelings confused him — baffled him, really. She certainly was not the type he was normally drawn to. Too particular and outspoken. Besides, he was still nursing old wounds, and he wasn't about to repeat that sad saga. Not after Mt. Joy. It wouldn't matter anyway. If Patience knew about some things from his past, she most certainly would have nothing to do with him.

He closed the door, returned to his desk, and swallowed the last biscuit down with coffee and satisfaction. Monty was right — he didn't think Hannah's biscuits could compete with Patience's — hers were lighter than a cloud. *Wonder how she learned to cook like that?*

He picked up his Winchester leaning against the wall by his desk. Time to make sure he had everything together before the town came to life. He hoped the jail cells stayed empty because he intended to get some much-needed shut-eye tonight.

Moonlight filtered through the bedroom window curtains, the gentle breeze lifting them with a soft sigh. It was long past midnight, and Patience couldn't sleep. Too many jumbled thoughts filled her head. The sudden arrangement with the marshal, Hannah's rather transparent pretense at matchmaking a very unlikely couple, preparations for tomorrow's duties.

And, she admitted, she was lonely. Would it always be like this? She went over to the window and stared out at the finally quiet town. She thought back to Russell, how his eyes had danced with excitement at the prospect of having his own ranch. *I believed*

in him, but did he believe in me? She shook
her head. It was all so very tragic, and the
thought that he'd come to an awful death
pierced her heart — one that was finally
beginning to heal, she realized. She mustn't
let the unfortunate memories get in the way
of living. That's what her grandmother
would say if she were here tonight. She
sighed and leaned on the window sill.

She watched a tall figure stroll up the
street toward her boardinghouse. Jedediah.
So he was up late as well. Where was he going? The man was ruggedly handsome in
the moonlight, his shoulders straight, long
legs moving purposefully, hat pushed back
to reveal his features beneath the brim. He
was a man to be reckoned with. She was
sure of that. But certainly not her type with
his brusque way of speaking and short
temper. A man like that could never hold
her the way she longed to be held, with
tenderness and loving whispers, could he?
Don't be silly!

Just as she was about to move away from
the window, he looked up, slowing his steps
until she thought he was going to wave. But
she quickly closed the window and pulled
the curtains together with shaking hands.
God forbid! He'd seen her in her nightgown!
Her face grew hot, and her hands flew to

her face, their coldness cooling her skin. What must he *think* of her? Hopefully he'd seen very little . . . although the full moon was bright tonight.

She hurried back to bed. After yanking the coverlet back and crawling in, she wrapped her arms around the pillow. With the wind whistling through the cracks in the window frame, she willed herself to go to sleep, knowing that she'd have to be up very early in order to have the lunches ready when Jedediah stopped by. Notions that he had the tiniest bit of interest in her flashed across her mind, and she almost laughed out loud at the very thought. The two of them mixed like a dark spot on a Sunday shirt!

5

Patience was ready when Jedediah rapped on the door at sunrise. His posse was lined up in the street behind his horse, saddlebags and guns strapped on their mounts, hats slung low.

"Mornin', ma'am," Jedediah said when she opened the door. The mere bulk of him filled her small foyer as he stepped inside with a jingle of spurs. He made a formidable presence, outfitted as he was in a long black duster, a large bandana around his neck, his six-shooter strapped to his leg, and steely eyes observing her from beneath a brown leather hat. *Sure wouldn't want to tangle with him if I got on the wrong side of the law,* she thought. However, thinking about their earlier sparring made her heart beat faster. Had he held her gaze a little longer than necessary just now . . . or not?

"Morning," she said, attempting to match his laconic tone. "The boxes are right here on the hall table," she told him. "I'll help you carry them out." But as she reached for them, his leather-gloved hand covered hers. "No need." He turned in the doorway to the men. "Monty," he called, "lend a hand."

She recalled the cowboy named Monty from the day Jedediah had arrested the attempted saddle thief. In a swift minute or two, they'd handed the boxes up to each rider. A couple tipped their hats to her.

"Much obliged, Miss Patience. Smells mighty good. Be seeing you before too long." Jedediah joined his waiting men, said something she couldn't hear, then mounted his horse. He thumbed a signal to his posse, leading them in a trot down the street toward the foothills. Just then the morning sun broke across the purple mountaintop, sending shafts of light through the trees.

Patience shivered and hurried back inside, deciding to have her coffee before the boarders came down. She'd make a double batch of biscuits and fry up some potatoes and eggs in a bit. But since she was up a little earlier than normal, she made a list of pressing items around the boardinghouse that needed attention. Staring down at her ledger and the total at the bottom of the page, it was obvious that the needs outweighed her meager income. She chewed on her bottom lip and closed her eyes, as if she expected an answer to suddenly appear in a vision.

Sometimes she felt like giving up and going back home, but the thought of living with her overbearing mother quickly redirected her intent. The miners who boarded seemed to come and go as fast as an apple pie at a church picnic — whether off to work at the next strike on a nearby mine, or moving on to a new town with the hope of becoming rich. Still, she was grateful for the boarders she had. If she only had one more, she might have enough income to hire someone to put a fresh coat of paint on the weather-worn front facade. The pantry was getting low on staples, but the money she'd be receiving from the marshal would help pay for additional groceries needed near week's end.

She closed the ledger and decided to see about paint and supplies first thing tomorrow. A fresh coat would brighten the outside and might bring in business. *Yes, that's exactly what I'll do.* Hearing movement overhead meant it was time to start breakfast. She hurried off to the kitchen.

"All right, men," Jed said, pulling his horse up after nearly a four-hour ride. "Let's take a rest here, have our lunch." The sloped meadow and outcropping of trees offered a respite from the trail. The sun was high in the sky now, the time well past noon.

"Be glad to." Monty sighed, sliding off his horse. "My stomach is eating my backbone. Sure smells divine, doesn't it?" The rest of the posse mumbled their agreement, taking only moments to find a seat on the grass before attacking the food Patience had prepared.

Kit devoured the fried chicken, licked his fingers clean, and exclaimed, "Why, the woman even tucked a miniature apple pie in mine!" He was the youngest of the group, still wet behind the ears, but Jed had agreed to let him come along.

A ripple of snorts and guffaws pealed out from the group. "Don't feel too special." Monty chortled from his place against a tree trunk. "We all have one in our box. Now if we just had a cup of fresh brewed coffee to go with dessert."

"I'll second that," Brady, sitting cross-legged on the ground, said in his Irish brogue between mouthfuls.

"Say, Jed." Bob, a scrawny old horse breeder, turned toward the marshal. "Ever think about those times we had a few years back, hanging those road agents?"

Jed slanted a look at Bob, feeling the pie turn sour in his stomach. "Not lately," he muttered. "It's best not to dwell on the past — can't change things." The words sounded good, but they didn't change his lie into truth.

Quiet settled over the group until James, a wiry, short fella and the more outspoken one of the men, said, "Well, if it hadn't been for you and the Montana vigilantes, those agents would've continued robbing and stealing the countryside bare."

Kit choked on his pie and coughed until James thumped him on the back. "You mean you wuz one of them vigilantes?" Kit said around another cough. "I didn't know that — why, you're a living legend! No one ever told me!" The young man was wide-eyed with amazement.

Jed clenched his jaw, not wanting this impressionable kid to put him on a pedestal where he certainly didn't belong. Even though he hadn't been here that long, most of the men already knew he never wanted to talk about those days. "Haven't missed much, Kit," he said, avoiding the boy's appraisal.

"Wonder what ever happened to Ned?" Bob continued.

Monty grunted. "I heard tell he took off

for Kansas. Said he'd had enough of Montana."

Jed abruptly stood, wadding the sandwich paper into a ball, ignoring their stares. "Enough lollygagging. Let's get back on the trail. If we don't find what we're looking for, we'll head back to town before dusk."

Late-afternoon sun danced across the worn porch, its nails pushing upward from the boards as Patience swept. She leaned her broom against the unstable railing, shielding her eyes from the setting sun to glance down the dusty road. But there was no sign of Jedediah and his posse. Was that a good sign or bad? She didn't know, but she hoped everything had turned out all right. She couldn't stay out here sweeping much longer.

6

The next morning she set off to buy paint and supplies at Foster's general store. She had to push her way through the other shoppers in hopes of getting waited on. Finally she touched the sleeve of a scrawny young clerk who didn't appear strong enough to hoist the five-pound sack of flour balanced on his shoulder. But before she could speak, he said, "Sorry, ma'am, this will only take a few minutes."

She pulled her list from her reticule, but he was already walking on.

"Hold on there, lad." Patience heard a raspy voice from behind her. "Is that any way to treat a lady?"

Patience turned in the direction of a tall man moving toward them. His black hair beneath the fine black cowboy hat was so long that it brushed the top of his broad shoulders. He was smartly dressed in a paisley tan vest under his leather coat and sported a blue silk neckerchief knotted at the base of his throat. "Won't you take a moment to find out what the young lady needs?" He stood waiting, feet spread apart in well-heeled boots.

Although the young clerk's face flooded bright red, no doubt taken aback at the man's intrusion, he stood his ground. "In time I will, but she has to wait like everyone else, mister." He gave Patience a curt nod, then hurried away.

The man shrugged. "I tried, but how he could pass up an opportunity to serve a comely customer such as you is beyond me." His blue eyes twinkled.

Patience felt her face grow warm. *Comely — me?* "Sir, I appreciate your efforts, but I can see the clerk has more than enough to handle. I shouldn't have prevailed upon him to assist me. Thank you all the same. I'll wait my turn and, in the meantime, see if I can locate some of these items myself." She stared down at her list. *Perhaps if I don't look up, he'll walk away.* But he continued to stand there.

She couldn't remember seeing him about town, but with so many coming and going daily, she'd be hard-pressed to remember every face — except for the fact that she wouldn't likely forget his handsome face or his deep, raspy voice.

"I could help if you'd like," he offered.

"That won't be necessary. I'm sure you have better things to do." She looked directly into his eyes, which crinkled at the corners. A slight smile parted his lips. Was he flirting or just being helpful?

He took a step closer and held out his hand, and she reluctantly placed hers inside his big, strong fingers. "Name's Cody. Cody Martin." He shook her hand firmly, holding her eyes with his.

She gave him a curt nod. "Patience Cavanaugh," she said, pulling her hand away.

He shoved his hands into his pockets. "I have nothing but time. To tell you the truth, I just got into town. I'm looking for a job, so I'm completely free and at your service."

"Well, that's all good and well, and I do hope you find employment. But from your manner of dress, I'd say you're more suited to ranching. Am I wrong in my assessment?" she asked primly.

He arched an eyebrow but smiled. "Matter of fact, that's all I know, but I haven't been lucky enough to snag employment in that field yet. May I?" he asked, motioning to her list.

Patience wasn't sure if he really wanted to help or was only toying with her. Her experience with the ways of men was very limited. But somehow after a moment she found herself handing the list to him.

"Ah," he murmured as he quickly scanned it. "I see you're planning on doing some painting."

"Why, yes. I own Creekside Inn, and I intend to spruce things up a bit."

His eyes narrowed. "Is that so? It just so happens that I'm looking for a room to rent, if you have any available. And I do know how to paint."

She shook her head. "Oh no, I couldn't ask you to do that. I do have vacancies, but I'm afraid I wouldn't be able to pay you for your services." She took the list back.

His chuckle reverberated from deep within his chest. "It was an offer to help you while I find a job. I can pay for the room and board. I'm also pretty good with a paint-brush. You learn to do everything when you're not out cattle punchin'."

Patience was hesitant. She wondered how he'd be able to pay rent. "I see . . . Well, I can certainly rent you a room, and as far as the painting, we'll have to see."

"Right! Now, let's see about finding the right paint and brushes, then you can lead the way to your inn."

He was so friendly and energetic that suddenly she was giving in to his offer to help gather the items. Within a short time, she'd picked out suitable brushes and a paint color and, after a short wait in line, paid for it all.

Patience led the way down the boardwalk in the direction of Creekside. Her heels tapped a singsong rhythm against the boardwalk with Cody beside her, swinging two buckets of paint. It was a fine, sunny morning, and their pace evenly matched. Suddenly she was in good spirits, anticipating an improved boardinghouse filled with boarders. The man next to her was at least partly responsible.

"I'm determined to improve Creekside Inn to make it more appealing," she told him. "I'm envisioning pale yellow paint out front to welcome boarders, then a fresh coat of paint for the parlor, along with new voile curtains that I can make myself to give the place a feeling of home and coziness."

"I'm sure your ideas will improve everything. I'll just be glad to have a place to lay my head tonight."

"I believe the more my boarders feel at home, the longer they will reside. By the way, I serve breakfast and dinner for an extra fee. You're on your own for lunch, and it's up to you if you want those two meals included." It was only half a block to Creekside, and soon Patience was swinging the front door open. "Mr. Martin, just set the paint pails here in the foyer for now."

"Please call me Cody — my friends do."

"Does that mean I'm your friend?" Patience caught herself, removing the silly smile from her face. *I sound like a flirt!* For goodness' sake, what was wrong with her — acting this way toward some man who came along and paid her some attention!

"I certainly hope we can be. I've enjoyed talking with you and helping select paint," he chuckled. His handlebar mustache nearly covered his upper lip, and it twitched with his smile. "Is it all right if I call you Patience?"

My, he was bold! She hardly knew what to say — she'd just met him! "I, uh . . . I think that would be all right." She felt her face go warm, and her tongue was thick, but Cody only smiled. *What on earth would Mother say?*

"I'll just need you to sign your name on the register, right over here, and I require the first night's fee." She removed her cape and laid it aside, then walked behind the small wood counter. She flipped open a green ledger, hoping she looked like a professional businesswoman. She heard someone clear his throat and was surprised to see a man sitting just inside the parlor open to the foyer. *Jedediah?*

"I didn't see you there, Jedediah." Patience nervously fingered a button on her blouse. "Have you been waiting for me? Or are you here inquiring about a room?"

Patience could see Cody watching Jedediah as he rose and made his way to the front door, then paused. "It can wait. Looks like you're a little busy at the moment," he said, his gaze on the paint cans by the door. "Go ahead with your customer. I'll be back a little later."

"If you're sure," she responded, feeling awkward and flustered.

He tipped his hat at them and quickly closed the door behind him without another word. She turned back to the ledger.

"Now, show me where you want me to sign," he said. "I'm used to sleeping in hard bunk beds surrounded by a lot of snoring cowpokes."

"I'm sure you will be comfortable here during your stay. Did you decide whether you want to stay by the day or week?"

"Since no employment has miraculously appeared, I'll pay for the week and then go from there. Maybe something will come up."

"Very well. The front door is locked after

ten o'clock in the evening," she told him, keeping her tone as businesslike as she could, "but you have your own key to your room. If you want me to clean your room, that's extra. But I can supply fresh bedding, even laundry services, upon request, for an additional charge."

She pondered briefly why this man seemed to make her so . . . so discombobulated! He paid the amount she quoted for the week and accepted the room key. "I'm going over to retrieve my bags from the train depot where I left them," he told her. "Thank you for your charming company. We'll talk later about getting started on painting the outside. I can help with that at least until I find work. It'll give me something to do."

"You're most welcome, and I appreciate your willingness to help me . . . Cody." Her tone was matter of fact, but she fumbled with the register book and quickly looked away.

It wasn't the first time Cody had had that effect on a woman, but he was no womanizer. It'd been a while since there was a woman in his life. He spent too much time going from ranch to ranch the last few years.

But she was attractive in a down-to-earth way. Nicely put together — not some frail slip of a girl who couldn't lift a mop bucket. Sensual, though, without realizing it — an even better attribute when a woman wasn't aware she had it all. She had a quick mind, he could tell from their brief time together, and he liked that.

He sure was curious about the man obviously waiting for her when they'd returned from the mercantile. "Jedediah," she'd called him. Was he a suitor? He looked at her in some way that made his visit seem like it was more than simply to call on some kind of business matter.

Actually, the man seemed familiar somehow, not so much his looks, but maybe his voice? And the man was wearing a badge — the town marshal?

Well, anyway, he mustn't get tangled up with a woman . . . or with a marshal. They both usually spelled trouble. Besides, he didn't plan on being in Nevada City that long. Best that he stick to finding work and continue with his plans.

Jedediah's thoughts perplexed him as he left the Creekside Inn. Patience had seemed a little shy while she'd been chatting with her customer. It was surprising, but appealing. The two seemed to know each other, by the sound of their conversation. Well, it was none of his business. But he wondered what it would take for him to cause her to blush so prettily? *Easy now . . . She's too rigid and perfect for someone like me. I can't be hemmed in like that — even if she'd want to be!*

A hint of cinnamon wafted on the breeze. He headed down to The Star Bakery, his belly rumbling in response. Fragrant mixtures of cinnamon and other spices filled the tiny bakery and made his mouth water. Hannah was busy at her wooden table, kneading a big batch of dough he knew would be fresh bread by noon. Behind the glass-fronted counter were all those baking delights to tantalize his senses.

"Howdy, Jed." Hannah paused to wipe her hands on a cloth, then hurried over.

"Morning, Miss Hannah. I would love to have one of your cinnamon rolls. But," he bent to peer through the glass at the shelves, "I don't see —"

"My earlier customers wiped me out, but I always save one for you just in case." Her round face beamed at him like he was her son.

"Aww, Miss Hannah, you didn't have to do that."

"I know I didn't have to, but I wanted to." She reached under a linen cloth and placed the cinnamon roll on a piece of paper. "Want me to wrap it or you gonna eat it here?"

"I think I'll take it with me and make myself some coffee. I always have work I should be doing."

"No need to make your own. I just made some fresh. In fact, I'll take a break with you, now that it's finally settled down around here this morning." Ignoring his protests, she poured two mugs of coffee. She carried them and he picked up his roll and followed her over to one of the small wooden tables.

"How's life been treating ya, Jed?" She always got right to the point. "I heard you took the posse out. Anything I should know about? Robbers, criminals? You know I live alone here, and there's plenty o' no-accounts passing through."

Jed laughed. "Why, Miss Hannah, I don't think you have a thing to worry about. In fact, I'm pretty sure you can handle whatever comes your way!" He took a bite of the roll and a swig of coffee, looking into the older woman's eyes. *She's a keen one, that's for sure.* In this rugged country, women — especially widowed women — learned survival skills or the worst could happen.

"To tell you the truth, we trailed that no-good outlaw until we reached the border of Idaho, then lost him. Just as well. Let the authorities there apprehend him."

She gave him a serious look. "Can't say as I blame you there. You have plenty of drunks and minor lawbreakers to keep you busy right here in town. Seen any more of Patience?"

He finished his roll, giving him time to consider how to answer. "Why do you want to know?"

"I guess you need lookin' after, and I'm just the one to do it." She gave him a wry smile. "Someone should."

"Miss Hannah, don't worry your wise gray head about me. I'm not worth worrying over."

"Now, don't say that, Jed. I know better. So, have you seen her lately?" She leaned forward expectantly.

"Well, yes and no. She agreed to pack boxed lunches for me and my men, but when I dropped by to pay her today, she was . . . well, otherwise engaged."

Her brows knitted in a deep line above her nose. "Ya don't say? Tell me about it."

"Can't rightly tell you. Some cowboy checking in as a boarder, I guess." He flicked the crumbs he'd left on the table with his thumb.

"Mmm . . . That doesn't sound like she was otherwise *engaged,* Jed."

He snorted. "If you could've seen her face, you'd understand what I mean."

"You're beginning to sound jealous, but it doesn't surprise me none. Patience is a fine catch. She lives by the Good Book and when she can get there, goes to church —"

Jedediah's head jerked up and he slapped his thigh and forced a laugh. "That's just the problem, Miss Hannah. She's *too* perfect. Besides, I'm not looking for a woman, and she sure isn't interested in the likes of me."

Hannah's eyes squinted. "You listen here, young man. You have plenty to make a woman happy, and a little religion rubbing off on you can't hurt you at all!" She began gathering their cups.

"Give it a chance, Jed," she said in a low voice, "before you go making up your mind about how perfect somebody is. There's *no one* perfect in this world, and that's a fact. Even me." She laughed at her little quip, then leaned down and planted a kiss on the top of his head. "I'm watching out for you."

"Well, thanks anyway, but I don't need looking after." He pushed his chair back, pressed a quarter into her apron pocket, and gave her a pat on the arm when the bell at the door's entrance jangled.

"For all that tough exterior you put on, I know there's a tender spot buried somewhere in you, and I aim to find it." With a quick wink, she turned to greet her customers.

He greeted a few of the good townsfolk and stopped briefly to chat with the Larson family, who were in town for the day. The two youngsters hugged their father's pants leg while the mother's hip held their baby girl.

"Stop by sometime for Sunday dinner, Jed," the woman told him. "No need for an invitation. Just stop by. We're always home after we get back from church on Sundays. You're welcome to come along to church too — just a short trip over to Virginia City. What do you think, Pete?"

Church again! he grumbled to himself. *Glad we don't have one in town or I'd be nagged to death.*

Pete Larson was nodding. "Sure, and we'd be right honored for you to eat with us." He grinned. "If you can stand the noise."

"I'd be glad to, and I appreciate the offer." He tousled the two boys' heads and gave each of them a shiny penny. They grinned happily, pocketing the coins.

"What do you say to Marshal Jones,

children?" their father prompted.

The boys shyly stammered their thanks.

"Go buy yourselves a stick of peppermint," Jed told them. He reached over to the little baby and stroked her chubby arm. "My, she's growing up fast. And thanks for the invite. I better get going now." He tipped his hat and headed for the office.

Later this afternoon, he decided as he settled in behind the desk, *I'll go pay Patience for the box lunches before I forget.* But he had a hunch the cowboy would still be hanging around.

After a dispute about a claim jumper was easily settled, the rest of Jed's morning went by fast. He settled back in his chair to read the newspaper after lunch. When he heard a high-pitched cry, he leaped up and ran out onto the boardwalk. Just as he feared, two doors down and high up on a ladder was Patience, paintbrush in one hand, pail in the other, tangled up in her skirts. She quickly lost her footing and fell, screaming and hitting hard on her back. Fortunately, the ladder careened the other way.

Jedediah had almost reached her when the man he'd seen at Creekside earlier began to lean over her. But Jed charged straightaway to where she lay, very still. He pushed the cowboy to the side.

He knelt beside Patience. Her dress was torn, and the skirt was in some disarray. He pulled it down over her legs, knowing she would be humiliated beyond belief if she knew it was askew.

"You! Go get the doctor!" Jed barked at the flustered cowboy, who paused, then took off at a trot. Jed turned back to Patience. "Patience, can you hear me?" His heart banged against his ribs. She wasn't moving. Had she injured her neck or head?

A few passersby drew close, forming a semicircle around them.

"Is she dead?" someone asked.

Irritated, Jedediah didn't answer but leaned in close to feel the pulse in her neck with his two fingers — something he'd learned during his years of chasing outlaws. He felt the pulse throb against his fingertips. He was close enough that her rosewater fragrance was perceptible, and he moved back, unsure of his feelings.

Yellow paint splattered her pale face, so he took out his handkerchief to gently wipe the traces of paint from her cheek. Paint also clung to her hair on the same side, now unwound from its pins.

He didn't want to move her until he knew how badly she was injured. Then he heard a weak moan and her eyes fluttered open, trying to focus. She took a deep breath, and her hand moved to press against her right side. *Thank God.*

"Take it easy now. You might've broken something. I've sent for the doc."

Her eyes opened and she blinked, attempting to sit up. He slipped an arm under her shoulders. "What — I . . . ?" she murmured, looking up at him, her face furrowed into a frown.

He shifted onto his knees, supporting her back, and patted her hand. Something had unexpectedly moved him when he saw her fall, rendering her helpless, frail, and unassuming.

Where in tarnation is that doctor?

7

Patience blinked until her eyes finally focused on the face hovering above hers. The pain in her shoulder and head made her feel woozy, disconnected. *Is that Emily?*

"Oh, thank God!"

Patience could see the anxiety in the young woman's face. "You gave us all quite a scare," Emily said.

Patience tried to push herself up, but the throbbing in her head made her wince, and when she moved, her right side felt a sharp stab. Emily gently pushed her back against a pillow.

"What happened?" Patience asked, her voice sounding to her like it was coming from far away. "The last thing I remember is painting . . ." When she tried to look up at Emily, the room spun, and she felt slightly nauseated. She was in her bed, fully clothed minus her shoes. A quilt was draped across her legs. Late afternoon shadows fell across the room. How long had she been lying here?

"You hit your head when you fell off the ladder." Emily's hand rested on her shoulder. "You stay right there. Let me tell Doctor Gordon you're awake." With an anxious pat and a long gaze into Patience's face, Emily hurried out the door.

Moments later Emily returned with the doctor. He introduced himself and examined her — looking into her eyes, then listening to her heart. He asked if she had any pain, and she pointed to her side. He carefully felt around the area and stopped when she winced.

Finally he straightened after a pat on her shoulder and gave her a reassuring smile. "You'll be fine with a few days' rest. You have a mild concussion and a few bruised ribs, but I'd suggest not climbing a ladder anytime soon," he told her with a little chuckle. "Actually, no ladders at all for you, and only light activities for the next couple of days."

"Thank you, Doctor," Patience mumbled in a daze.

"Emily, if she throws up or seems confused, please come and get me." He snapped his bag shut. Turning back to Patience he said, "That includes any visual disturbances, all right?"

Patience nodded her agreement, but even the slightest movement of her head caused pain and nausea. She was sure she would have plenty of reminders about her mishap with her body's cautions to take it easy.

"I'm leaving some headache powder you can easily mix with water, to make your headache tolerable." He walked to the bedroom door. "You were very fortunate, Miss Patience. I don't need to see you again unless you get any of the symptoms I've just discussed with Emily."

Patience couldn't seem to think clearly. "Of course. Thank you for coming."

"I'll walk you out, Doctor," Emily said, following him from the bedroom.

When Emily returned, she carried a fresh pitcher of water. She poured a glass, then sprinkled the powder into it, giving it a whirl with a spoon. She slipped an arm under Patience's shoulders to lift her slightly, then handed the drink to Patience. "I'm going to let you rest, and I'll tell the others that dinner will not be served tonight. The boarders will make other arrangements for a day or two."

"But — but I can't let you do that." She tried to protest before swallowing the bitter-tasting water. "I can't run the boardinghouse if I'm lying here, and I'll lose the boarders I have . . ." Her voice trailed off weakly.

"Don't be silly. They'll understand," Emily said briskly as she pulled the curtains together. "They're boarding at the nicest, cleanest establishment in Nevada City," she said as she turned back to the bed. "Perhaps it's best if you try to sleep. You'll feel so much better after you rest."

"Thank you, Emily," Patience said through a wobbly smile. Were those violets on Emily's dress? Hard to keep her eyes focused.

"Do just as the doctor said. I can help you as much as I'm able, except for the time I'm at the café, of course." Emily pushed Patience's hair away from her eyes. "I'll come back in a little while, rustle up some soup or broth for you."

Patience was suddenly too tired to say any more. Her eyelids closed, and she felt her body beginning to relax.

Painting the inn would have to wait for a while.

When Patience opened her eyes, there was a fire in the grate, and it was dark beyond the curtains. She couldn't believe she'd slept. Then it came rushing back — her fall from the ladder, and coming to her senses

85

in her own bed.

She struggled to sit up, then carefully swung her legs over the side of the bed. She sat very still, waiting for a wave of dizziness to subside. The door opened, and Emily entered with a tray and a cheery greeting. "Hello, Emily," Patience said. Her side felt mighty sore. She supposed she was very fortunate not to have broken her neck since Emily had told her she was nearly at the top of the ladder. *My angel must've been watching over me.* She couldn't help but smile at the thought. For years her grand-mother had told her that Patience had her very own guardian angel. She liked to believe it was true.

"I thought you might be awake by now," said Emily. "I scrounged around the kitchen and found some leftover soup and bread. I hope this will do."

Patience's stomach growled in response, and they both laughed.

"I guess that was your answer." Emily placed the tray in Patience's lap. Taking a seat on the bed, she removed the linen napkin.

As Patience began her supper, Emily told her what she knew about the incident. "It appears that one of the rungs on that old ladder was cracked, and your dress must've gotten tangled in a piece of split wood when you tried to step down. The marshal heard you scream and ran to you."

"Mmm . . . I vaguely remember seeing someone, but I thought it was Cody. Maybe my mind's befuddled, Emily." She took another bite of the bread, butter liberally spread on it.

"Well, Cody was there too, but the marshal took over and sent him to fetch the doctor," Emily explained. "I heard the scream and got here just as Cody left."

"Nice of the marshal to help." She took another bite of bread and looked over at Emily. "What? Why are you giving me that look?"

"Oh, I'd say that the marshal was doing a little more than just a nice thing. I think he's interested in you," Emily answered, eyebrows arched. "I saw his expression when he was feeling for a pulse in your neck — fear, then relief."

"You must be joking. It's his duty to help. He was probably wondering if I'd be bringing him breakfast biscuits again," she tried a little chuckle but quit when it hurt her side. *So it was Jedediah who took care of me.*

Emily was shaking her head. "No, it was more than duty, Patience. He carried you up here after the doctor said you could be moved. He was very attentive and has already come again to check on you. I told him you might be able to receive visitors in the morning if he wanted to stop by then."

Patience felt warmth spread to her face. Jedediah's arms had lifted her, carried her right into her bedroom. "I'm sure he thought I was nothing more than a clumsy fool. Emily, I can't thank you enough for being my nursemaid. But I feel pretty good now that I've had something to eat."

They continued talking, finding out they shared more than a few similarities. Patience told her new friend about her family and her near engagement to Russell, then his death, and Emily shared how after her parents had died from an outbreak of diphtheria she'd become the ward of her uncle, who gave her everything she needed growing up. She had the sense that Emily was about as lonely as she was.

"Oh, goodness! Look at the time. And I have to be up early." Emily stood, lifting the tray. "Do you need help getting ready for bed?" At Patience's shake of her head, Emily said, "Fine then. If you need anything — anything at all during the night — just give me a holler. I'm sure I'll hear you across the hall. I'll stop by in the morning before I leave for Longhorn's."

Patience gave her arm a squeeze, then slowly stood and followed her to the bedroom doorway. "Emily, thank you again. I enjoyed getting to know you better, even if the circumstances were not the best. If there's anything I can do to repay you, please let me know."

Emily shrugged. "It's what friends do for each other. Don't forget, you don't need to get up early to prepare breakfast — everyone has been forewarned." She slipped from the room, and Patience closed the door to prepare for bed.

She soon found herself between the covers and allowed the warmth to envelope her like a cocoon. She thought about what Emily had said concerning Jedediah's interest in her. Her friend had seemed pretty certain about it, but Patience wasn't. *Jedediah? Interested in me?* Emily must be mistaken. Still . . .

Jedediah had trimmed his mustache, splashed on a bit of toilet water along his newly shaven jawline, and donned a clean chambray shirt. Outside he spied a patch of blue bachelor's buttons growing alongside the stage depot. He looked around to see if he was observed, then quickly bent to pick a bunch. It was mid-morning by then, so he'd decided to check in on Patience. He did need to pay her for the boxed lunches, so he had a good reason for the visit.

He sauntered down the boardwalk past his office, but slowed as he neared the Creekside Inn. The cowboy — he'd forgotten what he'd said his name was — stood high up on a ladder, slapping yellow paint on the outside of the inn. The same yellow that was matted in Patience's hair. *What in tarnation is he doing that for? Is he a good friend of Patience?* Jedediah intended to find out more about the stranger. Why hadn't he offered to finish the painting for Patience? After all, that was part of their agreement.

Feeling silly with the wildflowers in hand and an observer up on the ladder, he turned back in the direction he'd come and saw Hannah sweeping the sidewalk in front of her bakery. He'd have to give Patience the money later — when Mr. Cowboy wasn't around.

"Mornin', Miss Hannah. Maybe you'll find a place for these," he said, thrusting the bouquet in her hands. Her mouth dropped open as he strode on past her.

"Thanks, Jed, but where ya off to in such a rush?"

Jedediah heard the exasperation in her voice, but he didn't look back.

■ ■ ■ ■

By the time Emily peeked in on her, Patience was slowly getting dressed, careful of the bruise on her side. Though she was still stiff, she was grateful her headache had subsided.

"I'm leaving now," Emily told her, "if you're certain that you can manage getting your breakfast. I didn't want to wake you earlier." Emily stepped into the room and helped Patience with the buttons on her dress.

"I'll be just fine," Patience assured her. "Maybe I'll have just a piece of toast this morning, and I can easily manage that. In fact, I feel quite well, except for the soreness in my shoulder and ribs."

"Good! Now, don't overdo, and I'll see you after supper or as soon as I can get away from the café."

Patience assured her she would be careful. After she left, Patience tried brushing her hair up into its usual chignon as gently as she could. Tenderness from a bruise and swelling on the side of her head caused a sharp intake of breath. Instead of her comb, she used her fingers to make a loose knot at the back of her head. It would have to do for now, even if Jedediah stopped by, as Emily had indicated he might. She pinched her cheeks to add a little color and was glad for the green sprigged dress that brought out her eyes. Patience sighed. If she couldn't be tall and willowy like Emily, with her golden hair and honey-colored eyes, she could at least be bright and cheerful.

This kind of thinking got her absolutely nowhere.

After downing another two cups of coffee, Jedediah leaned back with his boots propped against the porch railing and surmised that he was simply confused. Considering how he'd reacted earlier, it all made no sense. Patience, with her lovely eyes and witty tongue, along with her deep faith, left him bewildered and wondering. He believed in God, but she seemed to take her faith a step further — writing "devotionals," whatever they were, and spouting off about them. And then, of all the nerve, suggesting he might have regrets in his past. Why would she presume such a thing about his life? She didn't know him from Adam. Why should he care how many devotionals she wrote? They meant nothing to him, and there was nothing between him and Patience.

Except for some reason or other, she stuck

in his craw. He knew little about her — who her parents were, where she came from — and maybe he didn't need to. Forget whatever Hannah said or thought. He and the Patience woman would mix like grub worms in a tomato patch — pure disaster. *Especially if she knew me for what I really am.*

He'd walk over there now and pay her what he owed her, then leave it at that. At least until he needed lunches again.

Patience was sitting in a rocker on the front porch, chatting with that cowboy still up on the ladder, when Jedediah walked up. Hadn't this dude finished yet? For goodness' sake! He could've had the entire front painted by now. *Cowboy's slow. Or maybe he wants to paint at a snail's pace to hang around longer.* He hoped the slowpoke wasn't charging her for the job.

"Why, Jedediah, good morning. It's good to see you this beautiful day. I wanted to thank you for coming to my aid yesterday." She gave him a little smile. "Forgive me if I don't stand. My head still feels somewhat strange at times."

Her usual rosy cheeks were pale, and her eyes seemed dull as she gazed at him. A dark blue bruise swelled the side of her face.

"I'm sorry it happened, but glad you're

93

up and feeling better." He placed one foot on the top step, removed his hat, and leaned an arm across his knee.

A light pink now bathed her face. "Thank you. Emily said you sent for the doctor and — and carried me inside." She nervously fingered the fringe on the shawl draped across her shoulders. "I hope it wasn't too much of a bother."

Cowboy cleared his throat and turned to them from the top of the ladder. "*I* was the one who went after the doctor for you, Patience."

"Sure 'nuff, you did. Because I asked you to, cowboy," Jedediah drawled.

"*Cody.* My name is Cody." He flashed an annoyed look at Jedediah.

"Got it. Cody." Jedediah winked at him, then handed Patience an envelope. "This is payment for the lunches you made. Everyone said to tell you they were delicious," he said, fully aware that Cody had one ear cocked to their conversation. Wasn't he way too young for Patience?

She nodded, glancing inside the envelope. "I'm glad you all enjoyed the lunches. Just let me know when you think you'll need them again."

"I'll do that. You take it slow for a few days." Jedediah could have sworn her eyes softened when she looked into his. He smiled at her, watching her full lips lift at the corners with a sweet smile.

"Oh, don't worry. Emily's making sure of that," she said. "I'm not cooking for the boarders for the next day or two."

"Do you need for me to get you over to Longhorn's for supper then?" *Now where did that come from?* he berated himself. But it was asked, and now he couldn't back out without looking ridiculous.

"No need — I'm taking her myself," Cody called down from his perch.

"Did I ask you?" Jedediah straightened, irritated, and stared upward. "The lady can speak for herself."

"I don't *require* anyone to take me to supper," Patience announced archly. "But Cody was nice enough to ask me earlier. Maybe you'd care to join us?" Her smile was sweet and, Jedediah thought, genuine.

"I'll pass," he told her. "I've got to get back to work. Riffraff passing through Nevada City are always keeping me on my guard, you know," he said with a quick glance at Cody. He put his hat on and noticed Cody eyeing his badge, the muscles in his jaw flinching hard. Maybe he hadn't seen it yesterday. *Good! At least he knows who I am now.*

Patience stood and reached over, almost touching his arm, but drew her hand back. "Perhaps another night . . ."

"We'll see." What the devil was wrong with him? Eating alone was becoming tedious and lonely. However, Cody had his eye on her, and who was he to get in the way of that?

Patience chuckled, though it sounded forced. "I wouldn't want to twist your arm."

"You're not. It's just that I've got a lot of things to do . . . and it looks like you won't be needing my help with painting now."

Patience was looking down at her shoe tops. "I see. Well, in that case, thank you again for your help. Cody was free for now and wanted something to do and offered to do some painting for me. I'm on my way inside to rest now." She slipped through the doorway and disappeared, leaving him to wonder.

Was it something he'd said? He never could understand the workings of a woman's mind. Who could?

Cody lifted the brush from the pail with a distinct harrumph, and Jedediah stared hard at him, then stalked off. *Good luck, cowboy. Maybe some of her manners will wear off on you.*

8

Throughout supper at the Longhorn, though Cody was both handsome and attentive, Patience's mind kept wandering back to Jedediah. She was embarrassed to have her invitation to join them turned down, especially in front of Cody. What was she thinking? She'd clearly mistaken Jedediah's interest in her accident for romantic notions. She shook her head briefly, and Cody looked puzzled. At least he seemed interested in their friendship, and she forced herself to pay attention to what he said.

The Longhorn was the nicest place to eat in town, and any other time Patience would have thoroughly enjoyed it, but not tonight. The decor was homey, with blue-checked tablecloths and blue spatterware. This was the first time she'd eaten here, and she could see how it could be a cozy place to enjoy eating with friends. But even though their dinner of thick steaks and potatoes looked delicious, her inward turmoil distracted her.

She leaned back in the comfortably upholstered chair with a sigh.

"Your appetite seems to have disappeared. Are you sure you're feeling better?"

Patience laid her fork down. "Yes, I am. But a steak as large as this one is more than I can manage." The truth was, her jaw hurt when she chewed. It was a wonder that she hadn't lost her teeth from the fall.

Patience tried to take the focus from herself. "Tell me, have you had any jobs of interest materialize yet?"

"Not yet, but I'm not too concerned. When I'm finished painting, I'll help you out with a few things that you need done around the inn. If I don't find something soon, I'll move on to the next town. That's the life of a cowboy. I'm used to it." His eyes held a certain melancholy when he looked into hers. "I have some money saved to tide me over until something turns up."

If he stayed in Nevada City, Patience knew he'd have the ladies swarming around him with his dark good looks and affable personality. "Tell me about your family, Cody."

His shoulders stiffened as he cut into his steak. "There's not much to tell. My pa taught me how to handle cows and horses at a young age, but he fell on hard times after my mother died, so I struck out on my own, working here and there. What about you?"

"I inherited the Creekside from my grandmother after she died. At first I wasn't sure I'd want to stay, but it seems preferable to living with my mother."

Cody arched a dark brow. "She wants to be in charge?"

"Yes." Patience didn't feel compelled to share details with him.

They were interrupted as Emily stopped by their table. "How's your dinner? I asked the cook to make sure your steak was especially tender for you, Patience."

"It's really wonderful, but I'm afraid it's more than I can eat. Please thank the cook for me, will you? I'm going to take the rest home with me, if that's all right."

Emily's face looked tired, but she managed to smile at them, assuring Patience that would be fine and she'd wrap it up as well as pass along her thanks to the cook. She'd been on the job for hours, and Patience knew her feet and legs must be very weary. She felt sorry for her new friend, making a promise to herself to have a nice cup of tea and biscuit ready for Emily when she returned tonight.

Emily glanced over to Cody. "Will you be having dessert?"

He gave her a smile. "Sure. Do you have vanilla custard? That would be easy for Patience to eat."

"Coming right up. I'll take these plates if you're through." At Patience's nod, she began clearing the table.

"Emily — perhaps coffee too?" Patience suggested.

Emily nodded, and after she left, Cody asked, "Why aren't you married?"

His rather direct question took her by surprise. Swallowing hard, she answered, "I came close to it . . . or at least I believe I was about to become engaged, but a tragedy occurred."

"Do you want to talk about it?"

"The man I hoped to marry was hanged for cattle rustling," she blurted out, and all the pain and memories of Russell's death came flooding back. Suddenly the room was stifling hot — whether from the heat that rushed to her head or heat from the kitchen mixed with the summer air, she couldn't have said.

Shock registered on Cody's face and his brows creased into a tight line. "You don't say? You don't look like the type of lady who would be . . . well, would be involved with someone like that, if you don't mind me saying so."

She heard regret in his voice. "That's because he wasn't that type of person."

He gave her a curious gaze. "Do you know that for sure? Sometimes we can't always see the real person. Do you know who — well, who hanged him?"

This kind of talk was making her as uncomfortable as her corset. "Cody, if you don't mind, I need to get back to the inn. I'm suddenly feeling very tired." She moved her chair back. "Please tell Emily I'm sorry about the dessert. Maybe she can take a break and enjoy it with you — looks like she could use one."

Cody's eyes narrowed with surprise. "I'm sorry you aren't feeling well." He stood and reached for his hat. "I'll be glad to walk you back and skip the pudding myself."

"No, no. I'll be fine. It's only a block. Really, just relax and enjoy your dessert. Perhaps I'll see you in the morning?" she said, gathering her shawl about her.

"Yes, of course. Try to get some sleep, and thank you for having dinner with me." He bowed his head slightly.

"You're welcome." She hurried out of the restaurant, gulping in the much-needed evening air, hoping to clear her fuzzy thoughts.

She needed to get out of this corset that threatened to shut off her breathing entirely. She'd laced it as tight as she was able to without causing more pain, to give the appearance of a smaller waist. And she'd wanted to wear her favorite green dimity dress from last year that seemed to have gotten smaller.

Thankfully, the sun already had slipped behind the mountains, and the fresh air cooled her face and neck. She dabbed at her upper lip and picked up her pace. She lifted her head and saw Jedediah walking toward her.

He tipped his hat, slowing his steps. "Evening, ma'am. Going to a fire or running from someone?" he asked with a sardonic grin.

"Don't jest with me," she scolded, suddenly feeling strange. She pulled her shawl tighter about her, and marched right past him, her heels ringing against the boardwalk.

Jedediah paused with his hands on his hips and stared at her stiff-backed form receding down the boardwalk. Snubbing him only confirmed that something he'd said or done had upset her. *Probably didn't like me joking about her evening with Cowboy not going like she'd hoped.*

He went on his way, walking through the small town as he did every evening. Wallace Street still had folks coming and going about their business. He liked his job of keeping order and peace in Nevada City, knowing winter meant the number of miners would dwindle due to the cold and snow. That's when he would catch up on his reading and paperwork, or clean his collection of guns, or keep up his target practice.

He'd only walked a few steps when he heard a thump from behind. He spun around to see Patience crumpled on the boardwalk. He was at her side in two shakes.

"Can't . . . breathe . . . can't . . . ," she barely whispered, and she fumbled with the buttons on the front of her bodice. Her face was pale and glistening in the moon rising behind them.

Mumbling a mild curse, Jedediah did the only thing he knew to do for someone with the vapors. He whipped out his bowie knife and quickly slit the tight cords holding the front of her lace corset together. Patience took a deep breath, and the color began returning to her face.

He took the shawl bunched up behind her

back and covered her delicate white skin. He scooped her up in his arms, muttering, "Why do women wear such contraptions?" He did not expect a reply, but he noticed how she'd naturally slipped her arms around his neck.

"I . . . just . . . wanted . . ." But her voice drifted away.

"Don't say anything more, Patience." He strode quickly toward the Creekside Inn, conscious of townspeople staring with open mouths as he stalked past. Reaching the inn, Jedediah shoved open the front door with a kick of his boot. He carried her over to the couch, gently laying her down, and placed a needlepoint cushion under her head for support. She opened her eyes long enough to gaze up at him in disbelief and embarrassment.

He stood a moment looking down at her. "I think you'd better get back to bed. That concussion has affected you more than you realize." He turned on his heel and walked out into the night.

Moments later, Jedediah saw Cody and Emily in conversation in front of the Longhorn. Well, what was it? Was this Cody attracted to Emily too? Maybe the cowboy was the kind of man that liked to keep the ladies guessing. Jedediah was painfully reminded of years before, when he was younger and better looking and the woman he'd planned to marry had jilted him. He'd never gotten over it. *Reason enough to remain a bachelor,* he thought as he kicked an errant stone out of his way. Which is why it disturbed him that Patience crept into his daily thoughts lately.

He touched the tip of his hat to a couple who walked past. Cody eyed him and Emily said, "Good evening, Marshal."

No doubt they were heading back to Creekside where they both were staying. "Evening, ma'am. If you're heading back to the inn, you might want to check on Patience."

Cody frowned. "She said she wasn't feeling well at supper and left before dessert. I fear that concussion is worse than she thought."

"Maybe," he said tersely.

Emily held up her skirts and hurried toward the boardinghouse. "I'll go see to her."

Jedediah continued on his way, keeping an eye out for any indication of trouble. He was grateful he didn't have to separate a drunk or two tonight. He'd had more than a handful of difficulties already, and grinned wryly at the memory of scooping a woman up in his arms . . . for the second time in a week.

Before '65, he knew, the only law in the territory had been miners' law. By the time he'd arrived as marshal, the town had drastically reduced in size due to the stripping of placer gold from the Alder Gulch strike. It was dark now as he approached his office, and he glanced up at the full yellow moon. A peculiar loneliness swept over him. Shaking off the feeling, he trudged the last few steps to spend yet another night in his dismal, cramped room above the jailhouse. Except now he was haunted by the memory of Patience's soft, limp body against his chest.

After a night of tossing and turning, Jedediah rose, washed his face, and slipped on his jeans and shirt. He stared back at his face in the small mirror above the pitcher and basin. *How could anyone love this face?* he wondered. He shook his head crossly. What was Cody's purpose in Nevada City? He'd ask around about this cowboy today, see what he could find out. He pulled on his boots, and made for the stairs.

By the time his boots hit the last step, he saw Hannah through the glass door front, her usual basket on her arm. He moved to the door, reached over to unlock it, and the lady sauntered in, full of vim and vigor.

"Good night, woman! Can't a man wake up first before you deliver breakfast?" he growled.

"My, my — aren't we grouchy this morning?" she teased as she placed the basket on his desk. "I can't stay but a minute or two before I need to open up the bakery."

Not a minute too soon, he groused silently. He went to light a fire in the potbellied stove while she assembled the coffeepot, filling it with water and coffee. She brought it over and placed it on the stove.

Jedediah had a moment's regret for his dark mood. He actually appreciated that she was comfortable being with him like a mother. He noticed the prominent blue veins on the back of her arthritic hands. No doubt they'd seen a lot of hard work in her lifetime.

She waited for the coffee to boil. "I wasn't sure if Patience was going to be bringing you her delicious biscuits or not."

"Unlikely, since she's not cooking right now. But those biscuits were merely a peace offering anyway. Nothing more." Now the woman was starting to get under his skin again.

Hannah moved to the other side of his

desk and sat down, much to his dismay. "Mmm . . . Well, what I really wanted to ask was, who were those wildflowers for — Patience?" Her eyes twinkled and she pursed her lips together, waiting.

He sighed. "They were, but I thought better of it. Did you hear that she fell off a ladder?"

Hannah sucked in a breath. "Oh, no, I hadn't heard. Goodness gracious — was she hurt?"

"A mild concussion, says the doc. She had no business being at the top of a ladder, trying to paint her place on her own." Smells of coffee filled the room, and he walked over to the stove to slide the cast-iron lid over the grate, then pushed the pot to one side to stay warm.

Hannah harrumphed. "Well, I call that mighty industrious for a young lady," she said, rising and bustling over to the stove with a mug. "She's being a responsible new owner for the boardinghouse. I tell you, I do miss her grandmother. Sometimes she'd come to the bakery for a dessert, and we would chat over a cup of coffee. Seemed like a fine lady, and so is Patience." She handed the mug to him.

He plopped down in his chair behind the desk, took a sip of the hot brew, then pulled the basket over and selected a biscuit. He closed his eyes and savored the first bite.

"So, why were you taking her flowers in the first place?" Hannah had returned to the seat across from him.

"Miss Hannah —" he blew out a long breath — "can't you leave it alone? There's really nothing to tell, other than I saw the flowers as I was on my way to pay her for the boxed lunches."

"And?" She cocked a brow.

I also cut her corset strings with my knife last night. But it wouldn't do to add that detail. "Patience was otherwise engaged with some cowboy called Cody, so I didn't want to interrupt." He wrapped his hands around the steaming mug. "Want a cup? Help yourself."

She shook her gray head. "No, I've had my morning coffee. You've hardly given her a chance, don't you think? How do you know for certain Cody's sparkin' her?"

Jedediah laid his second biscuit back down. "Chance for *what*? Did I say I was interested in sparkin' her? No, I didn't."

"A man doesn't bring flowers to a lady unless he's interested in her. So why don't you just admit it."

He sighed and, defeated, shook his head. "I did ask if she needed me to take her to supper since the doc told her to take it easy for a few days, but she flat turned me down."

Hannah tsked a response. "I suppose that's your way of answering me about sparkin' her. I declare, Jedediah, you're about as thickheaded as a buffalo. If that's how you asked her, then that's the reason she turned you down. She wanted a real invitation, not you asking if she *needed* to be taken to supper. Don't you get it?" Hannah folded her arms. "A woman wants to be made to feel she's special in some way."

He let her words sink in a minute. *So that's why she rebuffed me last night?* "Listen, Miss Hannah, I don't even know if she's all that special —"

"Well, you're not gonna find out if you don't spend some time with her. Tell you what, there's a barn dance next Saturday night at the Hargroves'. Everyone's welcome. Why don't you ask her to go with you?"

Jedediah now remembered that Frank Finney had mentioned the Hargrove dance to him last week. He cleared his throat. "I'm not sure she has any interest in knowing me any better than making boxed lunches for my crew."

Hannah picked up the empty basket. "I

see customers lining up waiting for me to open," she said, peering out the window. "As my late husband used to say, 'Wanderin' around like a pony with his bridle off don't get you to the end of the trail.' Think on it. I've got to hurry now."

He couldn't help but chuckle as he watched her scurry out the door. He shook his head. "Thanks for the biscuits!" he called out to her retreating form. *And maybe for the advice.*

9

A few days after her fall, Patience was back to her old self, and the bruise on her cheek had turned yellow and green. She tilted her bonnet to help conceal it, along with shading her face from the summer heat. She wanted to make curtains for the parlor, and since it was afternoon, she shouldn't have any trouble getting waited on at the general store.

She still felt chagrin that Emily and Cody had found her lying on the couch in total disarray after she'd collapsed and been rescued by Jed, and she'd had some explaining to do.

Emily had rushed to her side. "Are you all right, Patience?" she cried.

Cody eyed her with curiosity but hung back, and Patience was glad that he hadn't come too close. She finally was able to get herself to a sitting position and pulled her shawl more tightly over her. She patted her hair back into place with as much decorum as she could muster with the two of them staring down at her. Emily had straightened Patience's dress down around her ankles.

"So you really were sick. I was beginning to think it was my company," Cody commented with a little chuckle. "Should I send for the doctor? Is it your head again?"

"I'm going to be fine. I got a little faint, that's all."

"Thank heavens you didn't pass out and hit your head again," Emily said. "One time is quite enough. Is there anything I can get for you? Water?"

Patience waved her hand. "Truly, I feel perfectly fine now."

"Then I'll just be getting on up to my room," Cody said. "If you should need anything, send Emily for me," he said and excused himself.

Patience nodded and murmured her thanks, mortified that any of this had happened at all.

Emily stared at her friend. "Now you can tell me what *really* happened," she said, taking a seat next to Patience.

Making sure Cody was safely out of earshot, Patience explained, "It's all because I was vain enough to think I could squeeze into last year's summer dress."

113

"Don't be so hard on yourself. You look fine to me," Emily answered.

Patience was grateful she didn't laugh at her. "Thank you, Emily. That's what I get for trying to impress Cody."

"You were? I had a notion that you might like Jedediah." Emily arched a brow.

"I do like him, but not in the way you suggest. We can't seem to get along for more than five minutes at a time."

"I see. Well, Cody *is* handsome . . ." Her voice trailed off.

"Yes, and he's already been a big help to me, but I don't think he'll be around much longer."

"Why is that?"

"He's looking for a job, preferably on a ranch. He said he'd move on to the next town if he didn't find work soon."

Emily shrugged. "It would seem to me you'd be more interested in someone with a steady job. I know I would."

"True. However, we can still enjoy his company while he's here, can't we? I noticed he walked you home tonight."

Emily blushed. "Hardly that! I think he followed along because Jedediah told me I'd better check on you."

"He did?"

"Yes. Did he find you when you were sick,

Patience?"

Patience debated on whether or not to tell her what actually happened, then decided there would be no harm it in.

Emily giggled like a schoolgirl after Patience told her that he'd cut the strings of her corset with his knife so she could take a deep breath. "I declare, my friend, you do seem to get tangled into the most unusual situations!"

"See what I meant by being vain? That's what it got me!" They'd both laughed and decided to enjoy a cup of hot chocolate before bed.

Patience was awfully glad she'd become friends with someone close to her own age, someone so *nice.* Finishing her reverie, she stepped inside the general store to make a beeline for the fabric. She enjoyed even its smell as she fingered the bolts of cloth lined up on the table.

She knew what she wanted — something fine and light, suggesting homey comfort to her guests. There was plenty to choose from, and her eyes fell upon a bolt of lovely purple brocade material that would make a beautiful gown for a special event. Patience fingered the beautiful material but sighed. No need for her to wish for something that would be a luxury — at least not until the boardinghouse was thriving.

Near the bottom of the bolts on the table, she spied what might be exactly the delicate cream-colored lace she was looking for. It would be perfect for her parlor, if the price was reasonable. She found matching thread and carried the entire bolt to the counter to wait for a clerk, but they were busy with other customers.

Glancing around, she realized she didn't know any of those milling about the cheerful store, and she suddenly felt a wave of loneliness. All had their own shopping lists and were taken up with finding the items. Since coming to live here, she'd met a few people — a few at church in Virginia City too, though most did not shop in Nevada City. Miners were so transient that every week it seemed new faces appeared . . . and disappeared. She was getting to know Hannah, she mused — but then her thoughts were interrupted by the scrawny clerk who'd waited on her before.

"Can I help you, miss?" His smile broadened in his freckled face, and his red hair curled down into his collar, beads of perspiration dotting forehead and upper lip.

"Yes, please. What's the cost per yard for this fabric?"

He openly stared at her until she wondered if there was something on her face, then remembered the faint bruise. He eventually picked up the end of the bolt and pulled the material away from its end, exposing a tag. "It's fifteen cents a yard."

Patience chewed the bottom of her lip, adding the yardage in her head. She might have enough to pay for it. "I'll take ten yards, then."

"Alrighty, miss." He began to unroll the material, holding it against a yardstick nailed to the counter as his guide. When he finished, he cut the fabric and folded it in half. Looking over the counter at her, he grinned. "There ya go. Didn't I help you last week with paint? In spite of that cowboy?"

"Why, yes — matter of fact, you did."

"My name's Harold. Harold Osborn." He thrust his hand across the counter toward hers and she hesitantly shook it. His palm was damp and his handshake limp.

"Nice to meet you, Mr. Osborn. I'm Patience Cavanaugh, and I run the Creekside Inn. I've only been here a few weeks."

"I'm so glad to know you. Please don't think me bold, but I wonder if someone is taking you to the Hargroves' dance next Saturday?"

117

"I'm sorry, but I know nothing about that."

"You do now. I thought . . . well . . ." His Adam's apple bobbed and his hands shook holding the material. "Maybe you'd like to attend. It's a big affair here every year, and Mr. Hargrove spares no expense. It could be a good way for you to meet some of our town folk, since you're new." He pressed her for an answer while he wrapped her purchases in brown paper and tied the package with twine.

Patience handed him the money. He seemed somewhat younger than her, but not so young that he minded asking her to the dance. He may be a nice man who at least had a steady job, but she felt no appeal for him whatsoever. "I appreciate the invitation, but I hardly know you."

"Then this could be your chance to do that." His freckled face heightened with color.

She picked up the package, not wanting to hurt the young man's feelings. "Thank you, but I must run. I — I have a lot to do." Patience scurried out the door, passing two older ladies who turned to stare after her.

"Maybe I'll see you at the dance," he called.

■ ■ ■ ■

Patience decided she had time for a cup of coffee at The Star Bakery this afternoon. She liked Hannah with her cheery disposition — and the woman seemed to genuinely care about Jedediah. Someone needed to tame him — that was certain. Patience had always been gratified by the fact that she normally was very tolerant, but somehow she became less patient when Jedediah was around.

Hannah was pouring batter into muffin tins when Patience greeted her.

"Good afternoon, Patience," she said, wiping the batter from her fingers. "You look fit as a fiddle, so you must be over that awful fall from the ladder."

"Oh, yes, ma'am, I am. I thought I'd stop in for a cup of coffee and maybe one of your famous cinnamon rolls. I could smell them from the sidewalk."

Hannah reached into the glass case, picking out the largest roll. "Come have a seat and I'll pour us some coffee." She hurried from behind the counter to a small table by the window with the roll on a plate. "I need to slide the muffins in the oven, and I'll be right with you."

Patience took a seat, glancing out the window as she waited. Her heart lurched. Jedediah was across the street chatting with a pretty, dark-haired lady rather flamboyantly dressed for daytime. She wore a large black hat with a tall black feather and a cream bustled dress with black stripes — very stylish but a bit much for Patience's taste. She didn't remember seeing her around before, but then she didn't know everyone in town.

"Here we are." Hannah carried two beautiful rose teacups with steaming coffee over and took a seat opposite her. "Cream and sugar right here if you use it — I like mine black." Hannah followed her gaze beyond the window. "Ah, Jedediah with Millie. She's a widow. I believe her husband left her with a king's ransom, and she lives extravagantly for the likes of Nevada City."

"Mmm" was all Patience said. She added cream and sugar to her coffee, then took a bite of her cinnamon roll. "Delicious, Hannah."

"I'm glad you like it. Jed's favorite, you know."

"No — I didn't know."

"Well, maybe you should get to know him better. He's softer than he comes across."

"I'll believe that when I see it." *Although*

120

he did rescue me from making a fool of myself on the sidewalk.

Hannah laughed. "He needs a woman's gentle touch on his heart, I wager. Maybe he'll ask you to the Hargroves' dance."

"Humph," Patience responded. "I rather doubt that." She wanted to change the subject. "Hannah, did you know my grandmother?"

Hannah put her cup down. "Yes . . . yes I did, and we were good friends. She never had an unkind word to say about anybody. You're a lot like her. Even resemble her."

"I could only hope to be as wonderful as she was. I . . . oh, never mind."

"What, dear?"

"My grandmother was much more like a mother to me than my own." Patience stared down at her coffee.

"How well I know. Your grandmother wondered what she did wrong that your mother turned out to be so self-centered. Oh, I shouldn't have said that." Hannah pursed her lips.

"It's true, so don't worry. You haven't offended me. I do miss my grandmother and wish I could've spent more time with her."

Hannah paused and looked directly at Patience. "A young woman like you should be out there enjoying life, surrounded by

121

friends and suitors!"

"I don't think that'll happen. I'm already twenty-five, and no suitors have come calling."

"I've seen you with Cody. Don't you enjoy his company?"

"We're friends, that's all." She glanced outside again and saw Jedediah parting from Millie.

"Are you sure you're not interested in Jed? I've seen how you look at him." Hannah lifted a brow.

Patience's heart fluttered. "Even if I was, he doesn't seem interested in me."

"Oh, no, dear — that's just Jed's way. I've told him by the time he makes his mind up to do something, it's always too late. I think his self-confidence suffers. You're younger and attractive, and he thinks you wouldn't like him that way."

"Attractive? *Me?*" Patience was flabbergasted. No one had ever told her — that she could recall — not her mother, or even Russell. "Uh, well . . . thank you."

"Of course! Don't you ever look in the mirror?"

"I don't like what I see. I think I carry more weight than I should for my height. I mean — well, look at Emily." Patience frowned.

"Humph! Don't compare yourself to others. It's what's on the inside — in your heart — that matters. None of us are perfect. We are only made complete when we rest in the Good Lord. If Jedediah asks you to the dance, why not give him a chance?"

"Where is the dance?"

"The Hargroves' place. They throw one every year, and —"

"Maybe, but I should be going," Patience said, standing to her feet. "I have to get supper started. I have a number of boarders now, and it's keeping me pretty busy."

Hannah stood with her. "What do you do in your spare time, Patience?"

"I read or sew . . . and I'm writing a collection of devotional readings."

"You don't say? That's wonderful, and I'm sure the Lord appreciates it. But don't neglect to have a little fun in life. It's all over too soon." Her eyes misted and she walked Patience to the door. "Think about what I said."

"I will." She leaned over, giving Hannah a quick hug, then handed her coins for the roll and coffee. "I hope to see you again soon."

Patience hurried back to the boardinghouse, contemplating what Hannah said. If

Hannah thought she was attractive, could Jedediah think so too?

10

Nodding at a few customers, Jedediah strode inside the general store looking for Benny Foster, the store owner. The man smiled when he saw him. "Be with you in a few minutes, Marshal," he called with a little wave, turning back to the customer he was serving.

Jedediah folded his arms and leaned against a big barrel by the front door. From where he stood he could see Patience hurrying up the walk, her head held high and her homespun bonnet shading most of her face. *Quite a contrast from Millie's fancy do and hat,* he mused. He wondered if Patience had ever owned anything as . . . well, as nice. Probably not. He admired how determined she'd been the last few weeks — running the boardinghouse and sprucing it up, trying her best to make a go of it.

His heart couldn't help but soften as he thought about her. Where was her family?

I'll ask her to the dance, first chance I get.
'Course, Millie would be an easier one to ask, but he'd never felt his heart go all mushy over that one.

"Sorry to keep you waiting, Marshal," Benny said at his side.

"No problem," he said, pitching his voice low. "I want to ask you if you know anything about that new fella around town, Cody."

"Can't say that I do. Seen him a couple o' times, and noticed him painting Miss Patience's boardinghouse. He's friendly enough, but mostly keeps to himself, far as I can tell." Benny rubbed his bearded jaw.

"That's what the blacksmith told me. This Cody keeps his horse stabled there. No one seems to know where he came from."

"He in some trouble?"

"Not that I know of. Well, I best get out of your way so both of us can get back to work." The two men grinned at each other, and Benny walked him to the door.

"I'll let you know if I hear anything," Benny said as he held the door.

Jedediah nodded. "Appreciate it." He left, his mind toying with why Cody stayed in Nevada City. The man didn't have a job, and no one seemed to know where he came from. Jed gave his head a shake. He'd just have to keep his eyes peeled for any signs of trouble in the making. He'd developed what he figured was sort of a sixth sense about people through years of law work, and something definitely rubbed him wrong about Cody . . . besides his flirting with Patience.

While supper simmered on the stove, Patience slipped out to the front porch to her rocker, hoping for a cooling breeze. The kitchen was always warm, even with all the windows open. She unfastened the button at her throat and loosened her collar, glancing over at Cody finishing up the last of the painting on the front railing.

Soon she might have to hire someone else to help her with the workload, she concluded as she fanned her face with a discarded *Montana Post.* She now had eight residents, give or take one or more on any given week. There was room for only four more. *Hmm.* An idea for the help she needed popped into her mind. *Cody isn't going to want to change beds and do laundry, but maybe there* is *someone else . . .*

She fanned harder as she watched him work. "Cody, why don't you take off that big neckerchief and loosen your shirt?" she suggested. "I don't know how you stand the awful heat today."

"I'm used to it," he told her. "The necker-chief catches the sweat. Besides, I'd feel funny without it."

Patience shook her head. "Whatever you say. I do like the fresh white paint on the railing. Everything looks so clean now. Thank you for all you've done. I do appreciate it."

"I have an idea for how you can thank me, Miss Patience," he said, lifting a foot to the edge of the porch. "I'd like to take you to the dance Saturday night. What do you say? Would you care to go with me?"

Patience stopped rocking. When he grinned at her like that, the man was most charming. She recalled Hannah's words — yes, she needed to get out and have a little fun. "All right, Cody, I'd love to go. I think it will be . . . will be rather enjoyable," she finished primly, her cheeks feeling even warmer than the sun was making them.

He grinned and went back to his painting. "Good, that's settled then, 'cause tonight is my last night. I got a job today as a ranch hand."

"Congratulations, Cody!" she said with genuine admiration. "I know you're tired of these little odd jobs of mine." But she did briefly wonder once more how she'd get everything done that needed doing. And did this mean he'd no longer be boarding with her?

"Not a problem, Patience. Your assignments gave me something to do until a job came my way. Glad I got the painting done." He was brushing the last rungs of the railing.

"Well, I am grateful, all the same." She rose from the rocker. "It's about time for supper. You'd better clean the paintbrushes," she said over her shoulder, a twinkle in her eye, as she reached the door. "That is — if you're planning on eating here tonight."

"I think I'll do both — clean the brushes and eat here — since it's my last night. Be there in a few minutes."

So I guess he will be staying out at the ranch, she concluded as she went back to the kitchen, fastening once again the top button of her shirtwaist collar. She wasn't sure how she felt about that.

Some evenings the residents enjoyed a game of checkers or a chat with other boarders in the parlor. Patience liked the lively conversation. It was good to have laughter and more people in the house. It all kept her from feeling so alone. However, she wasn't able to sit there at her desk with so many of them

129

in the room tonight, so she excused herself to go to her room with her Bible and notebook before it got very late. Emily was close behind, acknowledging how tired she was.

As she and Emily walked upstairs, Patience dropped her notebook. Emily hurried to pick it up for her, but held it open, staring at the page. " 'Seeking to Forgive Others,' " she read out loud. "What are you writing, my friend? A book?"

Patience smiled and gave a little shrug. "Something like that. I'm working on a collection of my thoughts that I call *Devotional Readings for Every Day.*" She watched as Emily continued to read silently.

"This is really good, Patience. I'm impressed." Emily handed her the notebook.

"Thank you. I try to write one every few days, when I can. I don't know what I'll do with them, though," she said as they continued down the hallway.

Emily paused in front of Patience's door. "Well, I have an idea. My uncle works for a publishing house in New York. I'll help you get them to him."

Patience laughed. "I don't think he'd be interested in publishing devotionals by someone he's never heard of — and a woman at that. But I have to admit, Emily,

I hope to get them published someday."

"Then you will. Let me know when you've written as much as you intend for the collection, and we'll mail it off."

"You really think he'd take a look at them?" Patience swallowed, butterflies spreading in the pit of her stomach.

Emily smiled. "With a little bit of persuasion from me, I think so. I'm his favorite niece."

"Do you have a few minutes, before you retire? I'd like to talk to you about something that's been on my mind."

"Of course. I'd probably only lie in the bed counting sheep anyway. The main thing I really wanted was to get off my feet."

"That's good. Come with me then." Patience unlocked her bedroom door and motioned Emily inside.

"Please, sit here." Patience pointed to the overstuffed chair, then turned her desk chair around to face her friend. "As you know, I'm continuing to get more boarders, and I'm almost full to capacity — a lot to handle on my own. I've been thinking . . . well, I've seen how hard you work and your long hours at the Longhorn, and I'm wondering if you'd like to come to work for me. I haven't thought through all the details yet, but we could split the chores —"

"Are you sure?" Emily's face lit up with a smile. "I thought you wouldn't be able to hire anyone right now. I don't want to put any further strain on —"

"No strain at all," she quickly assured her friend. "With more boarders, and the little extra I get paid for doing the marshal's boxed lunches, I'm doing pretty well presently."

Emily reached over to grab her hands. "Then I accept gratefully!"

"If it all works out, maybe I can make you an equal partner, if you're interested."

Emily clapped her hands. "Oh my, Patience! I hope we can. I think we'd enjoy working together."

"I think so too." Patience smiled back. "I hope you don't mind my asking, but you mentioned an uncle. Wasn't he in a position to give you a job or at least let you live with him and his family?" Emily visibly stiffened and Patience rushed on to say, "I'm sorry. It's really none of my business."

"It's a long story. Perhaps sometime I'll share it with you." Emily stood. "But it's getting late, and I need to get to bed. I'll give the restaurant my notice tomorrow, but I'll work there the full day. They won't have any trouble finding a replacement. Every day we have someone coming in, looking for a waitress position. Mostly miners' wives. If they don't yet have little ones, they hope to make a bit of extra until their husbands strike it rich." Both women chuckled, and Patience walked her to the door.

"I'm so glad you accepted, Emily. I think we can put our heads together soon and work out an arrangement of the daily schedule that suits both of us. And I think we'll both have a little more free time. For now, I'll match the wage you're earning at Longhorn's. Then later, I hope to be able to increase it — as soon as I can."

Emily suddenly was sniffling tears away, and she wrapped her arms around her new employer. "Thank you. You won't be disappointed," she whispered.

Patience hugged her back. "I'm sure I won't. Now run along and get your beauty rest. Not that you need any," she added with a laugh.

While Patience changed into her nightgown, she wondered if Emily would tell her more about her background . . . maybe about the uncle too. Patience wanted to be sure the publisher was reputable and would appreciate her writing.

Jedediah saddled Charlie and headed out to John Hargrove's ranch, the Cross Bar, glad to leave behind the overcrowded town on this warm summer day. It was always refreshing to quietly ride alone, though his eyes automatically scanned the surrounding woods for any sign of movement. Somebody had stolen Hargrove's cattle, he had found out just this morning. But he was sure whoever it was wouldn't have hung around — either driving the herd on to the nearest town and railroad or hiding them in a coulee. But where?

Today he'd try to gather some clues about it. He wanted to discover the rustler before he — or he and his cohorts — hit other ranches.

The Cross Bar was one of the larger ranches by comparison to others in the area. John Hargrove was one of the first in the territory and had a decent head of cattle and ranch hands to help run it. He and his wife, Judith, had invited him over to supper once — *as much to get on my good side as anything else,* Jedediah thought with a wry grin. Like now — John was expecting immediate capture of the rustlers and retribution. Well, so much for wishful thinking.

Jedediah knew all there was to know about road agents — enough pilfering of homesteaders and rustling to last him a lifetime. And he also knew it was unlikely that anything would be settled anytime soon . . . if ever.

Cow dogs, barking loud enough to raise the dead, ran to meet him after he secured Charlie and sauntered up the lane to the ranch house. He saw John's wife walk out onto the porch steps, shading her eyes with her hand.

"How do, Miz Judith. John around?"

Jedediah knew John had done himself a favor by marrying Judith. Not only was she a pretty woman, he found her to be just as sweet as she was pretty. And now that she was with child, he could've sworn she was even prettier. *Will I ever be lucky enough to have a wife that looks like that?* All he knew was that he wanted someone in his life with whom he could share the day's events, accomplish things together, and if he was fortunate, appreciate a lot of cuddling. He'd never had much of that in his life growing up. He figured that's why he had a harder edge to him. *Human touch matters a lot . . . a whole lot.* Which he of course wouldn't say aloud.

"Hello, Jedediah. Why don't you come up here in the shade? That sun is powerful hot today," Judith told him as he approached the porch.

"Thanks, but I wanted to speak with John

if I could. Do you know when he'll be back?" Jedediah was hoping he'd be close by. Although he'd enjoyed the ride alone, he would hate to have made a trip all the way out here for nothing.

"He didn't say, but I don't think he's too far down the property. Probably toward the south," she said, pointing. "He and a couple of ranch hands are out checking for any breaks in the fence line. Has anyone else had trouble with the cattle thieves?" she asked, stepping back under the protection of the porch's roof.

"No, ma'am. Not that I know of yet. I'll mosey on in that direction, but if I don't catch up with him, will you let him know I stopped by?"

She nodded with a sweet smile. "I surely will. Come back and have supper again soon now. Particularly if you have news on the rustlers." She laughed, and Jedediah turned away with a smile and a wave.

He had gone a couple of miles and was about to nudge Charlie back toward town when he spied John and his men. A couple of ranch hands stood next to a fence post, rewiring a section of the barbed wire, and John was still on his horse. Jedediah called out to him, and John waved his hat in greeting. He pulled up alongside the other man's horse.

"Hope you're here to tell me you've found the rustler," John grumbled in greeting.

"I haven't yet, but I'm wondering if I could ask you and your men a few questions. It might be helpful," Jedediah said. The ranch hands stood about, listening.

John was chewing on a wad of tobacco and spit a long string on the ground. "Ask away."

"Were any of your men around that night when the cattle went missing?" He looked at the group of rugged cowboys. A couple of them shook their heads and two others answered yes.

"Where were you two at the time?" he asked them directly.

One of them, a shaggy mustache and beard hiding his mouth, shifted on his feet. "Both of us was up at one of the line shacks on the other end of the prope'ty."

Jedediah directed his gaze to the other two. "Did you see anything unusual about the time you heard the shots? The ones John said were fired?"

"Can't say I noticed anything," a younger fellow answered. "Did you, Bob?" he asked, turning to his companion.

Bob squinted his eyes. "You know, 'fore I

heard the shot and the cattle scattered, I noticed a flash of blue color — maybe the man's shirt?" He scratched his chin. "I thought it was mighty purty for a man to be wearin'. But other than that, it was dark enough I ain't sure he had somebody helpin' him or not."

The other guys guffawed and one crowed, "That flash o' blue was prob'ly the lights in your brain from when you fell off that high-strung stallion the other day!" There was another round of laughter and elbow poking.

"All right now — cut out the shenanigans," John commanded sternly.

Jedediah filed the information away. "Were the shots, then, only fired from one direction?"

The younger man answered, "I believe so, Marshal."

"Thanks for answering a few questions. Appreciate your time." Jedediah nodded at the men.

"Jed, why don't you stay for supper? I'm sure Judith would like to see somebody else's face across the table — hear what's happening in town," John said.

"I'd like to, but maybe some other time, John."

"You got it. Let me know if anything

develops."

"I will." He swung Charlie around. "By the way, where was Monty during all the ruckus?"

"You'd have to ask him. He rode over to Virginia City this morning."

"Sure enough, next time I see him." Jedediah galloped off, leaving the men to get on with stretching barbed wire.

Monty must've been off seeing a lady friend. *At least he has one.*

11

The summer heat built to near sweltering during the day, and thunderclouds slowly formed over the dusty town. Patience and Emily had the windows wide open to catch any cooler breeze that might happen along.

"I do smell rain in the air, and it will be a welcome relief from this heat," Patience noted with a glance outside. She and Emily were at the dining room table going over the list of boardinghouse tasks.

"I agree. The only good thing about summer in Montana is that it usually cools down after dark." Emily was copying the list in longhand for her personal use. "I'm not much of a cook, but I can make beds and dust," she said, glancing again at the list.

Patience laughed. "And I'd much rather be baking, although the kitchen is not the place to be with the heat like it is."

"I've heard nothing but compliments from

boarders when it comes to your cooking, Patience. Maybe some of it will rub off on me." Emily smiled, tapping her pencil against her cheek. "We could both do the shopping for the pantry."

"Good idea. That way we can have a respite from our usual work. I plan to start cutting the fabric for the parlor curtains this afternoon. Do you sew, Emily?"

"I've done some, but I'd be glad to learn more from you."

"After I get the curtains done, I want to rearrange the furniture — what little we have. I've been squirreling away money to save for one or two more dining room chairs. You can help me decide what will go well in that room."

"I'd enjoy that. What we need is music! Music is great entertainment — perhaps a piano."

"Now hold on there a minute." Patience giggled. "One thing at a time. I doubt I'll ever have enough money for such an extravagance."

"I'd love to learn to play the piano. It's possible that we could find a used one. Oh!" Emily clapped in her excitement. "We could sing Christmas carols and place ivy and candles all around the parlor, have an old-fashioned Christmas party —"

"Decorating the room, yes, but a piano?" Patience inserted quickly. "I'm afraid that's out of the question for a very long time."

"Do you know how to play a piano?"

Patience closed the writing tablet. "Oh, yes. My mother insisted that I learn, and I hated it at the time, but I learned to love it. I like singing too. Do you like to sing?"

"Yes —"

The doorbell chimed, and Emily pushed her chair back and went to answer the door. A few moments later she called from the hallway, "Patience, you have a visitor."

Patience reached up to pat her hair into place, hoping she was presentable. *Too late to remove my apron. Perhaps another boarder?*

"Is this a bad time?" Jedediah said as he removed his hat and walked into the room. "Looks like you're working."

Patience had stood to her feet. "Hello, Jedediah. No, it's not a bad time. We were just finishing. Is there something I can do for you? Are you about to hit the trail again?"

"No, not yet, though I may have a posse rounded up in a few days . . ." He didn't explain further.

"Are you interested in a room?" Patience teased. Of course she knew the answer to

142

her question.

He chuckled. "No, no I'm not. But it does sound better than the cot upstairs above the marshal's office. I'm afraid my position doesn't pay well enough for such a nice place as you have here, though."

This was a more courteous, amenable tone than what Patience was using to hearing from him. "Won't you have a seat, then?"

He pulled out a chair and placed his hat on the table.

Patience caught Emily's glance from Jedediah to her and gave her a little nod.

"Would you care for some refreshment?" Emily quickly offered, making to move toward the kitchen. "A cup of coffee or tea perhaps?"

"Don't mind if I do. Coffee sounds good, if you have some ready."

Emily smiled and told him they did. She slipped past them to the kitchen.

"Now, Jedediah," Patience said, cocking her eyebrow, "if it's not boxed lunches and not a room you need to rent — or some crime I'm guilty of — what brings you here this afternoon?" She began clearing the paperwork and pencils to make room for their coffee. She hoped he knew she was only teasing.

Jedediah leveled a gaze at her for a moment. "Not cattle thieves, I can assure you."

"Well?" The word hung in the quiet air except for the ticktock from the clock in the parlor.

"I came to ask you to the Hargrove dance on Saturday," he blurted out, his mustache twitching and his gaze skittering away in the direction of the big china hutch.

Her breath caught and she mourned silently. If she'd only known he might ask, she never would have accepted Cody's invitation! "I'm so sorry," she began slowly, but then her words stumbled over each other. "I have — have already been asked. I have an escort for the dance. But I do thank you." He had turned back to face her, and their eyes seemed to lock. Why was he looking at her like that? *Say something . . . anything.*

He cleared his throat as Emily returned with the three cups on a tray.

"I brought us a couple of sugar cookies also," she said cheerfully. She eyed Patience with an arched brow, her expression asking what was happening. But Patience avoided Emily's gaze and held the plate of cookies over to Jedediah, who merely shook his head. Emily gave them each a cup and sat down again.

Trying to break the silence, Patience told

him, "Emily is my partner for the boarding-house. She's already proved to be an asset."

"And I'm excited about working here and thrilled Patience made me a partner." Emily bit into her sugar cookie around a smile.

Jedediah grunted and took a long drink of coffee. "Then it's the restaurant's loss, for sure." He looked over the rim of his cup at Patience. "I thought money was tight right now."

Ah — there was the suspicious man she knew. "Not that it's any of your concern, Jedediah," she answered tartly, "but I have nearly a houseful of boarders now, and that's helped a great deal."

A rumble of thunder sounded outside.

Jedediah's jaw muscle twitched. "Good to know you're making a go of it, Patience." He downed the rest of his drink, then stood, reaching for his hat. "Better get on my way now. Sounds like we might be in for a storm."

"I'll show you out," Patience offered. "Emily, will you clear the table so we can cut the fabric?"

"Yes, of course. Goodbye, Marshal." He murmured a goodbye and followed Patience to the door. When she opened it, rain was beginning to fall, and people hurried up and down the boardwalk for shelter. Jedediah gave off a pleasant scent of leather and shaving soap as he walked past her. She couldn't remember him ever being so quiet.

"I do hope I will see you at the dance," she said quickly, "and I did mean it when I thanked you for thinking of me."

He paused at the doorway, and his nearness unnerved her. "Don't mention it." He donned his hat and pulled up his collar against the rain and wind. "By the way, who's the lucky man?"

"Cody," she answered. "He — he asked me just this week." *What's wrong with me?* she thought, licking dry lips. But she knew it was his penetrating eyes that now held a softness she didn't know he was capable of.

"Then tell Cody that you're saving a dance for me!" He turned and strode into the storm.

That last comment to Patience was forced, and Jedediah tried to rein in his disappointment as he headed up the boardwalk to his office in the downpour. He'd worried all morning about asking Patience to the dance, planned what he might say, imagined her response, and had finally gotten up the nerve to ask her. He felt foolish now. He walked with his Stetson pulled forward, head down, to avoid the worst of the stinging rain in his face. And so it was he walked smack-dab into Millie, who was fighting to open her umbrella in the wind but getting drenched in the process.

"Sorry, Millie! Here, let me help you," he said, steadying her by the elbow.

"Jedediah! We meet again. I declare," she said, still struggling with the umbrella. "This thing is stuck — just plain hard to open."

Jedediah took it in hand and in a second had popped the umbrella up and held it over her. "It won't do you much good now with all this blowing wind." He avoided looking at her soggy dress clinging to her shapely form.

"Thank you so much, Marshal. Please, won't you step inside Hannah's and have a cup of coffee with me? Let's get out of this miserable storm."

"I'd love to, Miss Millie, but not this time," he said as he passed the handle of the umbrella to her. He paused a moment, then looked under the edge of the umbrella into her face. "Uh . . . but since we meet again, would you care to go to the Hargrove dance with me? That is if you don't already have an escort. I'm a bit late asking . . ." Maybe this way he could keep an eye on Cody and get his chance to dance with

147

Patience. Besides, Millie was a good-looking woman. Maybe Patience would notice, wish she was the one on his arm.

"Well, Jedediah, I'm flattered." Millie was dabbing raindrops from her face. "Yes, I'd love to go with you. I wouldn't miss all that fun and frivolity." She batted her eyelashes, her brown eyes full of merriment.

He pulled his collar up higher. "Good! I'll let you get outta this rain before you get washed away."

"Yes, let's do that. See you soon." She hurried on her way, leaving him wondering if asking her to the dance had been that good of an idea.

Back at his office, he ran upstairs, toweled off, and quickly changed. He spread his wet clothes across the foot of the bed to dry. He smacked his wet hair down, trying to tame the waves. He hadn't many clothes, but he took out his black coat to examine it for moth holes. About the only time he wore it was to church — the few times he went. There was a small hole near the first button, where some type of bug had eaten through. Hopefully, if he wore a dark shirt underneath maybe it wouldn't be noticeable. He heard the door open below, so he left his coat hanging on the wardrobe to air out and went down to the office.

" 'Bout time you showed your purty face, Jed." Joe peered over at him from the doorway, dressed in his usual — dungarees caked with mud on bowed legs tucked into the tops of heavy boots, and a beat-up old hat folded back along the front brim. He also dripped water all over the floor.

"Now, Joe, I know you just walked in 'cause I heard the door open. What's up?" Jedediah eyed him for signs of liquor, but decided he was sober for now.

"Not much, really. Got tired o' working on the claim that's 'bout near petered out. I'll either have to move on or call it quits — which at my age is sounding better 'n better all the time." He pulled on his long gray beard, looking like his mind was somewhere else.

Jedediah chuckled. "You know you're not about to leave this town, Joe. You've threatened me with that before."

Joe snorted. "There's a possibility I'd stay if I had a good woman for those long winter nights."

"You? Aren't you a bit long in the tooth for such?"

Joe rolled his eyes. "Not long as I can still breathe, I ain't! What about Hannah at the bakery? She's a nice looker and a widder to boot. She's prob'ly thinkin' 'bout next winter too —"

"You don't stand a chance, Joe, unless you can clean up your act. How 'bout a cup of java?"

Joe licked his lips and Jedediah wondered if he was considering something stronger. "Guess I could manage a cup."

"You know that other stuff is going to rot your gut, don't you?" Jedediah looked him square in the eyes.

"Now don't you go to preaching at me. I ain't got a whole lot to live for in the first place. Or nobody." He shuffled over to the coffeepot, dripping water behind him.

Jedediah knew the man's past — how he'd lost his family to an Indian attack on the Bozeman Trail west. Joe had never talked about it to anyone but him. How he'd earned that trust, Jedediah wasn't sure. "Oh, come on now. Don't go feeling sorry for yourself." He took the coffee mugs from Joe and filled them from the pot. The rain continued hitting the tin roof with loud pings. *A dismal day indeed,* he thought, handing one cup to Joe.

"You gonna go to the dance with that purty Miss Patience?" Joe asked over the brim.

"No . . . no, I'm not — at least not with her. I'm going with Millie. What about you?"

Joe grinned. "I reckon a man don't need a lady to show up at a dance the whole town's invited to." He drained his mug.

"If that's your plan, then you'd better clean up some."

Joe rubbed his jaw thoughtfully. "Well, I might give my beard a trim."

Jedediah knew it was going to take a whole lot more than a beard trim to get Hannah to give Joe a second glance.

12

The heavy rain had washed away the dust from the boardwalk. However, the streets were now a muddy mess, Patience noted as she looked down from her bedroom window. She could have sworn she heard a faint crying, like an animal in distress. Donning her robe, she decided she'd check out the sound before she put the coffee on. She knew some of her boarders left at daybreak, but others would be eating here before going about their usual business. The Burtons, Liza and Will, slept in, as lovebirds will do, but came down for the breakfast that Patience kept warm on the sideboard for any late risers.

The sound was louder by the time Patience got to the door, but when she opened it and looked around, she didn't see anything but the usual daybreak activity. As she turned back, she spied a little creature behind her rocking chair at the far end of the porch — a young yellow tabby cat, its fur soaked and paws caked with mud. "Where in the world did you come from?" Its meowing grew louder, and Patience reached down to pet the cat. The meowing stopped, replaced by a loud purring.

"My goodness! Are you hungry? You're as light as a feather," she said, scooping up the yellow ball of fur. She was glad she had donned her apron before she stepped outside. "I wonder where you belong? It sure looks like you're all alone in the world, like me. Why, you're so yellow I think I'll call you Buttercup!" The cat snuggled against her elbow. "Let's go inside and get you some warm milk."

After walking back to the kitchen, Patience dried the fur as best she could, set out a small bowl of milk, and watched the cat lap it away in no time before curling up on the floor near the stove. She smiled and decided it was a stroke of luck that the animal had showed up on her doorstep. Buttercup could keep the mice at bay in the rambling house. Besides, she would be a good companion. She hoped the little animal was simply a stray with no home. Humming a tune, Patience concluded it was a fine morning for flapjacks.

"Good morning —" Emily stopped short when she saw the cat by the stove. "What have we here — a new boarder?" She chuckled and bent down to get a closer look at it.

"We do. I kept hearing a noise this morning and found her on the porch." She started making the batter. "She's a mite dirty from all the rain and mud, but after breakfast I'll try to clean her up."

Emily chuckled again, stroking the cat's back. "Cats don't like to be bathed, but we can wipe her down with a wet cloth."

"I've named her Buttercup. What do you think?"

"I like it. Buttercup, welcome to Creekside." Emily stood, then washed her hands. "I'll get the dishes stacked on the sideboard."

"Perfect!" Patience poured nice rounds of batter onto a sizzling griddle. "Emily," she called, "can you turn the pancakes once bubbles begin to form? I'll go up and get dressed before anybody sees me."

She and Emily worked very well together, she thought as she removed her apron and hurried up the stairs. And it was certainly easier to share chores of running the boardinghouse. She would have the afternoon to finish sewing the parlor curtains. Her day was all planned, and she was feeling happy.

Buttercup was lying in the windowsill, soaking up the slanting afternoon sun, while Patience hand-hemmed the last panels of the curtains and Emily ironed the ones already finished.

"Did I tell you that Monty invited me to the dance?" Emily asked.

"No, you didn't tell me. I'm glad you'll be going — at least I'll have someone to talk to besides Cody. I know so few folks in town yet."

Patience glanced up as Emily blew a curl out of her line of vision. "Ironing is making me even hotter than it is outside," she complained.

"We can swap and I'll iron if you'd like."

Emily shook her head. "No, thank you. I couldn't manage a straight hem if I had to, but when you have time I'd like some simple things to try with you looking over my shoulder." She looked up from her work. "I take it Jedediah asked you to the dance when he dropped by."

"Yes, and I was surprised. I — well, actually, I felt a little sorry for him."

"Why on earth would you feel that way? I'm sure it's not the first time he's asked a lady who had to decline — or is it because you'd rather go with him?" Emily placed the iron on its metal plate and stared at her.

"Mmm . . . maybe. I'm not really sure. I

think the manner in which he asked me — not with his normal brashness — appealed to me. By the time he left he was already asking me to save him a dance."

"It's as I said before — he likes you, Patience." Emily lifted a hot iron from the stove and placed the one she'd been using back on the stove to heat. "However, Cody seems very charming," she noted, looking cunningly over at Patience above her ironing.

"I confess that I too think he is handsome. I've been praying the Lord will send the right man my way. I see how Liza and Will are totally absorbed with one another and truly care about each other's happiness, and I feel I'm missing something. Don't you long for that, Emily? I know I do," Patience finished with a sigh.

Emily handed Patience the panel she'd finished and took the next one to be ironed. "Of course I do. I want to have a family someday. I worry that I'll end up a spinster."

"That isn't too likely," Patience hurried to assure her. "But I know what you mean about children. I want little ones to fill my heart and life. A good man of faith can provide the kind of life I hope for, but they are rare here."

"That's true, but neither can we give up."

Emily pressed the last panel as Patience began putting away her sewing supplies.

"I guess that's what's nagging at me. I'm drawn to Jedediah, but I really don't know much about him. He mentions God, so I think he does believe, but there's something he's hiding behind that tough exterior."

"Then you'll have to find a way to get to know him better. The Lord will warn you, tell you, 'Here's the way — walk in it.' "

"I know you're right . . . we'll see." Patience smiled at her friend and motioned toward the couch. "Let's rest for a bit." The two women settled side by side, Patience fanning herself with her handkerchief. "I have something to ask you, Emily, if you don't mind." At Emily's nod, Patience said, "When you spoke of your uncle in New York, I . . . well . . . I got the feeling that something wasn't quite right. If he's so successful, why would he not be able to provide you with a job?"

Emily sighed. "To tell you the truth, there's not much to the story. He was my guardian and very wealthy. I worked as a clerk in my uncle's publishing house, and I could've lived a very opulent life — servants and never having to lift a finger — but after reading about the West, I craved something more that I couldn't explain. Living here seemed like a challenging adventure I needed to see for myself. So here I am." She shrugged.

"Living in a mining town like Nevada City is hard and challenging — certainly very little in comforts or the finer things in life. That must have been a hard decision for you."

Emily pursed her lips together. "In some ways it was, but it was more important to me to see what life had to offer away from the crowded streets of New York. With God's help I survived traveling across the country, and I met some interesting people along the way."

"I'm so glad you did, Emily." Patience reached over to squeeze Emily's hand and saw tears in her eyes.

"So am I, Patience. So am I," she whispered.

"All right, shall we get started on the next part of this endeavor?" Patience carried the panels to the living room window. "Now, let's get the curtains hung, then I'll prepare supper. Or are *you* cooking tonight?" she teased. Emily laughed since their agreement was that Patience would retain the official cooking duties for Creekside.

"Let's see how our handiwork looks," Emily said. "I did help you cut them out, remember, and ironed them up so nicely."

Now they both were laughing. After a few attempts, Patience had the rods over the hooks already attached to the wall, and they slipped the lacey curtains into place and evened out the gathers. They stood back to admire their handiwork.

Patience clapped her hands. "Oh, they're perfect! They give the parlor a cozy, finished feel, don't you think?"

Emily nodded. "It changes the mood of the entire room. Your guests will enjoy relaxing here now — not that they didn't before, but curtains provide a feeling of home."

"Exactly my purpose, Emily."

Emily beamed at her, then hooked her arm through Patience's. Together they marched toward the kitchen in mutual satisfaction.

Jedediah was about to begin his usual night patrol when Joe stomped through the door. "Joe, what are you doing here?"

Joe swayed on his feet as Jed watched the older man's eyes try to focus. "Jed, it's like this . . . ," he said, slurring his words, "I want you to lock me up for the night in a cell . . . think —" he hiccupped — "it's just what I need."

"What the dickens are you yammering on

about?" Jedediah stood with hands on his hips and watched Joe stagger over toward an unlocked cell.

"Go on ahead and lock me in for the night!" Joe hollered. "Can't ya hear?"

"Have you gotten yourself in some trouble tonight, Joe? I haven't seen you like this in a while."

"Well, it's nothin' like that . . . I'm a peaceful guy. You know that." He belched, and Jedediah stepped back, waving his hand at the odor.

"For heaven's sake, Joe!"

"Sorry. Lock yer door." The man hiccupped and swiped a hand over his mouth. "I'm gonna stay th' night till I sober up. My nerves got to me when I commenced to thinkin' 'bout askin' Miss Hannah to that there dance."

Jedediah turned his head away to cover his laughter, then recovered enough to say between chuckles, "Well, that's one way to keep you from the bottle. Are you sure you want me to do this?" He reached for the keys on his desk.

"Sure as that key fits this here lock. Now, do it and go on 'bout your business." Jed swung the cell's door open, and his guest stumbled over to the cot and fell forward on it. He was snoring loudly within moments.

Jedediah was happy to oblige his elderly friend. It was an unusual solution, but maybe it'd work. Jedediah was glad that he never imbibed — he'd seen what it did to many good men, and it was not a pretty sight.

Brilliant rays through the cell window played across the floor and bed, and Jedediah saw the old man's whiskered face twitch. "Rise and shine, old man!" Jedediah called. "I've got your coffee ready."

Joe groaned, then rolled to his side and opened one bloodshot eye. He finally got himself up to a sitting position. He leaned over, head in his hands. "Just let me be for a minute, will ya? My head's a poundin'."

"Nope, we gotta get going, Joe," he said as he opened the cell door. "Here's some coffee that'll help." Jedediah held the mug lower, and the fragrance wafted up into the man's face.

"Yeah," he mumbled, "does smell good." He held out trembling hands, and Jed placed the mug into them. Joe took a sip, then another. "Tastes good too," he added. "Ya got anything in this place ta eat?"

"Nope. If you can pull yourself together,

we can go grab a bite at the café."

"Got yerself a deal, Marshal. Give me a minute or two." Jedediah took his second cup of coffee and waited on the porch.

He loved watching his town spring to life — shopkeepers opening their shades and flipping over their signs to OPEN. He was happier in this mining town, working to keep order, than in any of the places he'd been. Certainly better than traipsing across the country trying to find meaning to his life.

Joe finally walked outside, his face still dripping from his attempts to wash up. "Could we go first over to The Star Bakery?" he asked, avoiding eye contact with Jedediah.

"Why? You want to eat there?"

"No." He looked up at the marshal, then quickly away again. "I want to ask Hannah to the dance, but I need your support."

"Me? Come on, you're a grown man, Joe. I don't think —"

"Maybe so, but I need ya there. Please."

"Well . . ." Jed considered it for a while and grinned. "I guess it'd be a shame to miss out on seeing how this conversation's gonna go — sure, I'll come." He held Joe's arm down the steps.

They walked in silence to the bakery.

Jedediah opened the door to the jingle of the bell. "Go right ahead. I'm right behind you," he said with a sweep of his hand.

Hannah was sliding pans of biscuits in the oven and looked over her shoulder. "Howdy, Jed." She nodded to Joe. "Biscuits are baking now, so you'll have to wait a few minutes for a nice hot one."

Jedediah nudged his friend inside, and Joe straightened his shoulders. "Go ahead," Jedediah told him through barely moving lips.

"Uh . . . mornin', Miss Hannah, . . . uh, we're not here for a biscuit. I . . . uh . . ." Joe turned to look at Jedediah, despair written all over his wrinkled face.

"Well, what is it?" Hannah questioned. "You want something different? I have cinnamon rolls too, but they won't be ready till eight o'clock."

Jedediah walked over to the counter and leaned against it, arms folded, as he watched Joe struggle.

"Naw . . ." Joe removed his hat and nearly wadded it up in his hands. "I wanted to find out — well, I'm askin' if I can . . . escort ya to the Hargroves' dance. Before you say no," he rushed on, "I jus' want ya ta know I'd sure be honored."

"Land o' Goshen!" Hannah exclaimed.

"You reek of alcohol and Lord knows what else. Before I'd even consider it, Joe, you'd have to get yourself cleaned up — in more ways than one."

"I admit I have a drink or two sometimes, but I'm no drunk —"

"Humph!" Hannah put in, arms akimbo on her ample hips.

"So I take it that's not a no?" He gave her a lopsided grin, then glanced at Jedediah.

Jedediah watched Hannah roll her eyes toward the ceiling. "It's not a direct no, Joe — but I expect you to shave, wash up, and find some decent, clean clothes. I know you're not a pauper!"

He looked at her for a moment. "I never had much reason to dress up for nobody before."

"Then you need to change your way of thinkin' and do it for yourself! And last but not least, not a single drop between now and the dance. You think that over when you've got your wits about you again. Now, I've got lots to do this morning, so come back later after you've had a chance to clean up, and we'll talk."

Joe clapped his hat back on his head, smiling broadly. "I'll do that . . . yes, ma'am, I will!"

"Come on, Joe. Let's get out of Hannah's

way," Jedediah said. The two of them left, and once they were out the door, Jedediah clapped his hand on Joe's back. "I'm right proud of you, friend, mustering up the courage. At least she didn't say no."

Joe held out his hands. "Lookee here, Jed. My hands are shakin', and it ain't from no alcohol this time."

"The worst is behind you now, Joe. You'll just have to wait and see what her answer might be. It seemed to me her face went all soft when she was talking to you."

Joe stared back. "Is that right?" He rubbed his jaw, looking incredulous. "Well, I'll be jumpin' Jehoshaphat! I just could have me a chance yet. Let's go eat. My stomach is 'bout to gnaw my backbone —"

"And we've got some work to do before you see Hannah again," Jedediah said. "I imagine we'll have to change the water in the tub a few times." That got a chuckle out of Joe.

Jedediah doubted most of Hargrove's ranch hands even had a suit, but they all tried their best to clean up well in order to impress the young ladies. The one thing he was not comfortable in, though, was his Sunday-go-to-meetin' suit. Comfort to him meant jeans, worn boots, and a flannel shirt with his badge pinned on it. But tonight he'd do his part to follow accepted dress codes. He wrapped a black string tie around his collar, redoing it so it wasn't too tight, put on his Stetson, then stood back to stare at his reflection in the old mirror. Best he could tell, he didn't look too sorry, and with his hat on, one might even consider him good-looking. *At least my mother would,* he told himself with a wry grin.

He couldn't help but chuckle, though, at the face staring back at him. Who was he trying to kid, with his leathery skin the color of bark, and the deep crease between his eyes from frowning at the sun too long? *Let's face it — I'm not a looker. The only reason Millie accepted my invitation was so she could attend the dance.* And if he was honest, the only reason he'd invited her was because he'd been miffed that he hadn't asked Patience before Cody did.

He knew there'd been some murmured rumblings around town about "Millie's past" in Kansas City, but was there anybody in Nevada City that didn't have a past — including him?

He'd stalled long enough. Time he left to get the rig harnessed up and go get Millie.

Millie chatted the entire way to the party,

leaving Jedediah little chance to get a word in edgewise. He didn't really mind, though. He didn't have that much to say anyway.

She wore a bright red gown with a rather daring neckline exposing her creamy neck and shoulders. She carried a shawl, placing it in her lap instead of around her bare shoulders. The dress was startlingly bold, he'd thought when she'd answered the door, and her cheeks held a dusting of rouge, but not too much, he figured. She talked mostly of the places she'd been and the different odd jobs she'd worked.

"So what exactly do you do now, Millie?" he finally ventured when she stopped for a breath. "Why, I thought you knew," she replied, turning to look at him. "I know the rumor has it that I am a wealthy widow, but that's far from the truth. I'm a companion to old Mrs. Brock. She fell and broke her hip. She ain't been right since." She fiddled with the bows on her gown. "But she pays me well, and so she should. Not many could put up with all her demands. It's a pity her husband passed first, I tell you."

He was surprised she spoke so frankly of her employer. "Why's that?"

"Well, he was a darling and had plenty of money from his mine. I think he would have been a lot easier to work for." She shrugged those smooth shoulders. "I don't mean to complain. At least I have decent employment." She moved closer to him on the seat until they were almost touching. "And a handsome man to escort me to the dance." She blinked at him with long, pretty eyelashes.

Jedediah stiffened and swallowed hard, suddenly uncomfortable with Millie's too-close proximity and overly friendly personality. Maybe he'd made a bad judgment call.

He flicked the reins across the horse's back, anxious to get on to the Hargroves'.

13

Music could be heard long before Patience and Cody arrived at the dance. As they drove up in the rig Cody had rented for the event, lanterns glowed in the twilight, and everything looked festive and inviting. Cody ran around the buggy to help Patience step down while she looked around in delight. She was sure she'd never seen so many people at one time or so many horses and buggies arrayed in a row outside the barn.

"Folks from Virginia City were invited too," Cody said, "since not much separates the two towns but a short ride down the road, Mr. Hargrove told me." Cody held out his arm to Patience. "Did I tell you yet that you're looking most lovely tonight, Patience?"

"No, you didn't, but I thank you for saying so." She glanced down at her hand on his arm, feeling a bit awkward since she was not used to receiving compliments.

The Hargroves stood at the entrance to the barn, smiling and greeting each of their guests as they arrived.

"So glad you could come," Mrs. Hargrove said in her genteel, southern drawl. "I'm Judith Hargrove, and this is my husband, John." She held out a gloved hand to gently shake with both Cody and Patience. "And you are the young lady that runs the Creekside Inn, aren't you, my dear?"

"Yes, ma'am, I'm Patience Cavanaugh," Patience answered over a warm handshake from John.

Judith gave her a warm smile. "From what I've heard, you're doing a fine job too!"

"I'd like to think I am," she murmured.

"I'm glad to see you made it back with a woman by your side, Cody," John remarked with a grin at his newly hired ranch hand.

"Yes, sir. I wouldn't miss this dance since it's been said on good authority it's the best in these parts." Cody placed his hand at Patience's back. "Shall we go inside?"

"There's plenty of food and dancing. I hope you young folks enjoy yourselves tonight." Judith motioned them into the barn with a wave of her hand.

"I'm sure we will," Cody replied. Patience quickly caught sight of Monty and Emily dancing and smiled at Emily as she whirled by. The smaller guests were running about the perimeter, entertaining themselves with a game of hide-and-seek, and older ladies managed the refreshment tables, keeping the long tables inside and out filled with an array of delicious food and desserts.

Cody swept Patience out onto the floor. "The food can wait until we kick up our heels, right?"

Patience had never had much opportunity for dancing, but she gamely tried to keep up with Cody. Several dances later, a gentleman with white hair and a big smile stepped over to the little group of fiddlers and called for the crowd's attention.

"Folks, Mac here will rosin up his bow and start to fiddle us a quadrille. Now grab your partner's hand, and let's make up four couples into a square."

"I don't know how to do this dance," a young cowboy called out.

The older man laughed. "You'll get the hang of it — learn as you go."

Patience wasn't sure herself what was about to happen, but Cody led her to a group of three other couples and they all formed the square. *Maybe Cody has done this before,* she hoped. He saw her questioning look and whispered, "Just follow my lead."

Patience heard lots of laughter and clapping from folks standing off to the side, cheering them on. Soon everyone was having a good time just trying to figure out the next steps — or the next "call," as Cody explained to her.

Jim, the caller, slapped his thigh in time to Mac on the fiddle. "Bow to your partner! Now prom-e-nade your partner, boys," he sang out while all the couples stepped around the two lines they'd formed.

"Now swing your partner, round and round," Jim called out in rhythm.

The couples finished the move exchanging partners. Patience found herself holding the new partner's sweaty palms, but she was sure she was more nervous than he was.

"Now allemande left," Jim called above the fiddle's music and the laughing couples who either went the wrong way or fumbled catching their next partner's hands. But Jim smiled and kept right on going. "Do-si-do . . . now back to back." Patience was getting dizzy, overly warm, and confused, but found herself laughing along with the rest of the dancers. She was enjoying herself until she looked across the room and spotted Jedediah. Millie, who was in a bright red dress, was laughing gaily as she held tightly to his arm. She was sort of pretty in an unusual sort of way. Jedediah locked eyes with Patience for a moment before the next dance move required their full attention.

Jedediah was clothed very differently than his usual attire. Tonight a black frock coat and tie, with his hair all slicked down, made him seem rather genteel compared with the rough-and-ready marshal she was used to seeing. Patience missed a step and turned back to Cody and the dance.

Jim was calling out, "Allemande right. Now swing your partner down the middle," as the fiddler kept up the tune. "Now pass through," Jim instructed, grinning at the dancers, and the couples crisscrossed the floor, arm in arm. "Circle right. Now prom-e-nade your partner." Patience enjoyed his singsong style. Despite her nerves, this was the most fun she'd had in a very long time.

After all that, to Patience's surprise the couples ended up with their original partners, and Jim then called the whole dance all over again. After the second set, she and Cody agreed they were both out of breath and in need of a break and something to drink.

Millie kept a firm grasp of Jedediah's arm throughout the evening, even while they were getting their refreshments, and it made him wonder if she was afraid he was going to abandon her. He didn't care all that much for a woman clinging to him tighter than a bat in daylight — seemed too desperate for his liking. Millie might be attractive, but he was beginning to think there wasn't much going on in that space between her ears. All those heavy curls piled nearly to the beams of the barn probably took all her concentration to keep upright. He almost chuckled out loud at the thought.

"What are you smilin' 'bout, Jedediah — or can I call you Jed?" She leaned closer and looked up at him with a come-hither expression.

"Aww, nothing. Just thinking how we were all stumbling around out there on the dance floor. I do hope I didn't step on your toes too much. And, yes, you may call me Jed. Most folks do."

"Oh, I was hopin' it could be my special name for you," she said coyly. When he didn't respond, she added, "Why don't we go have somethin' to eat? Most of the food tables are outside, and it won't be so crowded —"

"Sounds like a good idea to me," Jedediah agreed quickly and escorted her through the crowd. They walked straight into Patience and Cody, coming close to upsetting their plates of food.

"Excuse us," Jedediah said, reaching out to steady Patience's plate. She gave him a smile, then glanced at Millie. *Wonder if Patience is admiring or comparing.* Jedediah wasn't sure.

"No harm done," Cody said. Jedediah noticed the other man's eyes sweep the length of Millie, and he thought she gave the man a friendly smile.

"This is my friend Millie. Millie, these are other friends of mine, Patience and Cody."

"How do you do." Patience nodded without offering a hand since she was holding apple cider in one hand and a plate in the other.

If Jedediah hadn't been on his best behavior, he might have stood stock still at Patience's appearance. Her gown was a lovely green — *Her best color with those eyes,* he thought — trimmed in black at the demure bodice, with black embroidered swirls circling the skirt like feathers. But unlike Millie's more revealing gown, Patience's had long sleeves and an appropriate neckline for both femininity and modesty, as well as nights that were always cool when the sun went down.

"Hello. I enjoy meeting new people," Millie said, barely glancing at Patience but taking the moment to throw Cody a broad smile.

"Are you from around here?" Cody asked. "I don't recollect seeing you in town, Miss Millie."

"No, I'm not. I'm here working as a companion to Mrs. Brock for the time being or until something better turns up."

"Millie, why don't we get out of the way and let these folks settle down with their food?" Jedediah started to move away.

"Would you care to join us?" Patience asked. "We're going over to sit with Hannah and Joe."

So Hannah came through for old Joe, Jedediah mused with a little smile.

Millie waved her hand. "No, that's all right. You go on ahead. Jed and I already have a place picked out, right, Jed?" She looked up at him with a coquettish smile and drew his arm closer.

Jedediah could see Patience's lips press together, and as he passed her, he whispered, "Save a dance for me." Patience flushed with pleasure, making her even more appealing.

Jedediah found he didn't mind at all when a tall cowboy asked Millie to dance. In fact, he was relieved. Cody was nowhere in sight,

176

and after the cowboy had left, he noticed Patience talking to Emily. He'd spoken to Monty and Emily earlier, and it was obvious they made a handsome and lively pair.

Now or never, he decided, and walked up to the two ladies as the announcer hollered out that the next dance would be a waltz.

"I see you're without a partner for the waltz, Patience. How about we give it a whirl?"

"It's the one dance I'm familiar with, Marshal." He saw her give a quick glance around, no doubt for sight of her errant escort. She turned to Emily. "You don't mind if I excuse myself, Emily?"

"Of course not. I'll watch you two and wait for Monty." She smiled at them both.

Jedediah held out his arm, and Patience laid her hand on the top of his as he led her onto the crowded dance floor. He knew how to waltz, but not as deftly as Patience, apparently. They twirled this way and that, and soon the steps seemed as smooth as a Vermont maple syrup. Emily waved and smiled as they swung by her.

This was the closest Jedediah had been to her since he'd carried her into the house from her collapse on the boardwalk. Ever since, he'd felt like putting his arms around her again — *at least most of the time,* he amended with a quick grin. Her green eyes sparkled like emeralds under the lights, along with the jeweled combs holding her dark hair in a fancy upswept style — just the right touch for her green gown. He caught a whiff of her scent as they swung around.

His throat felt dry as he searched for something to say. "Are you enjoying the dance, Patience?"

She tilted her head back to look up at him. "Yes, Jedediah, I am . . . or should I call you 'Jed' like Millie does? But maybe you're saving that for your *closest* friends?" There was a twinkle in her eyes.

He hurried to correct her. "For one thing, she is not my closest friend by a long shot, just someone I asked to the dance since — well, since my *first* choice was already taken," he said meaningfully. "But I'd like it if *you'd* call me Jed."

"Then I will . . . Jed. It's strange, but when I was a child my mother only called me Patience when she was angry with me."

"Is that so? Then what was *your* nickname?"

"It was . . . well, it was 'Patty.' "

"Would you like me to call you Patty?"

"Actually, no. When I'm special to someone, I'd rather that person decide on a nickname for me."

Jedediah was quiet for a moment, knowing they weren't special like she meant. *But given the chance, something might develop,* he thought hopefully. "I hope you don't mind if I tell you how . . . well, how different you look tonight."

"And that's a good thing?"

"Oh, absolutely! With your hair done up . . . and no apron and work dress on . . ." He stumbled around for the right words. "I hardly recognized you. You do look very pretty," he managed to choke out, surprised he'd been able to say it at all.

"Why, thank you, Jed. That's not a word I'm used to hearing. I've never expected much of my appearance, whether dressed up for an occasion or not. My mother wasn't one to waste a compliment."

"I don't mean to offend you, Patience, but sometimes a mother can be wrong. Beauty is external, but don't underestimate the inward qualities that can make one beautiful. And you have both."

Her face flushed, and then she said, "I must say you look rather handsome yourself."

Me? The woman must be nearsighted. The thudding in his chest had finally slowed before he admitted to himself that she was the first woman he'd been attracted to in years. Holding Patience this close made his hands tremble and his legs feel like they'd turned to jelly. He hoped she didn't notice, and took a deep breath to steady himself.

He sure did wish she'd come to the dance with him, but unfortunately he was stuck with Millie, at least for this event.

But then again, maybe not. He saw Cody and Millie standing near the barn door. Cody leaning against the wall, and Millie bending closer each time he said something. She'd laugh, and he would smile back. Mutual flirting, Jedediah determined, and fine with him.

"Your escort seems to be having a good time with Millie," he finally worked up nerve to say as Patience swung about with the rhythm of the waltz.

"Mmm . . . I noticed that too, and now they're dancing. I wonder if he'll have to provide transportation home for *two* women tonight." When she laughed merrily, Jed joined in, assuring her that she needn't worry about it.

When the waltz ended, he escorted her over to Emily and Monty, and the four stood and watched Hannah and Joe dancing the next waltz. Jedediah was amazed how well Joe had cleaned up. He'd obviously bathed and washed his hair, trimmed his beard, and pressed his worn but clean pants and stiff white shirt for the occasion. He'd even added a string tie — from where, Jedediah had no idea. He watched the little miner moving stiffly about, holding Hannah around the waist while they danced, but she was all smiles. *Guess I'll have to eat my words — looks like she's actually giving the man a second glance.*

When Hannah and Joe walked over to the little group, Hannah gave Patience a quick hug. "My, but you're a fine dancer, Patience. I saw you out there, turning and twisting and swinging back and forth."

Patience laughed. "Thank you, but you should have seen me on the earlier dances. I had two left feet."

"Have you met Joe?" Hannah nodded to her partner.

"No, I haven't. Nice to meet you, Joe."

"Likewise, I'm sure." The six stood talking for a while, Joe standing next to Hannah with a grin on his grizzled face. At a lull in the conversation, he pulled her back onto the dance floor. "See y'all later," he said around another grin. Jedediah couldn't help but smile at this highly unexpected development.

"I don't see Cody anywhere," Jedediah

commented when he saw Patience looking around. She seemed embarrassed that her escort was nowhere in sight. "Guess we'll have to dance again," he said lightly, offering his arm.

"But what about Millie?" she asked as she slipped her arm through his.

"I don't want you to feel bad, Patience, but I figure the two of them are probably off together someplace. Millie can take care of herself though."

"And I can't?" she cocked an eyebrow at him.

He shifted his feet. "That's not what I meant. It's just that I feel Millie knows her way around men, if you know what I mean."

"I see. Then I'd rather get some fresh air, if you don't mind."

"Not at all," he said, turning her toward the door.

They strolled away from the barn and onto the immaculate stretch of lawn, lit only with occasional lanterns and a partial moon. They soon found themselves away from the other guests and in a fragrant rose garden.

"How lovely!" Patience exclaimed. "Judith must enjoy gardening. I'd love to have some roses like these."

They paused in front of the bushes, Patience inhaling the scent from the different varieties, and Jedediah was amazed at how much Patience knew about them all.

"Oooh. I love these pink ones," she breathed as she lowered her head to the beautiful bloom.

Jedediah pulled out his pocketknife, reached over her, and snipped the rose to place in her hair. "Looks better there."

In the moonlight, he wasn't sure if she blushed or not. Her eyes seemed all soft and glowing, her lips the color of the pink rose, slightly parted and tempting him. Before he knew what he was doing, his arms had circled her in a swift embrace. Heat filled his face, and his heart pounded so hard he was sure Patience could hear it. Would she let him kiss her?

But she was already pulling away, visibly shaken. Her fingers touched her hair, patting it into place, and her eyes, large with surprise, looked into his, then quickly away. "I . . . Jed . . . I think we'd better go back inside and join the party."

"I'm — I'm truly sorry, Patience. I don't know . . . I'm not sure what came over me just now. It must be the moonlight and the roses." *And you,* he said only to himself.

14

Patience could still feel the warmth of Jedediah's arms around her as his hand pressed the small of her back, guiding her inside the barn. She felt quite flustered and looked around the dance floor in a daze. She noticed Cody come off the dance floor with a young woman, and Patience saw him return her glance while he continued to talk with his most recent dance partner. *Not Millie, I see. I'm glad he was far too busy to miss me,* she told herself with a little shrug.

Cody said something further to the woman, then strode over to them. "Where have you been?" His eyes narrowed. "I was looking all over for you." He looked from Patience to Jedediah.

"Just getting some fresh air — it was getting rather close with all these people in the room." Patience caught Jedediah's eye.

"I probably should go find Millie," Jedediah murmured. "If you'll excuse me." He bowed and walked away.

Before Cody could say another word, Harold Osborn, the clerk from the mercantile, joined them. "Please, Miss Patience, may I have this next dance?"

Patience almost said no, but feeling slightly sorry for the awkward young man, said, "Yes, you may. Excuse us, Cody." She nodded, and Harold took her hand and led her onto the dance floor.

She held herself erect as Harold tried to pull her close. *I sure don't want him to get any ideas into that red head of his.* She sighed in relief as the dance ended. He thanked her, led her back to the side of the room, then reluctantly left when she purposefully turned away.

Cody finally had the opportunity to spin Patience around the dance floor with a waltz. "So how do you like your new job, Cody?" Patience asked.

"It's all right . . ." He paused a moment, then added, "John's a good man. I hope someday to be a rancher's foreman so I can quit having to wander from place to place, depending on the season."

"Are you sure you can't find that around here?"

"Nobody trusts a stranger in these parts. I can't blame them — I don't trust anyone either. Too many road agents left bad reputations, so folks don't want to get burned." His jaw clenched, his lips forming a tight line.

"Sounds like you've been misused before."

She felt his body stiffen. "Let's just say I was in the wrong place at the wrong time," he finally told her. "Someday, I'll find the vigilante who had it in for me for no good reason."

"Why? Were you in trouble? Maybe jailed by him?" She was getting curious about the reason for his anger and mistrust. It wasn't the first time Patience had observed that faraway look, usually when he thought no one was looking.

"Something like that," he said. "Let's not waste our time talking about it. Not now."

"All right, but you might consider forgiveness, Cody. If you have resentment in your heart, it will only eat away at you. Besides, you're still here and enjoying life, it seems." She squeezed his hand.

"I don't think forgiveness is likely," he muttered. The dance ended, and after another glass of punch, Patience said, "I'm about ready to get back home — how about you?" She looked around at the other guests beginning their departures.

"Really? All tuckered out? I'm not, but I'll

take you home," Cody abruptly responded.

"It *is* getting rather late, and I promised Emily we'd go to church together tomorrow. I'd better get home. But if you'd rather stay longer, I can catch a ride with her and Monty."

"Aww . . . I hate for you to do that . . ." But even as he said it, he was glancing around the dance floor. *Is he looking for Millie, or one of the other ladies?*

"Oh, it's no problem," she assured him. "You stay and enjoy the rest of the dance."

He turned back to Patience. "If you're sure. I *am* having a good time . . ."

Yes, and it doesn't include me! I don't know why I thought he was attracted to me. I should've known better. "Truly, it's not a problem," she said, taking a step toward the door.

"Okay. See you soon." And before she could respond further, he hurried away, making a beeline for Millie.

Well! He could've at least walked me to the door. Apparently I don't begin to compare to Millie. Slightly miffed, she gathered up her skirts and hurried away to find Monty and Emily.

She was just about to give up when Jedediah approached her. "Are you looking for someone?" he asked, an eyebrow cocked.

"Cody's inside dancing with Millie," he said with a grin, apparently not too worried that she would be perturbed.

"Silly, I know that! I was looking for Emily and Monty," she told him, eyes still searching the room.

"Sorry, but you just missed them. They left about five minutes ago," Jedediah said.

"Oh, dear! I was hoping to catch a ride home —"

Jedediah laughed, and pointedly looked over at Cody, still dancing. "A lovers' quarrel?"

Patience rolled her eyes. "Hardly. I've told you before we're only friends. I wanted to leave, but Cody wanted to stay longer. Neither of us was with someone special tonight," she added, looking at Jedediah, then quickly away as she felt her cheeks warm.

He pushed his hat further back on his head. "Well, you're in luck," he said with a grin, obviously enjoying her discomfort, "because I'm just about to pull out of here. Millie seems to be enjoying Cody's company more than mine. You're welcome to hitch a ride with me. Or of course you can stay here and wait for Cody. But I have a gut feeling he's going to be leaving with somebody else tonight."

Patience pretended to consider his offer. "Well . . . I suppose you're right. Yes, and thank you," she added, her formal tone belying her rapidly beating heart.

Moments later, in Jed's carriage, Patience draped her shoulders with her shawl, crossing her arms to her chest — to protect her shoulders from the cool air or from Jedediah's closeness? She wasn't certain. He had a magnetic pull on her that she couldn't quite explain. She wondered what he was thinking. *Is he feeling — ?*

"Are you comfortable?" his voice interrupted her thoughts. "If you're cold, I have a blanket in the back of the wagon I can put over your legs," Jedediah said.

"No, thank you. I'm perfectly warm." She peered through the darkness at him, his profile outlined in the lantern's light.

He clicked to the horse, and they headed toward Nevada City, the bright lights from the ranch fading into the distance behind them.

"Did you enjoy the evening?" Jedediah asked in a conversational tone.

"It was fun," Patience told him, also keeping her voice neutral. "I admit that I had two left feet when it came to the square dancing. But it was loads of fun trying to learn the calls." Patience glanced at him again but couldn't tell much about his expression in the dark.

A great horned owl startled her with hoots from its perch, and she looked to her right in time to catch a glimpse of those bright yellow eyes staring back at them. "What a beautiful creature!" she couldn't help but exclaim. "His eyes seem to pierce right through to my soul . . ." Patience twisted in her seat as they drove past the bird perched on the limb of a ponderosa pine.

"Right you are. I've felt the same way." Jedediah turned to look at her. "Have you ever sat below a wonderful ponderosa pine?"

"I can't say that I ever have," she answered, wondering if he would continue.

"In the hot summer, the tree smells like a mixture of citrus and turpentine, but the bark smells like vanilla. It's very pleasant." He looked back at the road, then added, "Maybe we could have a picnic beneath one sometime so you can experience that."

Patience's next breath caught in her throat. "How interesting," she finally managed. "I like your idea. Yes, perhaps we can have a picnic soon. I could put together a basket . . ."

"Unless, of course, you and Cody have an understanding . . . ," Jedediah put in, obviously trying to hide a grin.

Patience chuckled. "Cody and I are only friends, as you might have noticed tonight. It would be — would be nice to have someone to do things with." Her voice sounded rather lame to her own ears.

"You do, Patience," he said, a smile in his voice. "You've got Emily."

"Jed, is it possible you might be just a bit . . . well, a bit envious of my time spent with Cody?"

"Nah," he said easily. "But maybe since Emily works with you now, you two could find plenty to do together." He looked at her, his grin making clear he was purposefully acting thickheaded, then added, his voice now gruff, "It seems to me Cody's just about worn his welcome out, hanging around the Creekside."

"He was looking for work and helping me out too. He did have a room at the boardinghouse until he got his ranch job. He's not renting a room there any longer." She chuckled softly. "I hardly think he's got any designs on me — at least not any longer. You're right, Jed. I saw how he flirted with all the eligible ladies at the dance."

"In that case," he responded carefully, "do you think I was out of line . . . with the embrace earlier tonight?" He'd slowed the horse's pace to a walk, then did a half turn in his seat, the reins resting across his legs.

Patience could feel her heart beating faster. *Oh, what do I do, Lord? I don't want my heart broken again. But I do think I'm beginning to care about him.*

She swallowed hard, then answered, "Uh . . . not exactly. It was a surprise though. I didn't realize you had any feelings . . ." But she couldn't finish.

Jedediah steered the horse to the side of the road and pulled back on the reins. Only the lantern shone through the darkness surrounding them, silent at the side of the road.

Her eyes were large and luminous in the lantern's light but held a softness beneath those long lashes. They also held uncertainty, and Jedediah, who yearned to kiss her, knew she wouldn't want that right now.

It had been a very long time since he'd allowed himself to even imagine that any woman might be drawn to him. Was it possible? He turned away with a ragged breath and looked into the darkness, then back at her. But she simply sat there staring at him. Finally she straightened her shawl over her shoulders, looked away, and brushed at her eyes.

Was she blinking back tears? He hoped they were good ones. "Patience, I hope you don't think me too forward," he said, his voice low.

"I don't know what to say. We haven't known each other very long, and I don't want to get ahead of myself or the Lord. I am coming to . . . to care for you, but I think we should take our time, get to know each other better before . . ."

"I didn't mean to make you uncomfortable," he said when she didn't finish. "I think I understand what you are saying. Please forgive me." His brow felt damp in the summer night, despite the cooling air. He picked up the reins, and the horse began to move forward. "But I'm glad you have been honest with me about your feelings," he managed to say, his throat tight with emotions, his mind crowded with thoughts. After a while he asked, "Does this mean I may court you in the proper manner?" When she didn't answer right away, he was sure he'd made a huge mistake. He glanced quickly at her. "Well?"

Patience sighed. "I'm not sure I'm ready for anything that serious."

"Who said anything about serious?"

She gave a small ladylike cough. "Well, doesn't 'serious' go along with a man who asks about courting?"

Jedediah was thoughtful for a moment.

"Sometimes . . . but not always. Courting, at least at the beginning, gives two people time to get to know each other, see how well they might fit together . . . sort of like a puzzle."

"I see."

"We could start with that picnic next week under the ponderosa pines, if you're willing." He couldn't believe he had worked up the nerve to ask her again. He'd spent a few sleepless nights thinking about just such an outing.

The lights from the town were getting closer. "Let me think about it," she finally answered.

Jedediah sure didn't want to push what seemed to be a glimmer of good fortune. To fill in the time during the remainder of the ride, he asked, "Do you have any siblings?"

"No. I was an only daughter. Mother has a weak heart. Gradually it was more and more clear to me that she had wanted a son . . ." Her voice trailed off, and he saw her hand once again wipe at her eyes.

"Mmm . . . I'm glad you turned out to be a daughter. I don't think I'd be interested in picnicking with a son," he said, trying to lighten the moment.

He heard her small chuckle, then a sigh. "Sometimes I wonder. I basically took care of my mother with all her myriad ailments till I inherited my grandmother's boarding-house." She sighed again, then turned to him. "What about you? Have you lived here long?"

Jedediah didn't want to talk about his past, and she didn't need to know every-thing. "I lived in a few places before being appointed Deputy US Marshal when Mon-tana became a territory. Then I came to Nevada City."

"Have you always had positions with the law?"

"No, I didn't have much schooling, and I've tried my hand at several different trades."

"Really? Like what?"

Man, she's full of questions! Was she persis-tent or just plain nosy? "Well . . . let's see, I was a brick maker once and tried out farm-ing in Kansas. I even took up shoemaking, but that was a most tedious job. I didn't have the patience for it." He looked over at her and grinned. When she looked puzzled, he said, " 'Patience' — get it?" and she laughed.

"All very respectable trades, Jed," she told him.

"I suppose, but none seemed to fit me," he said, trying to end the conversation before she attempted to dig anything else out of him. By now they'd entered Wallace Street, he noted with some relief. "I'll bring you back to the Creekside, then get the horse and carriage on to the livery."

She nodded. "We can continue our conversation later. It's very late."

He was happy to hear that she seemed to want to talk again, though he hoped it would be a new topic. "I'll walk you to the door." He turned to step out of the buggy, but Patience put her hand on his forearm.

"No need to. I'm sure Emily and the others are back by now. I'm not afraid, you know."

"I know that for a fact, Patience, or you would've never come here on your own and lived alone. But a gentleman must walk the lady to her door." He stepped out of the carriage and reached his hand up to her.

"Even if she's not the one he brought to the dance?" she joked, eyebrows quirked.

Jedediah chuckled. "Even more so."

It felt rather odd to have a woman at his side, but he surmised that he could get used to it if given half a chance. He held her elbow up the front steps and turned to say good night, when a figure sitting at the end of the porch stood and moved out of the shadows toward them.

196

15

Patience gasped, and her hands flew to her mouth. "Mother! What on earth!" she exclaimed as the woman stepped out of the shadows. "Whatever are you doing here in Nevada City? And waiting here in the dark? You could have gone inside —"

"Well, dear, is that any way to greet your mother?" Charity Cavanaugh asked archly. "I couldn't very well go into the building this late without a key, could I? And it seems everyone has gone to bed — with the exception of you, of course." She turned her head to look at Jedediah, then back to Patience. "Don't you think it's rather late to be out? And without a proper chaperone?" She didn't wait for an answer but continued her chiding. "You certainly must remember, don't you, that this cool mountain air is bad for my rheumatism and my heart?"

No hug, nor even an "I've missed you." The same attitude and comments that had compelled Patience to leave home. "Mother, you should have told me you were coming, and I would have made certain I was home." Patience took a tentative step toward the woman.

Charity waved a delicate white hanky, dismissing Patience's explanation. "Please take me to a room with a nice, warm bed, and I'll be grateful. Much better than that dusty old stage ride to get here."

Patience sighed and silently prayed that the visit would be a short one. "Mother," she said, turning, "I'd like you to meet Jedediah Jones. He's our town's marshal." She motioned with her hand. "Jed, this is my mother, Charity Cavanaugh."

Her mother turned to take another look at Jedediah. "So, you're on a first-name basis with my daughter?" she said, the short, clipped tone all too familiar.

"How do, ma'am," Jedediah said, quickly sweeping off his hat. "Mighty nice to meet you." He reached out his hand, which her mother barely touched with her leather-gloved fingertips.

She's already passed judgment on him. Patience knew it didn't matter that her mother didn't know anything about him. Charity wanted to be the one to choose whom Patience would be courted by — or, for that matter, married to. Patience could feel a headache coming and wished somehow her daddy would appear.

"Right, Mother, let's go in and get you settled. We can talk further in the morning." Patience slipped her key out of her reticule and opened the door.

"Can I carry that upstairs for you?" Jedediah motioned toward the two bags next to the rocker.

"That won't be necessary," she snapped. "Patience is strong as an ox!"

Well, thank you, Mother, for pointing that out. But Jedediah already had the bags in hand, and he slipped inside and quickly moved up the stairs and deposited them on the landing.

"Humph," the woman muttered, and followed Patience through the door.

"Then I'll leave you two alone," Jedediah told them, stepping back onto the porch and putting on his hat. "I've got to get this carriage back to the livery now. Patience, thank you," he finished somewhat indirectly, touching his finger to his hat.

Patience ignored his attempt at discretion in front of her mother. "Thank you for bringing me home, Jed. We'll talk again soon. I must go now and see to my mother's needs." She breathed deeply. Her mother's presence seemed to have brought her scattered thoughts and feelings into some kind of order.

"My pleasure, I assure you." He tipped his hat, and Patience watched him climb into the carriage.

Patience led her mother up the stairway, then picked up the larger one of the bags at the top. What in the world did she have stashed in there? She lugged it toward the only empty room and leaned for a moment against the smooth wood of the door to catch her breath. Her mother cleared her throat.

"I must get the room key," Patience said. "Fortunately there is one room not yet rented."

"Oh, don't bother, dear. I can just share your room. I promise not to inconvenience you in the least."

"Oh no," she said over her shoulder, already heading downstairs for the key. "That won't work — I must be up very early. I'll give you the best room in the house," she called up the stairs, "the one at the front overlooking the main street. It's only two doors down from mine. I usually use that one for newlyweds or someone special."

Charity was nodding, looking somewhat

mollified. "Nice to know I'm special," she called back. "Show me the way then, Patty. I'm thoroughly exhausted. If it weren't so late, I'd have hot water for a bath brought up."

Patience brought the second bag to the room when she returned with key in hand. "Mother," she began, holding herself in check with some effort, "you need to know it's only Emily and I that work here, and with all the other things we must do, we are not able to draw baths for our boarders." Patience turned the key in the lock, pushed the door open, and deposited the luggage inside. "As I said, we have no assistants, but tomorrow I'll make time to bring up hot water for your bath."

Her mother leaned over to give Patience a peck on the cheek. "What a thoughtful daughter you've turned out to be. But who's Emily?"

"You'll probably get to meet her tomorrow at breakfast."

"I'll have mine on a tray in my room, dear, until I'm feeling more like myself," Charity announced with a "poor me" face.

Patience pressed her lips together to keep from saying something she might regret, such as the fact that her mother was quite capable of coming downstairs for breakfast.

She paused at the door. "Mother, how long do you plan to stay?"

Charity put a finger to her chin. "I haven't decided, but I *must* see how you are doing, since I haven't gotten more than a letter or two from you. If the answer is that things are going well, then I shall be satisfied. Daddy would want that."

"Yes, Daddy would. Good night, Mother."

"Ta-ta, Patty dear."

Patience could hardly wait to strip off her party dress and drop into bed. *What a shock to find Mother on my doorstep!* she thought as she pulled her nightgown over her head. Most likely she had come to see what Creekside looked like now.

Patience slipped under the covers, remembering that her mother had been very displeased when *she* hadn't been the one to inherit this boardinghouse. Patience sighed and closed her eyes. "Lord," she whispered, "help me to be kind and loving to Mother, even when she doesn't treat me the same way."

She hoped her mother would be pleased with all the improvements she'd made to the boardinghouse and that her visit would be pleasant. For now, she curled up with her pillow — Buttercup snuggled against her — and went to sleep with the memory of her special evening with Jedediah.

Patience couldn't have been more mistaken in hoping her mother would be gracious on this visit. On Monday morning, Charity glided into the dining room near the end of breakfast time, dressed in a skirt of light blue silk taffeta and bodice adorned with chenille fringe that matched her blue eyes, her best feature. Though middle-aged now, her mother had somehow maintained her slim silhouette, which made Patience feel poignantly aware of her own fuller figure. She could never expect to age as pleasingly as her mother.

"Good morning, Mother," Patience said, laying a place for her at the table. "Everyone, this is my mother, Charity Cavanaugh." Hellos and nodding of heads were the responses from the few still finishing their breakfast.

Her mother looked around, no doubt sizing up the guests. "Good morning to all," Charity said with an elegant sweep of her hand and a smile that quickly faded when everyone continued to eat. She sat down at her place and looked around uncertainly.

Patience nodded toward the sideboard holding the breakfast items, and her mother nodded in return, picked up her plate, and rose to help herself to what was left of breakfast.

"Patience, dear, were there any potatoes left this morning? I should love some with my sausage."

"I'm sorry, Mother, but I didn't serve potatoes today. There's still some oatmeal left next to the sausage."

Her mother removed the lid and spooned oatmeal into a bowl. "Then I shall put in my request for potatoes on the morrow," she said, her voice loud enough for everyone to hear. "We always had those at home, you know."

Patience winced at her mother's veiled rebuke as Emily came in from the kitchen to gather the dishes. She stopped short when she saw Charity. "You must be Patience's mother," she exclaimed. "I do see a resemblance between you. I'm Emily." The young woman held out her hand.

"Yes, I'm Mrs. Cavanaugh," she said, taking the outstretched hand. "I'm not that sure of the resemblance, though," she added with a shrug. She placed her bowl of oatmeal on the table, sat down, then looked up at Emily. "You do the kitchen work for my daughter?"

"Heavens, no! I can't cook at all. I'm Patience's partner in business," she said cheerfully. "Patience probably hasn't had a chance to tell you yet."

Patience didn't miss her mother's glance from Emily to her and then back to Emily. "No, I wasn't told. It seems my daughter has more than a few surprises in store for me." Her lips formed a smile but her eyes narrowed. "It's probably a good thing I was able to come in person. A few letters obviously aren't sufficient."

Patience's mouth felt dry. "We work well together, Mother, and our abilities are very compatible."

"I see," she said, and proceeded to eat her oatmeal.

The last of the boarders excused themselves and departed for the day. Patience began clearing the sideboard food with a large tray.

"Well, my dear, it appears your enterprise is beginning to flourish in a fairly short time. I will be happy to share some ideas with you."

Patience paused at the kitchen doorway with the tray balanced on her hip. "Yes, things are going well, and if you have some helpful ideas for further improvements, by all means, I'll want to hear them, Mother."

"Perhaps when you've finished with cleaning up, you can show me around the town.

It's been a while since I visited my mother here."

Patience eyed her thoughtfully. "And you're dressed to go out already."

"I try to plan ahead, dear. I'll be in the parlor when you're ready," she said. "Oh, and I'm sure you're planning to change from that drab housedress before we leave."

Emily gave Patience a sympathetic glance. "I'm the one who does the dishes, Mrs. Cavanaugh, while Patience makes us such excellent meals," she said. "One can't very well do that in beautiful clothing such as you are wearing."

Charity arched an eyebrow, and Patience almost laughed outright — her mother had met her match. Little did Emily know that Charity Cavanaugh never cooked or cleaned or washed dishes if there was anyone else around to do it for her.

"That doesn't surprise me at all. She learned to cook from me," Charity said with a smug little smile.

Yes, you left the running of the house to me because of your "illnesses." But all she said was, "I'll meet you in the parlor a little later, Mother."

Her mother dabbed her mouth with her napkin. "I think I'm finished here — Emily, is it? You can take my plate too. I have to

206

watch my figure, even at my age." She sent Patience a meaningful glance. "I believe I'll have another cup of coffee and take it with me to the parlor. Excuse me."

When the two were alone, Patience whispered to Emily, "I'm sorry about my mother. She likes to be in charge. But thanks for sticking up for me."

"No need to apologize, Patience. I understand," Emily told her with a smile. "I can finish up here. Why don't you go ahead and get ready for the outing with your mother." Emily took the plates from Patience. "I wish I'd had more time with my mother . . ."

Patience wiped her hands on her apron, then touched Emily's sleeve. "I'm so sorry. Hopefully your mother was a kind, gracious woman." Patience could tell Emily was suppressing the tears that filled her eyes.

Emily sniffled and turned toward the kitchen. "She wasn't perfect, but she was certainly a good mother to me. Don't forget to put on something nice — you know, for your mother's sake."

Patience shook her head. "She must assume I can run this place and cook meals dressed to the nines." She untied her apron, slipped it over her head, and laid it on the table. "Thank you, Emily, not just for the work you do here, but for being a good friend."

"That goes both ways. We all need someone we can talk to. Now shoo!"

"I'm going. I'm going," Patience said over her shoulder with a smile and exited the dining room. *What would it have been like to have a mother like Emily's?* she wondered as she headed toward the stairs. Maybe growing-up years would have been pleasant ones, and she wouldn't have had to struggle to even be seen and heard.

"My grace is sufficient for thee: for my strength is made perfect in weakness." Patience heard the familiar words in her mind. *I know, Lord, but I don't know what You're trying to work into me.*

The answering voice was clear in her heart. *Maybe you don't need to know, Patience. And may I remind you of your name, My beloved daughter?*

16

Patience hurried upstairs and quickly selected a periwinkle-blue street dress with cream-colored lace ties at the throat. She pulled the corset she'd mended with new ribbons as tight as she could so she would fit into the slender bodice cutting deep into the folds of the matching skirt. With the darker fabric-covered buttons running the length of the gown, she hoped she would seem to have a nicely smaller waist.

She smiled wryly as she gathered up her reticule. "Showing Mother about town" would mean passing by the saloons, looking into three mercantile stores, seeing the butcher's shop, the livery stables, blacksmith, maybe coffee in The Star Bakery, and a visit to two hotels. Most of the wooden structures had been hastily built with false fronts to give them the illusion of two-story buildings.

This won't take very long. What are we go-

ing to do with the rest of the day? she wondered as she caught her skirt up with one hand and hurried downstairs.

She paused at the bottom to catch her breath, then sailed into the parlor where her mother sat in an armchair near the fireplace, looking every bit the part of queen of the manor. She was sipping the last of her coffee while thumbing through an outdated copy of *Godey's Lady's Book.*

"Was there a fire?" her mother asked in a clipped tone.

Patience stopped. "Fire?"

"The one you're rushing from, my dear. It's not ladylike, especially when you're the owner of an establishment, to look so — befuddled." Charity's gaze swept the length of Patience's apparel, and the woman apparently approved.

"Yes, Mother. I didn't want to keep you waiting. Are you ready to take a stroll through our little town?"

"Indeed I am. But before we depart I want to suggest that you find some other drapes, dear, something more formal for the parlor."

Patience's heart pounded in her chest. "I — the truth is, I like them."

Her mother strode over to the window, fingering the material. She frowned. "They look . . . homemade —"

"They *are,*" Patience put in before her mother could say anything further. "Emily and I made them. Money is not very plenteous just yet, and this was the nicest material I could afford."

Her mother dropped the panel as if it were soiling her fingers. "I see. Once you're flourishing financially, I'll help you choose some stylish drapes more in keeping with a high-class residence."

Patience held her breath to keep from bursting out in anger. She finally said, "You'll soon see, Mother, that Nevada City cannot support a 'high-class residence.' This is a boardinghouse for people from all walks of life. Besides, Emily and I like these drapes. And we enjoyed working on them together."

"Well, then, shall we be on our way?" Charity responded with her most elegant shrug.

"Such a busy little town here." Charity chatted away as they walked along the boardwalk, with Patience pointing out the shops and introducing the occasional person she knew.

"And very transient," Patience explained, "as most of them are miners hoping for a strike."

"How will you ever be able to find an eligible man here, my dear?"

"Mother, I have plenty to keep me busy with running the boardinghouse."

"Maybe so, but I'm sure your evenings do get lonely — oh my, what's that on ahead? A bake shop?"

"Yes, Miss Hannah runs it. She was a good friend to Grandmother . . . and now me."

"I don't remember my mother ever mentioning her," Charity murmured with a frown. "But shall we stop in and say hello?"

"Yes, and you'll like her. She's very nice and has helped me get settled here. Let's go inside."

As soon as they stepped into the Star, Patience's mother began exclaiming about the delicious smells and variety of desserts. "I must have one of those rolls — no, wait! Make that two." She turned to Patience. "We can have them this afternoon with our tea or coffee."

Patience turned to her friend. "Yes, Hannah, please make that three. I'm sure Emily would enjoy one too. And may I introduce —"

"Oh, yes . . . well — of course," her mother inserted rather abruptly.

"Miss Hannah," Patience tried again, "I'd

like you to meet my mother, Charity Cavanaugh."

"How do you do, Mrs. Cavanaugh! I'm *so* pleased to meet you. You know, I knew your mother quite well. Please call me Hannah," she enthused in her own warm style.

"Yes, so I understand," Charity murmured, looking distractedly at the display of items. "I'm glad to meet you too."

Hannah lifted the cinnamon rolls from the glass-encased shelf and asked, "Will you want these packed up for later?"

"That would be perfect," Patience assured her when her mother did not respond.

"Your daughter has become quite the entrepreneur, you know," Hannah said to Charity, "and I should also add that she whips up a better batch of biscuits than I do any day!" She gave Patience a friendly smile.

"Is that so?" Charity said distantly. "Seems I have a lot to catch up on about my daughter. She must have felt her poor widowed mother's loss was not important enough to stay . . ." Her voice trailed off with so much self-pity that Patience felt she had to respond somehow.

"Mother, please!"

But Hannah quickly stepped in with her own comment. "Oh, I have a hard time believing that, Miz Cavanaugh! Your daughter is simply filled with spirit and adventure, probably much like we both were back in the day. Isn't that right?"

"I'm not as *old* as you might think," Charity said, staring directly at Hannah for a moment.

Hannah ignored the awkward exchange and handed over the bags of rolls. "That will be thirty-five cents, please."

"Oh my. I didn't think to bring any cash with me . . ." Charity turned to her daughter. "Dear —"

"It's fine, Mother. I have the exact change." Patience was already reaching inside her reticule and handed some coins to Hannah.

"Thank you, Patience. Did you have a good time at the dance? I certainly did." Hannah's cheeks turned pink.

"Oh, yes! Lots of food and fun."

"I saw you come to the dance with Cody, but I thought I saw you leave with —"

"Yes, yes I did," Patience put in quickly. "I was ready to go, but Cody wanted to stay, so Jed offered me a ride."

Charity drew back, eyes narrowed, as she stared at Patience. "Cody? Jed? Two different men at the same event? I'm astounded, Patience! That is not how you were raised."

She shook her head, still facing down her daughter. "And I thought you were too busy for courting."

"Mother." Patience blew out a breath and tried to calm her ire. "I am *not* being courted by anybody, and I *don't* have two men in my life — I *know* two men along with several others I have met here."

Hannah was trying to say something to make amends, but Patience gave her a quick look to assure her that nothing further would help at the moment.

"You must tell me all about them," Charity said, head lifted high as she took Patience's elbow and nudged her in the direction of the door.

The last thing Patience wanted to do was to talk with her mother about anything related to matters of the heart. Memories of her tragic experience with Russell and all the incriminations flung at her for choosing Russell in the first place filled her mind, and she closed her eyes for a moment as her mother almost pushed her out the door.

Patience walked straight into Jed's arms, her mother stumbling into her from behind. "Oh, please, forgive me! We — we are just on our way out." Patience caught her balance and stepped away from her mother's hand on her back.

Jedediah had already reached out to steady Patience. "I wasn't watching where I was going. Are you all right?" His steady eyes looked into hers until she glanced away. "Yes, I am, thank you. Please excuse us. We are heading back to the boardinghouse," she babbled on.

Once on the boardwalk, her mother said in consternation, "I didn't realize that — what's his name? — Jedediah Jones is the marshal! I just saw his badge. You realize, Patience, it's far best you don't get involved with a person whose life is in jeopardy at any moment."

Patience shook her head and forced a chuckle. "Oh, Mother, you're incorrigible. That's hardly the case."

Charity caught Patience's arm. "But even worse, men like him usually carry a past with them. I can tell just by looking at him."

"Why don't we stop in at the mercantile before we go home?" Patience suggested. "It's right up the street. Then I must get back to start our supper." She hoped these distractions would stay further discussion on the topic of Jedediah.

Jedediah stood watching the two women as they walked into the mercantile, deep in conversation. From his vantage point, mother and daughter were enjoying their visit. He guessed he wouldn't see much of Patience now that her mother had arrived.

"You through gawking after Patience? I saw you two on the dance floor," Hannah said from behind, giving him a wink as he turned to face her.

"Am I that obvious?" Jedediah growled.

Hannah bobbed her head. "Don't worry about it, though. Have you met her mother? I mean before just now?"

"Yes, I did. Seems like a proper lady."

"Proper? Or particular?"

"Can't say I know the difference. Haven't spent any time with her. You like her or not?"

Hannah moved back to the counter, wiping up crumbs. "Oh, she seems nice enough. A little hard on her daughter, though."

"What makes you say that?"

Hannah shrugged. "Something about the way she talks to her, I guess."

Jedediah chuckled. "I thought all mothers did that."

"She made Patience uncomfortable, seems to me."

"Well, I'm pretty sure Patience can take care of herself."

"You're right. So, what can I get you, Marshal, the usual?"

"Ah . . . you know me too well, Miz Hannah. Yes, then tell me about you and Joe." Jedediah watched a blush turn her cheeks pink.

"We had a good time, me and Joe did, and he kept his promise not to drink the three days before."

"That a fact? You just may be the woman to keep him from that poison."

"I'm not sure about that. I've heard alcohol is hard to cut loose from, but when he's sober, we have a lot to talk about." She took out a cinnamon roll, folded a napkin around it, and handed it to him. "It's on the house. I'm sure you're the one that got Joe to clean up his act."

"Well, thank you. I told him you wouldn't give him the time of day unless he did." Jedediah bit off a large chunk of the roll and licked the cinnamon sugar from his fingers.

"Not sure if his 'good behavior' will last, though," Hannah reflected. "I don't want to turn out to be an old fool . . ."

"I'm sure that's not going to happen. Joe's had his eye on you since he came to town. It's been hard for him to let go of his memories and find a new life. I think that's the reason he drinks — to drown his sorrows."

Hannah sighed heavily. "I know about them memories myself. It's very hard to turn away from all that and see where God might lead."

Something in her voice he hadn't heard before surprised him — a longing, a loneliness. Pretty much the way he'd been himself for a long time now, he had to admit. Hannah was always the cheerful one, but today was different. Maybe she was afraid to get too close to Joe because he might disappoint her.

"I hear ya," Jed assured her. "It's better to feel something than to feel nothing at all, Hannah. But I've never heard you talk this way before." Jedediah realized he truly cared what happened to the older lady.

She reached across the counter and pinched his cheek. "Don't mind me — I'm just an old woman that gets sentimental once in a while."

"You let me know if Joe doesn't treat you right. He really has a good heart, so I don't think that's likely."

After a few more pleasantries, Jedediah went on his way. The sun was very hot today, and the dusty noonday streets were not as busy as usual. Folks either sought a cool shade tree or stayed indoors. He stopped by the livery to pay for his horse's board, then back to work. In one way he was grateful for the hot weather — it seemed to keep trouble down to a bare minimum. On the other hand, though, it didn't give him a lot to do. Might be a good day to clean his rifles . . . and maybe ponder some more about Patience.

17

Patience sat at the desk, making notes and planning for what needed to be done. In a matter of just days, she had lost three boarders but gained two new ones. If she booked another one, she'd have to ask Emily to share her room, and she hated to do that. Emily had made her room homey with her personal things. But it'd certainly be preferable to having her mother in her room. *Heaven forbid. That woman could drive me clean out of my mind.*

Patience felt guilty for such thoughts. But her mother continued to be too intrusive, overbearing in her own "genteel" way. She had lists of items she wanted Patience to change at Creekside — like the menu, because it didn't suit her constitution, or the arrangement of the furniture throughout the house, because it *felt* better. She wanted to change the meal times, and on and on. Patience was too busy to get into discussions that she knew would turn into arguments. She'd simply return everything to how she and Emily wanted it after her mother left. For now, Patience would let her mother believe she was doing something productive.

She paused, tapping her pencil against the paper, and thought back to church in Virginia City last Sunday. It had proved to be the highlight of the week for both Patience and her mother, who had enjoyed her visitor status and being the center of attention. They'd stayed afterward for the church's Fourth of July picnic. It was a wonderful afternoon of potato-sack races, a three-piece band made up of church members, speeches, and fireworks. Jedediah had even showed up. He spent most of the time talking with his cronies, but he had shared apple cider with them during the fireworks. *Perhaps he feels like he's imposing with Mother here.* Her mother had liked Cody on the spot and was captured by his disarming charm. But then so was Millie.

Patience pulled her thoughts back to the work at hand — menus and groceries for the next few days. Then she must balance her ledger. She was hoping to save for a used piano, but from the looks of things, that would be many months from now.

However, her business was thriving, considering how difficult it had been to manage financially when she had first arrived. She was sure the improvements, though costly, had helped to secure additional boarders.

It'd been a while since she'd made any boxed lunches for Jedediah, but maybe that was a sign all was peaceful — though the rustlers still hadn't been captured.

Patience's quiet was suddenly broken by the frantic cry of her mother. "Patty!" Her mother burst into her room. "My diamond brooch — the one your father gave me for our wedding anniversary — is missing. Someone here has taken it, I'm sure! I've looked everywhere!"

Patience pushed back her chair. "Oh my goodness, Mother? What — ?"

"I'm telling you, it's missing!" Charity was wringing her hands. "It's quite a valuable piece, you know. Do you think Emily took it?"

"Mother! Please lower your voice!" she hissed. "How in the world would you come to suspect Emily?" She pulled her mother by the sleeve away from the door and closed it, thankful that no one else was around, particularly Emily.

"Because you and Emily are the only ones that have access to the rooms," she snapped.

"Who else could possibly get into my room?"

"Don't be ridiculous! Emily isn't like that . . . she would *never* stoop to steal. Believe me, I know that for sure."

"Well, I'm going for the marshal. He's the one who can legally check all the rooms." She marched over to the door and reached for the knob.

"Don't do that, Mother," Patience admonished. "We can look around and ask if anyone has seen it. Perhaps the clasp is broken, and it fell off your dress."

"You go right ahead and do that. I'm going to get *official* help." She opened the parlor door, and Patience could hear her heels sharp against the wooden floor as she stalked back to the stairs and her own room. Very soon Charity was heading down the stairs and out the front door.

Patience waited a moment, then went up to her mother's room and carefully looked around. She felt sure no one had stolen it. It must be here somewhere. She knelt and looked underneath the bed, felt around under the nightstand.

Emily walked by the open door with fresh laundry. "What are you doing on your knees?" She put the basket down at the door and came in.

Patience rose, banging her head on the corner of the nightstand. "Ouch! Oh, for heaven's sake!" She rubbed the spot as she stood. "My mother insists someone has taken her diamond brooch!"

"What?" Emily's eyes widened with alarm.

"Yes, I'm afraid so. I've been searching her room but haven't found it. Worse yet, instead of waiting to see if we can discover where it is, she's gone after Jed to search everyone's room and personal belongings."

"Mmm . . . I can understand her being upset. Was it valuable?"

"Yes, and special to her. My father gave it to her the year before he died — on their anniversary. Emily, please, we've got to find it."

"Let's go look on the porch and garden area, then the kitchen and dining room and parlor. Maybe we can locate it before she returns with Jed . . . unless someone indeed has taken it."

The thought did cross Patience's mind. "I sincerely hope not."

Patience and Emily were scouring the downstairs of the boardinghouse when Charity returned, Jed in tow. "I've filed a report," she announced, "but the marshal wants to take a look around and search the boarders' rooms." She pointed him to the parlor.

Behind Charity's back, Jedediah smiled wryly at Patience. He noticed she looked both serious and frustrated, which puzzled him. Did the cameo have a special meaning to her too? He kept his voice low as he said, "I hope you don't mind, Patience. Your mother insisted that I come and do a thorough search. Is that all right with you?"

"By all means. The sooner we find that brooch, the better." Her lips were compressed into a fine line. "We looked through the kitchen, the porch and garden, and the parlor and dining room, and of course, my mother's room. Here are all the keys to the rooms."

Jed turned to Charity, who was standing at the parlor window. "Ma'am, why don't you have a rest, while I have a look around?"

"Good idea," Patience said. "Mother, I'll fix you a cup of tea."

The front door opened and a couple of boarders came in, noticed the gathering, and asked what was going on. Emily briefly told them the situation and that Jedediah was there to look in everyone's room.

"Don't matter none to me. I've got nothin' to hide," a middle-aged miner said, and the other gentleman agreed with a nod of his head.

Patience nodded toward the kitchen. "I'm going to go fix us all some tea, if you'd care to wait in the parlor until the marshal has completed his search."

Jedediah liked the way Patience took over, efficiently directing her guests and her mother. The last thing he needed was to have a group following him around as he did his search. Emily followed Patience into the kitchen, and he excused himself and went directly upstairs.

He methodically scoured each room, amazed at how neat some folks' rooms were and how disorderly were others. It felt odd to be in Patience's room — he knew it had to be hers because one of the dresses he'd seen her wear was neatly hanging on the wardrobe door. He saw a notebook open on the bed and her bedroom slippers on the floor below. He looked at the carefully written page. *Must be the devotionals she's talked about.* He was tempted to pick it up, but that would be snooping. He glanced at her dresser and imagined Patience sitting there, brushing out her long hair in the evenings. He suddenly was overcome with an unusual feeling . . . foreboding? He hurried out, locking the door behind him.

In the parlor, Jedediah noted a few more boarders had returned and were standing about quietly talking, tea or coffee cups in hand. Patience rose as soon as she saw him. "Well? Did you find it?" she asked.

"No, sorry to say, I did not. Unless Mrs. Cavanaugh has any more specific evidence, or has seen something suspicious, then I must consider all the boarders as possible suspects." He looked around at their anxious faces. To his way of thinking, none of them looked like a guilty thief, but then who usually did?

There were murmurs and grumbles heard around the room. Jed raised his hand, signaling quiet. "I'm sorry, folks, to inconvenience you — but I must have a list of names of everyone who is boarding here, as a very expensive diamond brooch belonging to Charity Cavanaugh is missing. Patience, might I have a piece of paper so we can have each one jot his or her name down?"

"Yes, of course. I have some right here." She took paper and pen from a drawer.

"Why don't we just let everyone sign their name, and you can fill in those that aren't here right now. I assume you have the names listed in your register?" Patience nodded at him. "That would be a big help. I want to speak with each of you briefly," he added as he looked around the room. "After that you're free to go on about your business."

In less than half an hour, Jedediah had talked individually with everyone present. He asked Charity to describe the cameo.

"It's a mother-of-pearl brooch on black onyx encrusted with forty diamonds — the years of our marriage." She sniffled into her hanky and shook her head.

He gave her a pat on the shoulder. "There, there. Okay, folks, you all heard the description. Keep an eye out for it, in case it got misplaced or fell off Mrs. Cavanaugh's dress."

Everyone filed out of the room and went their separate ways, including Charity, while Emily began cleaning up the cups.

"Patience, may I have a word with you?" Jedediah asked quietly.

Her brow furrowed. "Certainly. Let's step outside. Emily, I won't be long. Please check the beans that are simmering."

"Yes, I will," Emily agreed.

Jedediah closed the door and they walked to the end of the porch.

"I want to ask you something, Patience." Jedediah pulled out a bright-blue neckerchief from his pocket. "Who does this belong to?"

Patience looked at it. "Oh, Cody must've left that behind. He always wore neckerchiefs like that."

"Do you mind if I keep it for now?"

Patience's face showed her puzzlement. "No, but why? Where did you find it?"

"On top of a high shelf in one of the rooms."

"Jed . . ." Patience moved closer, and Jed could smell a light fragrance of rose water. He wanted to pull her into his arms but this was not the time or place. "Do you believe someone staying here took my mother's brooch? At first she was accusing Emily, and I told her that was nonsense."

"Maybe. It's hard to know for sure. How would anyone other than you or Emily get into that room? I think it's more likely that your mother mislaid it."

Patience nodded, the sun shining on her brown curls. "That's true, but it's also possible she might've thought she had it securely pinned, and it fell off. Sorry this took so much of your time."

"No trouble at all. It's my job. Let me know if something turns up."

"I will, and I'll run the list over to you when it's complete." Patience moved to go inside. "Would you like to come for supper?"

Jedediah shuffled from one foot to the other. "Thank you, but not tonight. I don't fancy being under scrutiny by your mother and all the rest. And trying to figure out how to answer all their questions without actually answering them."

She looked disappointed, he thought. She simply said, "I understand."

He couldn't help but be encouraged. *She seems regretful that I couldn't accept the invitation,* he thought. He tipped his hat. "Good evening, Patience. We'll talk further soon," he added as he stepped off the porch.

18

A pall of uneasiness seemed to be hanging over the Creekside Inn ever since Charity had reported her diamond cameo missing — and no doubt word had gotten out that the woman was casting aspersions on the residents themselves. Patience was fully aware of more than a few cool stares among the boarders cast toward her and her mother. But no one spoke about the brooch, and neither had it been found. She couldn't bear to think that someone would have taken it. But she couldn't help but worry that the boardinghouse's reputation would suffer, regardless of who was the culprit. The thought concerned her — especially now that Creekside was doing well.

"You must be deep in thought," Emily said, dropping down in the chair next to her on the porch.

"Why do you say that?" Patience turned to face her friend.

Emily giggled, and her dimple deepened. "Because I was just talking to you."

"I'm so sorry. Did you need something?"

"Not really. I thought I'd take a break from housekeeping and have a cup of tea. Would you care to join me?"

"I would indeed." Patience sighed. "I was thinking about Mother's missing brooch." She sighed again. "I'm sure the whole thing will not be good for our establishment."

Emily gave her a caring gaze. "Oh, fiddledeedee," she said with a wave of her hand. "Don't worry about that. I don't think anyone will give it a thought . . . only the residents. Please stop worrying, Patience. I have confidence it will turn up."

"You do?"

"It has to. Try not to dwell on what you can't change. Whatever happens, we'll figure out how to manage," Emily said as she rose. "I'll put the teakettle on."

"I'll meet you in the kitchen — no need to carry it out here. It'll only get dusty from the street today with all the wagons passing to and fro."

Patience rose, noticing she still felt stiffness in her side though her accident had been several weeks ago. Was that Cody just down the block? She paused, hand on the doorknob. He waved and turned his horse toward her. What had brought him into town?

"Howdy, Patience," Cody said with a tip of his hat as he approached the porch.

"Hello, Cody. I wouldn't expect to see you here in the middle of the afternoon," she answered, her hand up to shield the sun's glare.

"Me neither, but the boss sent me to order a few things to improve the fencing. He wants to make sure the herd doesn't stray, I reckon, after what happened."

"Won't you come in out of the heat?"

"I expect I can visit a few minutes." He tied his horse to the post, and Patience returned to her rocker and gestured toward a chair next to hers. "How've you been?" he asked. "I should've taken you home from the dance instead of . . . well, instead of staying on. Forgive me." His voice sounded its usual raspy tone, but nonetheless sincere.

"There's nothing to forgive. I think we understand one another . . . Millie seems to have caught your eye." The last comment slipped out before Patience thought about it.

Cody laughed. "Aww, that didn't mean anything. Just having a good time dancing with her."

"It's really none of my concern," Patience

said quietly.

"Are we still friends then?" He smiled broadly and cocked an eyebrow at her.

"Certainly." The last thing Patience wanted was for him to think she was pining over him. However, she did enjoy his company and lively conversation. But was Cody merely a diversion? Had she already lost her heart to another?

Cody smiled again. "I'm glad. When I leave here, I'd like to think I made a few friends."

"You are leaving?"

"I told you that my intention wasn't to put down roots here — once I find the man I'm looking for."

"Oh, yes. You did say that someone had wronged you." Patience turned to look directly at him. "Have you thought about letting the Lord be the man's judge instead of trying to get even?"

He jerked his head sideways and stared at her. "That's letting someone get away with a crime."

She gave him a level look. "You never said a crime was involved." An odd feeling about Cody came over her. "Have you committed some crime?"

"Heavens, no! But someone needs to pay for the crime he did to me!" His eyes snapped with anger. "One man gave the order."

"And what was that, Cody?" His friendly afternoon greeting had changed from a tone of cheer to quick anger, and Patience didn't like this side of him.

"I was *hanged*! That's what!" Cody yanked off the blue kerchief at his throat, exposing a large, deep scar running from one side of his neck to the other. "*That's* what they did to me, and I won't let it rest till somebody pays."

Patience drew her breath in sharply. *Not again! Am I destined to run into hangings wherever I turn?* "Cody." Patience laid a hand on his arm. "I'm very sorry for whatever happened to you. But even I know a person can't be hanged and survive."

"Well, the truth is my neck didn't snap, but I'd passed out so they thought I was dead. They cut me down, and one of the vigilantes hauled me to the local medical school so my body could be used for scientific study. That's when a student discovered I was alive." Patience stared at him, her eyes wide with shock.

Cody continued his sorry saga. "The vigilantes had gone after some road agents, and they thought I was one of them. There was one man that gave the hanging order,

236

but I had a hood over my head so I've got little to go on." Cody's eyes narrowed, and his face hardened. "I never committed any crime."

"So that's why you have a raspy voice." She felt very sorry for him as she tried to imagine actually living through a hanging.

"Yes, it is, and it took a long time before I could speak at all. I thought my voice was lost forever."

"How do you intend to find that man?" Patience was more than a little interested after hearing Cody's dreadful story.

"I've tried several ways, but I won't give up — you can be sure of that."

" 'Vengeance is mine, says the Lord,' " she reminded him. "You are very fortunate to be alive after all that." She paused a moment, then said quietly, "Spending all your time trying to get even is going to be awfully unsatisfying, even if you find the man and somehow punish him." She guessed from the look he gave her that he didn't agree. "And whatever you do to him is likely going to land you in prison . . . or worse." She wanted to say, *Or hanging from the end of a rope once more,* but she didn't dare.

"It may be in the Good Book," he spit out, "but I'm not so sure that it matters to me anymore. Besides, didn't you tell me the

237

man that had courted you was hanged? How do you know it wasn't the same vigilante? Could *you* forgive *him*?" Cody suddenly stood. "Look, I need to be going. Sorry I went on about this. Forget I even spoke about it, okay?" He tied the kerchief back in place over the scar.

"Well, it may not matter to you, but you matter to the Lord, I assure you. Why not put all this anger aside and see what your future holds?" Patience suggested. She couldn't see how his bitterness would come to any good.

Cody started down the steps, then turned back to her. "Look, I know you mean well, but I've got to handle this my own way. Gotta skedaddle," he said with a nod.

"I'll be praying for you," Patience said as he left, but if he heard her, he didn't acknowledge it. Cody was right — would she be able to forgive if she knew the man who'd hanged Russell?

"I bet the tea is cold now, Emily," Patience said, back in the kitchen. "Cody dropped by, and I was talking with him." She poured herself a cup.

Emily looked up from a book in her lap. "I never notice the passing of time when I'm reading," she said with a grin.

238

"Is that *Jane Eyre*?"

"Yes. I'm enjoying it so much. When I take a break, I simply have to pick it up again."

"I've read it, so I know what you mean." Patience smiled, sat down, and sipped at her lukewarm tea.

Emily closed the book. "What did Cody want? From what you've told me, I didn't think he was interested in you."

Patience set her teacup down. "He isn't. I'm guessing he wanted to apologize for not bringing me home from the dance."

"Mmm . . . Maybe he's jealous of Jed?"

"Hardly that. We talked about other matters, including the reason he's in Nevada City." Patience's smile faded.

Emily's brows lifted. "Oh?"

Patience told her the little that she had learned about Cody but asked her to keep the information to herself.

"I won't say a word to anyone," Emily whispered.

"We better finish our tea so I can start supper. Have you seen Mother?"

"I believe she's in the parlor."

"I'd better go check on her, but I'll be back in a few minutes." Patience thought about the advice she'd given Cody, which made her think about her own attitude toward her mother. Perhaps she was a failure at taking her own counsel.

19

Stunning blue skies and a balmy breeze blew across the valley floor as if to say, "This is the Lord's day — I will rejoice and be glad in it." Patience, Emily, and Charity were rumbling back from church in a rented buggy, on their way to the Hargrove ranch for Sunday dinner.

"The pastor's sermon really spoke to me this morning about my attitudes," Charity said after a while. Patience frowned. *Since when has she ever cared one whit about her attitude?*

Emily responded, "I felt the same way, Mrs. Cavanaugh. I'm so grateful that we have a Sunday service to attend. Most mining towns and camps don't have a church of their own, you know."

Charity smiled. "Then perhaps a person with means could help build a church in Nevada City — like you, Patience."

Patience laughed. "Me? I have no idea

about such things, Mother, and I certainly don't have means!"

"The Lord used people in Scripture who had many vices and even no money. You're becoming successful, so who knows. This time next year, I'm sure you will be doing quite well."

Patience took a moment to let her mother's words sink in. She'd never heard the woman talk this way before. *My, my, wonders never cease! But me — build a church?*

"I think that's a wonderful idea, Patience — and you're just the one to do it," Emily said with an impish little grin.

"Mmm . . . I don't know . . . It's true that one is needed here . . ." She was already thinking of people who might be willing to invest in the labor. But she put those thoughts away as they approached Cross Bar Ranch for their meal with Judith.

"My . . . such a large ranch." Charity touched the top buttons of her throat. "I wish I had my diamond brooch —"

"Mother, you look fine," Patience put in quickly. She knew her mother would want Judith to think she was a person of means. "Besides, the brooch might be ostentatious on a cattle ranch in the middle of the day." Charity gave her a sharp glance while Emily hid a smile behind her hand.

Judith was at the door and came down the steps with hands outstretched as they drove up. She told Patience a ranch hand would take care of the horse and buggy and ushered them inside. The living area was large, furnished and decorated with a mixture of leather and wood. Oversized chairs flanked either side of an enormous stone fireplace, and beautiful carved wood bookcases with glass fronts held leather-bound volumes, which Patience yearned to peruse. She'd been inside only the barn the time she was here for their annual dance.

"You have a beautiful home, Judith," Patience told her hostess.

Judith's violet eyes coordinated with the lavender trim on her white linen day dress. She looked cool and comfortable as she greeted her guests. "I'm so glad you could come, and this must be your mother." Judith reached toward Charity.

"Yes, I am," she said, shaking the outstretched hand. "It's so nice to meet you, Judith."

"Right this way, everyone. John is not able to join us today, and I've asked the cook to serve us in my small rose garden. I thought you might enjoy that."

"I admired your roses the night of the dance," Patience told her. The roses brought to mind that unexpected time with Jed, and she felt her face growing warm at the thought. She was privately ill at ease when her mind kept straying to that evening, but of course, no one else knew it, thankfully.

Under the shade of a tree, they enjoyed a wonderful meal with friendly conversation around the small table spread with an embroidered cloth. Patience leaned back in her chair and breathed in deeply. It was the first time in a while that she'd felt truly relaxed. She was not surprised, though, when her mother brought up the idea of Patience starting a church building fund. She felt her insides tense. Her mother knew exactly what she was doing.

Judith clapped her hands. "I love the idea." She turned to Patience. "I'm sure that John and I would be able to help financially with some of the expenses, along with others, of course. A church has been needed here for some time."

Patience sat forward. "That would be wonderful, Judith, but I haven't said I was ready to initiate a church building fund — that was entirely Mother's idea on the way over here." Patience heaved a sigh. "It seems like an awfully daunting undertaking —"

"To be sure," Judith agreed quickly, "but you seem like a young lady capable enough to handle anything put before you."

Emily was eagerly nodding. "Of course she is — after all, she's her mother's daughter."

Charity glanced at Patience, then remarked, "We Cavanaughs have a fighting spirit that runs through our veins, and we can tackle just about anything we set our minds to. I'm very proud of the way she's turned Creekside around."

Patience sat and stared at her mother, stunned. Was she finally pleased with something Patience had done?

Emily sat up straight and clapped her hands. "Another idea — we could start a choir. I know Patience has a very nice voice. I've heard her singing when we're doing chores," she added.

Charity bobbed her head. "Of course she can sing, and she can play the piano too. A shame the boardinghouse doesn't have one."

"I'll talk it over with John," their hostess said, "but it's possible we even might be able to donate a piano for the boardinghouse so you could sing and play for your guests." Judith smiled at Patience.

"Oh my, I wasn't suggesting —" Charity began.

"Mother . . . ," Patience whispered and nudged her mother's arm.

"Why not, may I ask?" Judith looked between Charity and her daughter.

"Because . . . well, Patience has done nicely on her own and has worked on getting Creekside open for business," Charity said. "We Cavanaughs do not take charity," she finished with a spritely air.

Patience would have liked to kick her mother's foot under the table.

"Well, I wouldn't exactly call this *charity,* Charity," Judith said with a little smile. "I think of it as a donation to a good cause. Heaven knows our mining town could use more culture. And certainly if a piano might also be a step toward a church . . ."

"I agree," Charity said with a firm nod. "Patience has talents for getting things accomplished. Let's see what might happen, both toward a piano and a church, when she puts her mind to it."

Patience didn't know whether to laugh or cry. "Please, can we move on to another topic?"

"See there, Patty, you just took charge!" Charity said, arching her brows.

A smile twitched at the edge of Judith's mouth as she lifted her cup, and Patience shrugged in defeat. "Judith," she explained, "I had some excellent help sprucing up the boardinghouse. Cody painted the outside

246

for me, and I hired Emily, then made her my partner. I couldn't be happier with how it's turned out."

"I didn't know you had a partner," Judith exclaimed. "Two minds of like ambition are always better than one when it comes to business." She smiled warmly at Emily.

"I'm honored to work with Patience, truly. I couldn't ask for a better 'boss.' " She chuckled, and the others joined in.

Emily turned to their hostess and said, "Judith, your garden is lovely. Do you take care of the roses yourself?"

"Yes, I do because I enjoy it. I watched my grandmother pruning her roses and coddling them when I was a child, so naturally my own fondness for roses grew."

"I'd say you're doing a great job!" Emily enthused. "They're beautiful."

"John gave me my first rose bush, imported from Pennsylvania. Each year, he sees to it that I have another hybrid rose to cultivate."

Emily clasped her hands together and looked as though she would melt at Judith's story. "Oh, how very romantic!"

"Yes, my John can be a romantic at times, which only makes my heart grow fonder. I've decided our first child — if it's a girl — will be called 'Rose.' " Judith's gaze dropped and her cheeks grew pink, no doubt feeling a bit shy at sharing such a confidence.

The rest of the dinner continued with additional interesting topics, including the fact that Judith was planning on a hayride soon, which they agreed would be most enjoyable for Nevada City families. When it was time to leave, it was with an invitation to another Sunday dinner soon.

"And, hopefully, John will be free that time — although we'll need to find at least one other man."

They all laughed. They were waiting for the buggy to be brought around when riders in a cloud of dust came barreling up to the house, John close behind with several of his drovers. He pulled his horse to stop, dismounted, and walked toward them.

He removed his hat and gave them a nod. "Howdy, ladies. Judith, I hope I'm not interrupting anything, but I've just been told that more of my herd was stolen!"

"Oh, no, John!" Judith put a hand to her lips. "What are you going to do?"

"I'll tell you what I'm going to do," he said, his voice sounding taut. "I'm going to get Jedediah on this. I'm sure it has to be the same men who stole the others a few weeks back. I've had enough, and it's time the marshal got down to business and used

his skill to find these varmints — or else!"
His grim expression gave some indication
of what that "else" might be.

Monty, standing nearby, hands on his
hips, spit a wad of tobacco into the dirt.
"Those steers would've brought us a good
price come fall roundup time." Monty
looked over at Emily, and Patience saw him
give her a broad smile. Emily's face brightened in response.

"Is there anything I can do?" Patience
asked. "We're headed back to town now."

"No thanks, I'll handle this myself," John
told her and turned back to his wife. "I
wanted to let you know where I was going,
Judith. I'll see you at supper." He gave Judith a peck on the cheek, then turned on
his heel, mounted, and left.

Patience felt fingers of cold unfurl in her
stomach. John's tone had been threatening
— inferring that Jed had disregarded his
duty when the first theft had occurred. But
she was able to smile at Judith as she said,
"We must be going too, Judith, and I want
to thank you again for your hospitality."

"Please don't wait for an invitation to
come — any time at all. It gets lonely way
out here."

"We'll have you over for Sunday dinner
soon, Judith," Patience promised again,

drawing her gloves on. The three ladies got into the waiting carriage with smiles and waves, Patience picked up the reins, and they headed back to town.

Jedediah was determined to have a late afternoon coffee and read the *Montana Post* before supper. Miners had no sense of Sunday rest, and he'd spent most of the morning smoothing out miners' disputes about who was the first to stake their claim. At least he'd kept them from pulling out guns and shooting one another. With the current flood of incoming miners, it wouldn't be long before there wasn't any further placer gold to be found. But, he decided, that would be preferable to a town full of transients who most likely would never settle here but simply move on to the next news of a gold strike. He liked the idea of a stable town. He pictured a town square with festivities for families, and houses with white picket fences, and, yes, even a church — an idea that had circled through his head recently. *Might even find myself in a pew more often than I do now,* he mused.

He took his coffee and paper outside where he could relax and still keep an eye open for trouble. He'd barely got past the first paragraph when he spied John charging toward him, his horse's sides heaving and nostrils flaring. *Must be trouble,* he thought as he stood to his feet.

John slid to an abrupt stop and jumped off his horse. "Jed!" he bellowed. "We've been struck again!" He thumped up the steps, his face full of fury, and Jedediah put his paper down.

"Let's go inside to talk, John." John followed him inside, and Jedediah shut the door behind them. "Tell me about it —"

"I've had it up to here!" John spit out, indicating his chest with his hand. "You've got to quit sitting around reading the paper and find whoever it is that's stealing my herd. I've had my men on twenty-four-hour stakeout, but it didn't stop them from taking more of my prized stock!" His jaw muscles twitched in agitation.

"Sounds like you're trying to blame me, John, for this latest travesty." Jedediah didn't like being considered a slacker. "My men and I scoured the area for miles into the next county — and not my jurisdiction."

John wasn't even listening. "If you don't do something about it, Marshal, I'll have to take matters into my own hands." John's eyes narrowed.

"Is that a threat?" Jed's ire was rising too.

"Call it whatever you like! But I'd suggest

you track somebody down and bring 'em in or else you'll lose your badge. I just might have to make a visit to the territorial governor."

Jedediah's hands clenched, and he desperately tried to control his anger. "Your threats mean nothing to me. No one else wanted this job or had the guts for it. Okay, let's get the details now. Tell me when you discovered the steers were missing."

"This afternoon, when my men were rounding up the herd to move it to a higher pasture. The heat has parched a lot of my grass, and —"

"I'll call some men together," Jed interrupted, "and we can head out at first light. It's getting toward dusk. With this happening right on the heels of the first, they could be still hanging around to hit you again. Reckon they've been hiding out in the high country."

"I don't care where they're hiding out — I want them found and hanged!"

"Hold on now — don't go causing even more trouble by getting riled up. Neither of us wants you doing anything you might regret." *I know about regrets.*

"Trust me, I won't regret whatever it takes," the man growled. "It took me years to build my spread and make a home for

Judith. Those steers will be worth plenty on hoof by roundup time this fall. I'll be out looking for clues — I suggest you do the same." He turned to stride down the steps and swing back onto his horse, galloping away in a cloud of dust.

Jedediah shook his head. He'd get the word out to some men for another posse, let Patience know boxed dinners were needed pronto.

Just when he'd thought he might have a chance to relax.

20

Patience tapped her pen against her notebook, trying to concentrate on the devotional she was writing, but her thoughts kept
drifting to Jedediah and John — who
seemed to be at odds about catching the
rustlers. Added to that was her recent unset-
tling conversation with Cody. She admitted
she wasn't sure she could forgive the man
who'd hanged an innocent person like
Russell. But how did she know Cody was
innocent of the accused crime? Her instincts
seemed to tell her he was being truthful.
Maybe she should be telling *herself* to
forgive instead of lecturing Cody about it.
There certainly was room for spiritual
growth within herself.

"Lord," she whispered, "help me be the
person You want me to be . . . and please
help me sort out my feelings about Jed."

That evening after supper, everyone, including Emily, had gone to their rooms after a long day. The newlyweds, Will and Liza, always went for a walk before turning in.

Patience was back at the desk in the parlor, Buttercup warming her lap. She savored the quiet and slowly turned the pages of her Bible, contemplating what God might be teaching her, writing those thoughts down in her notebook. Soon she'd have a manuscript complete enough that she might have Emily send it to her uncle.

As she was writing, Buttercup leaped from her lap and ran up the stairs. Patience heard movement on the porch and saw a shadow through the window. Who in the world was out there in the dark? Her residents had their own keys, and she was glad that the door stayed locked after ten o'clock. A shuffling of boots against squeaky porch boards and a soft knock at the door didn't sound alarming, though.

Patience pulled her shawl about her, tiptoed to the door, and lifted one corner of the lace curtain. Actually, she wasn't surprised to see Jedediah there after how John had all but accused him of negligence today at the ranch. She quietly unbolted the lock, opening the door just enough to speak with him.

"Jed," she whispered, "I suppose you

know what time it is."

"I'm sorry," he said, keeping his voice low. "Yes, I know it's late, but something's come up. Can you step out here for a minute?"

Patience opened the door and moved out into the moonlight. "How did you know I would still be up?"

"I saw the light burning through the window and figured you were working on your writing."

"You are, in fact, correct, but I'm sure you didn't stop by to hear my explanation of forgiveness from the Word. I am happy to see you, though. So what's the matter?"

"You've probably heard there's been another incident at the Cross Bar Ranch," Jed said, motioning her to the rocker and taking a seat nearby. "More of John's cattle were stolen. Are you able to put four boxed lunches together on such short notice for the morning?"

Patience pursed her lips, thinking. "I may have enough from supper to make some sandwiches from leftovers. Will that do?"

"Anything will do. And thank you." He leaned back and looked at her. "By the way, Patience, it's awfully nice to see you in the moonlight after a hard day."

Patience was glad that he wasn't able to see her embarrassment. His face seemed very appealing in the moonlight too. All she could manage, though, was a low "Thank you."

Jedediah leaned forward, but she drew back. "Not even a little hug?" His smile faded.

"Not out here, Jed. We could be seen —"

His harrumph stopped her explanation. "I doubt anyone is up this late and peering out their windows. I've nothing to hide."

"You never know who might have insomnia tonight, and I don't want there to be talk."

He moved back in his chair. "Oh, I forgot you're a virtuous woman," he joked.

Her throat felt dry, and she wasn't sure if he was simply making fun. "Matter of fact, my goal *is* to be virtuous, according to the Scriptures, and I have a respectable boardinghouse to run and don't want anyone getting the wrong idea." She stood and reached for the doorknob. He quickly stood too and covered her hand with his own.

"Least of all me?" Jed's voice was husky.

His hand was large — warm — strong. It would be so easy to fall against his broad chest, feel the beating of his heart against her ear, but she mustn't. "Please, Jed. This is not the time or place. I'll have your boxes ready for you at six. We both need to get to

— to get our rest. Don't knock . . . better come to the side door of the kitchen. I'll see you in the morning. Good night, Jed," she whispered.

He squeezed her hand and lifted his hand from hers. "I'm looking forward to that picnic under the pines . . ." He backed away, walked down the steps, and started down the sidewalk.

She watched him disappear in the darkness, then hurried back inside. She shoved her notebook into a drawer and doused the light at her desk. She wouldn't be able to concentrate any further tonight.

Thunderation! I'll never understand the ways of a woman, he thought, shoving his hands in his pockets. *Is she interested? . . . Or not?* Maybe it was all in his head.

He didn't have time to dwell on it — not now. He needed to find whoever was stealing cattle right from under John's nose — and his own. He knew that John had the influence to see to it that he lost his job, but he wasn't all that concerned about that. He was more worried about some no-account rustler still hanging around. He'd been wrong thinking they'd fled further south.

As he climbed into bed, he muttered, "A good night's sleep, and I'll be ready to face down a rustler . . . or a woman who can't make up her own mind!"

The next thing he knew a loud rapping on the downstairs door roused him from deep sleep. Jedediah saw it was near daylight as he dragged on his pants and hurried downstairs.

Jedediah flipped the lock and swung the door open, and it was Monty that strode inside, breathing heavily.

"For Pete's sake, Jed, I declare you could sleep through an earthquake!" Monty complained.

"You're lucky I stopped long enough to pull my pants on! Now what in tarnation —"

"Jed." Monty stopped him with an abrupt movement of his hand. "John never came home last night after he spoke to you. I fear something bad has happened to him — a bear, or accident —"

"Give me a few minutes. My posse will be meeting me in fifteen minutes —"

"We've searched all over the Cross Bar with no luck, and Judith has worried herself sick."

Jedediah remembered how angry and hotheaded John seemed yesterday. He sure did hope John was holed up someplace during the night for a good reason. Jedediah didn't want to worry Judith unnecessarily.

"I'm leaving to go back to the ranch. I'll let you know if he shows up," Monty said, wheeling out the door.

"Good idea. Judith may need protection."

Monty whipped back, his eyes flicking back and forth nervously. "You know something I don't?"

"Nah . . . was just thinking out loud." But something about it all did not sit right with Jedediah. It might have to do with the rustlers, but until he knew for certain, he wouldn't speculate.

"Catch up with you later, Jed." Monty flew down the porch steps, mounting his horse before Jed could get back inside.

Jed hurriedly finished dressing, holstered his Colt, and grabbed his Winchester. In less than a half hour, he and his men were hightailing it out of town.

This time they'd travel south, looking for clues along the Cross Bar property line. They spread out in a wide fan, the early sun high enough to likely show up whatever might lead them to the rustlers.

Whoever or however many were involved, Jedediah found nothing of interest. He finally reined Charlie in, propping his arms across his saddle horn. It looked like they'd been outsmarted again, but at the same time he didn't want to rush to judgment. He didn't want to even think it, but he couldn't help but wonder if it could be Bob or Cody. They worked for John — it'd be easy to know where the cattle grazed, then tip off a partner in crime when the coast was clear.

Along about midday with the sun baking down on his back, he slid off his horse, reached for his canteen, and took a long swig. *Thank God for water!* he thought as he also watered his horse. He'd sure be glad when autumn set in. Just as he was about to mount again, he noticed grass compressed in an unusual way near some underbrush. It was strange enough that he cautiously moved in that direction.

He was not prepared for what he saw, and he'd seen many a dead body. John lay sprawled on his back, a trail of dried blood down his face and shirt. Most likely he'd seen his killer face-to-face. Jed thought how horrible that must have been as he crouched down for a closer look.

Scenes flashed across his memory — other times he'd seen men with no life left in them, faces slack or distorted in agony. He shook his head, as if that would dislodge the memories. It just wasn't right that men killed their own to satisfy their greed, their search for happiness. Or vengeance. But he'd pulled the trigger — or given the order — when it was required by western law and justice, just as it must be when soldiers in battle had no choice but to defend freedom.

Somehow it was all so very sad, like the stillness of the day, the sizzling heat, and the buzzing of flies about John's bloody head. He was glad Judith wouldn't have to see it.

He fired a shot in the air to signal the posse, and soon the others came riding up.

The two men stood in the yard at the Cross Bar. "Judith is taking it very hard, no family and all . . ." Monty's voice drifted off as he reported the situation to Jedediah. "I can't stand to see a woman cry," he said with a shake of his head. "John was a good man, good to all his ranch hands."

"We can't leave her alone here," Jedediah said. "I have an idea." He motioned to James and Kit. "James, take Kit with you and ride back into town. See if you can get Miss Patience to come out to the ranch and be with Judith. The woman could use another woman's touch about now, and I can't think of a better person to comfort her."

James and Kit galloped away as Jedediah contemplated what else to do. "Men, let's stick together and hunt down the killers that did this. They can't be too far away."

"I'm coming with you," Monty said, and Jedediah nodded.

Patience and Emily had finished the lunch dishes and were about to plan the supper menu when Emily hurried to answer the doorbell.

"Two cowboys in the parlor to see you, Patience," Emily told her quietly.

"Cowboys? The only one I know is Cody."

"It's not Cody, but they look like they have serious business," Emily said. "So I took them to the parlor."

"Mmm . . . okay. I'll go see what this is about. You could start on supper ideas."

When she entered the parlor the cowboys stood. *Cowboys or not, they have good manners,* she thought, *and they've also removed their hats.*

"What can I help you gentlemen with? Are you inquiring about a room?"

The young one looked at his companion and the older one answered. "I'm James and this is Kit. We're part of Jed's posse. Jed tells me that you know Judith Hargrove?"

"I do. Why? What is this about?" Patience was beginning to feel uneasy.

Kit looked down and twirled his hat.

James said, "John, her husband, was ambushed last night. They found him — they found his body — when he didn't return home."

Patience drew in a sharp breath, her stomach a knot of pain. "Oh, how awful! Is Judith all right?"

"I couldn't say for sure, but Jed wanted me to escort you to the Cross Bar to attend to her. She has no family here in Montana."

"Oh, of course I will!" She turned toward the kitchen. "Let me tell Emily that I'm leaving and I'll fetch my hat and handbag."

Kit finally spoke. "We'll wait outside for you, if that's okay."

"Yes, and I'll be out right away." Patience's heart felt like it was being squeezed by a giant fist. And to think they'd just had lunch with poor Judith!

By the time she had told Emily she was leaving and why, grabbed her handbag and hat, and returned to the parlor, one of the men had gone to the livery for a small buggy and had harnessed up his horse to it.

The three were quickly on their way back to the Hargrove ranch. Patience found herself leaning forward as if to spur the horse to greater speed. *O Lord, help me to know what to say to Judith, how to help her.* Then her thoughts went to Russell and her own terrible loss. What would have been most comforting to her back then?

As they drove up to the home where they'd enjoyed the lovely meal with Judith, Patience took a deep breath. James courteously helped her out of the buggy and up the steps to the double doors, already open. She took another breath, then stepped into the parlor. Judith was sitting on a large sofa, her face buried in a handkerchief, with Jedediah beside her.

"Don't you worry, Judith," he was telling her. "We won't quit until we find whoever did this."

The two of them looked over at Patience as she stood by the door. Judith was sobbing, and she tried to stand. Jed helped her to her feet, and Patience went straight to the poor woman. The two held each other tightly, and Patience soothed the devastated widow.

"I'm so, so very sorry, Judith," she whispered. Judith pressed her face into Patience's shoulder with heartbreaking cries. Patience looked at Jedediah and shook her head, tears in her own eyes. Instinctively she knew there were no words she could say that would console her new friend. Only time — a *long* time — would heal the wound. After several minutes, Judith pulled away to wipe her nose and eyes.

"Can I get you a cup of hot tea . . . anything at all?" Patience asked.

"No . . . nothing . . . I have a terrible headache." Judith blew her nose once again.

"Is there anyone I can contact for you? Someone from your family?" she asked.

"I haven't any family left." She hiccupped, staring out the window. "There's headache powder in the kitchen pantry."

Jedediah motioned to Patience. "Can I talk with you?" He mouthed the words and nodded toward the kitchen.

Patience said, "I'll bring you something for your headache." Judith didn't move a muscle but continued staring outside. Patience led the way to the kitchen. "This is all so very shocking, Jed. I feel *so* sorry for her. Do you think this has anything to do with the rustlers?" she asked him.

Jedediah's face was etched with his own sadness. "I think it has everything to do with the rustlers. Do you think you could take her back to Creekside to stay a couple of days with you? I'd feel better about her safety. This was a cold-blooded killer."

"Why, of course. I'll pack up a few things for her, and you go ahead and suggest that to her while I make her tea with headache powder."

"Yes," he answered quietly, his hand on her arm. "Thank you for coming so quickly. I was sure that you would." His eyes held hers in a steady gaze.

She blinked away her tears and covered his hand with hers. "I could do nothing less, Jed. I haven't lost a husband but I lost a dear father . . . and someone else I cared for. I feel deep sympathy for her." Patience squeezed his hand, and he turned his so their hands were grasped together.

"I'll go speak with her then." He turned and strode out of the kitchen. She dug around in the pantry until she found the powder, then brewed a cup of tea for Judith. *Poor soul. No family to share her grief with will be awfully hard.*

Patience was determined, though, to support her new friend through the very difficult days ahead.

21

The trip back to Nevada City was quiet and solemn except for Judith's soft weeping. Kit drove the two back in the borrowed buggy. He was thoughtful and gentle to Judith, helping her with her carpetbag and speaking in a quiet voice. It was obvious that Judith was well liked by the ranch hands.

Patience's mother and Emily were at the door when she helped Judith up the steps and inside. She gathered that news of the tragedy must have already spread through town. "I've just made a pot of tea, Judith, or if you prefer I'll make coffee," Emily spoke softly.

"It doesn't really matter . . . I — I can't seem to think." Judith pressed her handkerchief to her trembling mouth. "I'm sorry."

"I'm sorry, dear, for your terrible heartache," Charity put in, shaking her head. "I just don't understand how someone could

shoot a person in cold blood, then leave him
—"

"Mother," Patience said, trying to keep
her voice low yet firm without sounding irritated, "let's give Judith a little time to
herself, all right?"

Patience settled Judith on the settee.
"Don't you worry about a thing, Judith. You
can sit here or lie back on a pillow while I
prepare a room for you."

"Oh, there's no need, Patience," Emily
said quickly. "I'll share your room, if that's
all right with you, and she can have mine.
I've already changed the bedding and
dusted," Emily assured her.

"Oh, thank you, Emily. You're such a
dear," Patience said.

Judith spoke up from her place on the settee. "I don't want to put you out of your
room, Emily, especially since I have a home
full of rooms . . . and emptiness." Judith's
tears had started again from eyes already
swollen and red.

Emily leaned over to give Judith a loving
hug. "Have your tea, and then we'll take
you upstairs where you'll be comfortable."

"Comfortable . . . but alone . . . ," Judith
choked out and buried her face in her
hands.

Patience sat down beside her and held out

a cup of hot tea. "No, not alone. You have your friends, but more importantly, you have God who cares for you more than anyone." She put her arm around Judith's shoulder and looked into the face of her friend, so recently the beaming, joyful, and very poised mistress of a large ranch. In an instant she'd become a hurt, stricken woman with pain too enormous for her slender shoulders.

It was all too sad, and Patience prayed silently that someone soon would be brought to justice — one small step toward peace and comfort for her friend Judith.

The day had stretched to what seemed interminably long by the time Patience was finally able to slip on her nightgown and crawl into bed. She lay there wide awake, the numbing fact swirling through her mind that someone she'd seen just the day before was in fact now dead. *It's unfathomable . . . but that's exactly how it was with Russell.* She squeezed her eyes shut, not wanting again to be reminded of that awful day. It had been all she could do to maintain her composure in front of Judith as she had helped the grieving woman get ready for bed.

Judith looked so pitiful, about ready to

drop when Patience had assisted her up the stairs. Emily had already placed Judith's carpetbag next to the bed. Patience helped her with the buttons down the back of her bodice and skirt and slid a fine linen nightgown over her head. No words were spoken between them until she had Judith in the bed and tucked the blanket around her.

Patience had given her what she hoped was an encouraging smile. "I'm so sorry you have to go through this, Judith," she'd told her. "I feel sure Jedediah and his men will find the man or men who did this to John. We must believe and trust that God knows the pain in your heart and will carry you through, no matter what."

Judith said in a feeble voice, "In case I forgot to say thank you — bless you for caring for me in my sorrow. It means so much. I'm so tired, but I fear that sleep will escape me tonight."

"I understand. If you should need anything at all, I showed you where my room is right across the hall." Patience smoothed back strands of hair from Judith's forehead. "I will pray for God to give you strength," Patience said, giving her hand a squeeze. She hoped Judith would find some comfort in her care while she was here.

Emily slid into bed next to Patience. "I

hope this arrangement won't make you too uncomfortable for a day or two, but I was sure Judith needed some time alone."

"I've had worse arrangements," Patience said with a soft chuckle. "You did the right thing, and we'll make do until Jedediah thinks it's safe for her to return to the Cross Bar. I'm afraid it'll be hard for any of us to sleep tonight." As Patience finished the words, she could hear Emily's steady, even breathing. She'd left Emily to do everything this afternoon for their residents, including supper, so Emily was no doubt very tired also. *At least she doesn't snore!* Patience thought with a little smile.

Jedediah and his posse rode back into town more than twenty-four hours after leaving the Cross Bar, hauling one rugged-looking man, gagged and bound, on horseback. The town was busy as usual at the supper hour as wagons and people choked the main thoroughfare. Some pedestrians stopped to stare as the group rode past. News traveled fast in the small town, and most had already heard of John's unfortunate demise and were guessing at who the prisoner was.

Jedediah sure hoped he had the right man. It was James who'd tracked the man down and fired off a shot into the air, signaling to the rest of the posse he'd caught someone. After a few questions from Jedediah and a threat if he didn't cooperate, the man admitted to cattle rustling and begged them not to hang him. But that was not Jedediah's plan. He wanted the man to have a fair trial. He currently had no proof that the man had killed John Hargrove, but the confessed thief needed an attorney to represent him in any case.

So much for the blue neckerchief connecting Cody to the crimes. Had it simply been a ploy? So many unanswered questions. He shook his head, the memory of a man strung up for this kind of crime pressing again into his thoughts. But now Jedediah was trying hard to make the law fair and effective. He wiped his face with his hand as he wearily dismounted in front of the jailhouse, the others following suit.

Monty furiously yanked the man off his horse, then half dragged him up the steps and inside, where Jedediah promptly shoved him into a cell and locked it. The prisoner sat down on the cot with his head between his hands.

"Brady," he said to one of the posse, "can you rustle up some vittles from the café for our prisoner?" At the man's nod, Jed added, "Get yourself something to eat, too."

"Sure thing, Jed." He hurried out while James, Kit, and Monty stood about looking exhausted.

"The rest of you — go on home. Get some rest. I'm mighty proud of you all for keeping your word to bring the prisoner in alive." All Jedediah wanted now was a hot bath and sleep. "Kit, see that our horses get a rubdown and oats over at the livery."

Kit nodded, and James muttered good night and stalked down the steps to his horse.

Monty hung back. "You know he doesn't deserve living, not after what he's done." Monty leveled a dark look at Jedediah.

"Now hold on, Monty. He didn't admit to the ambush. He admitted only to the cattle stealing. We'll have to find more evidence —"

"If he said he was innocent, would you believe him?" Monty nearly shouted. "You know he couldn't've pulled this off single-handed. No way."

"I'm not sure, but I *am* sure this is what I was hired for — to give the man a fair hearing," Jedediah responded. He didn't need any more trouble than he already had, but he could tell Monty wasn't satisfied with his summation of the situation.

Monty's hands went to his hips. "You losing your nerve, Jed? I can't believe you!"

"Monty," he reasoned, "let the matter be. You need to let me handle this."

Monty turned on his boot heel. "We'll see 'bout that." He strode out, slamming the door.

Jedediah sighed heavily. He hoped some sense would sink into Monty's rather thick skull. If the man decided to get the town all riled up . . .

Jedediah decided to have a bath before grabbing a bite to eat. He took a clean shirt and pants from upstairs, and as he headed out the back toward the washhouse, he spied something on his desk — a white linen cloth over what appeared to be a plate. He lifted the napkin to find a complete dinner still warm underneath it. A note attached written in pretty handwriting read,

I pray you return without injury and with a criminal or two to pay for this heinous crime against Judith and John. I thought you might be hungry if you did return tonight. I know this is not our usual "arrangement," but I made an exception tonight.

Patience

Her note made him smile and warmth

275

flooded his chest. *Well, how do you like that? She's thinking about me.* He decided he would go ahead and eat now, but outside on the porch. Brady would return shortly with food for the prisoner. Not that the lowlife deserved any, but it was the law.

22

Strange as it seemed, Patience found herself somewhat reluctant for her mother to leave for her home. This last week they had seemed to find additional common ground. There was less sparring about how Patience should run the boardinghouse, although occasionally her mother would make a complaint — a "suggestion," she called it — about Patience's menu. There was either too much salt or not enough, chicken served too often, and couldn't they have more beef? This was cattle country, wasn't it? And on and on. There was no pleasing the woman completely, but for some reason she wasn't taking it to heart like before. They had even laughed together on occasion.

"I'm going to miss everyone here," Charity told her daughter as they worked together on packing. "I never knew that such busyness could be enjoyable. Living alone is very quiet, and even though I like that too,

I sure am going to find it rather lonely."

Patience didn't feel like the statement was an accusation. She paused as she folded another shirtwaist. "You can come back and visit as often as you like. You may have to room with me, though, if there are no vacancies." She looked at her mother fondly.

Charity folded her nightgown and robe, placing it in her case, and smiled. "I just might take you up on that. Maybe for the holidays?"

"Absolutely."

"Or perhaps a wedding?" A brow shot upward and her mother smiled knowingly. "I was wrong about Cody, Patty. It's apparent to me that Jedediah is more suited to your liking."

"I do care for him, but I'm not sure of his feelings for me." Patience hoped to change the subject. She lifted the two remaining dresses and began folding one, when something fell to the floor at her feet. She saw her mother's diamond brooch lying on the bedside rag rug. "Mother! Your brooch!" she called out as she bent to retrieve it.

Her mother's mouth dropped open. "Oh my!" she said, accepting it from Patience's hand. "I don't remember putting this in my pocket. I thought we all had looked everywhere. Now I feel truly awful that I accused

Emily of taking the brooch." She sighed heavily.

Patience laid a hand on her mother's. "Don't worry. I don't think Emily ever knew you had done so."

"You have a very nice partner here. The two of you work so well together. I've been meaning to tell you that."

"Yes, I agree. Emily has a good head and an even better heart. That's why I knew she would never take your cameo. No harm has been done, and you now have your brooch back."

Charity beamed. "I'm so happy that you found it, and from now on I'll be more careful with my valuables. Will you let Jedediah and the residents know that we found it?"

Patience nodded. "Yes, of course. We must get finished or you'll miss the stage."

Charity leaned over and kissed her cheek. "I'm very proud of you. I realize you had heavy responsibilities taking care of me after your father died. I don't think I ever showed my appreciation, but I want you to know I'm very thankful. I wish you great success."

Patience had a lump in her throat. She could never remember a time at home when her mother had talked to her this way. Maybe advancing age was softening her outlook. "Thank you" was all she managed to choke out as she put her arms around her mother's shoulders and felt the return hug. It was a new beginning.

After they had said their goodbyes at the depot and her mother boarded the Wells Fargo stagecoach, Patience stood and watched the mailbag being stowed on the top. She finally was mailing her compiled devotionals to Emily's uncle, and the package was going on the same stage as her mother. Emily had happily tucked in a note of introduction. A tiny spark bubbled in her heart with hope the editor might actually like it. She had dedicated it to her mother. She wondered what her mother would think if she knew. She smiled to herself as she waved the coach around the bend and out of sight.

Jedediah had the impression the townsfolk were giving him the cold shoulder — as if he were protecting the man guilty of John's death. John Hargrove had been admired and respected around the whole area, so it was no surprise that they wanted someone to pay. Jedediah decided the porch with his afternoon cup of coffee wasn't the place to be with folks casting hard stares his direction, so he went back inside.

He'd stopped by to pay Patience for the

lunches, but Emily told him she was at the stage depot with her mother. Tomorrow he'd be transporting the prisoner to Helena to see that justice was done, so he probably wouldn't see her for a few days.

He checked on the man — Nathan Watkins was his name — to be sure he was still in the cell, although there was no way he could've escaped.

"How long you plan on keepin' me locked up?" The prisoner glared up at him from the cot.

"I'm hauling you over to the judge in Helena for a hearing. Then you're his problem, and I say good riddance!" Jedediah growled back.

"So why didn't you just hang me like you did Russell Watkins?"

Jedediah froze. *How does he know about Russell? He said "Russell Watkins." Is he . . . ?*

"Why? He a friend of yours?" Jedediah tried to keep his tone nonchalant.

"More than a friend — he was my older brother, but you hanged him." The man dropped his face into his hands. "It should've been me," he said, his voice so low Jedediah could barely hear the words.

Jed grunted. Nathan was a decent-looking fellow. Should've been married with two kids bouncing on his knee by now, but instead he'd turned to stealing. Jed stared through the bars at the man.

Nathan continued to hang his head for a moment. When he finally lifted it, his eyes appeared vacant. "And now it'll be me," he said under his breath.

Through gritted teeth Jedediah responded, "Then you'll receive your just reward, if I have anything to do with it."

"I reckon, but I didn't kill John Hargrove," Nathan declared once more.

"Then who did?" Jed banged his hand against the cell bar and it rattled ominously.

"I don't know."

Jedediah tried to stare him down. "Know, but won't tell?"

"I may be a rustler, but I ain't no murderer!"

Jedediah stalked back to his desk, but he couldn't concentrate. With the grim looks he was getting from the townsfolk, he wasn't sure he should venture out to get their suppers. Maybe Joe would drop in. Besides, now his appetite had all but disappeared.

Jedediah awoke to Patience standing over him. He jerked upright and blinked at her. "I must have fallen asleep," he told her, "but what a nice way to wake up — your beautiful face right above me." She gave him a coy smile, then straightened, but he took her hand. "I've missed you," he admitted, and saw her sweet smile of surprise.

She whispered with a soft tone, "I missed you too." She looked down at his hand holding hers, and he chuckled at her discomfort over his compliment.

"I've never — well, no one's ever called me 'beautiful' before, Jed," she said, pressing her free hand against her face. "Do you really think that's so?" she whispered after a glance over her shoulder at Nathan in his cell.

Jed slowly stood and pulled her by the hand over to the corner, out of sight of his prisoner. "You sure are, Patience," he said, still holding her hand and staring into those green eyes. "You're beautiful in a lot of ways, not only in the way you look. I noticed it when you were taking care of Judith Hargrove, how gentle and caring you were." He put his arms around her, and he could feel her hug him back.

"Someone could come in any time, Jed," she finally whispered as she pulled away, and reluctantly he let her go.

"Is that food I smell?" he asked.

She laughed. "Is that all you can think about?" She led him over to the basket she'd placed on his desk.

He chuckled. But then he said, lowering his voice, "Hardly — lately all I can think about is you."

"I like to hear that, Jed. Thank you. Now, this is your plate, and I made one up for the prisoner."

"Sounds like a fair deal to me," he quipped. "Hope mine is bigger and better."

They stood in front of the cell door with the plate of food, and Jedediah unlocked it.

Nathan jumped up off the cot and stared through the bars, his jaw hanging open. "What the devil are *you* doing here, Patience?"

23

Patience reached out to one of the cell's bars to steady herself while Jedediah took the plate from her shaking hand. "What on earth are *you* doing here, Nathan?" she finally managed to ask.

Jedediah shot a look from Patience to Nathan and back again. "You *know* him?"

"Yes, I do," she croaked out. "Jedediah, can you leave us alone for a few minutes?"

"I don't know if that's a good —"

"Please, Jed," she said.

Reluctantly he agreed. "Five minutes, no more." She took the plate back from Jedediah and went inside the cell. Jedediah shut the door and walked back to his desk.

She'd have to try and explain it all to Jed later, but for now she handed the plate to the prisoner. He went to the cot and sat down, the dinner balanced on his knees. She took a seat on the other cot facing him.

Patience wasted no time. "Why didn't I ever hear from you after Russell died, Nathan?"

"I was hiding out and couldn't take the chance of being caught." Nathan ran his hand through his hair in extreme agitation. He placed the plate of food on the cot and jumped to his feet, pacing the distance between them.

"Why? Were you in trouble?"

The man stopped his pacing to stare at her. "Don't you know? Russell was hanged by Jedediah Jones, your own town marshal."

Patience felt her heart turn to lead. She could hardly take a breath. "How — why do you say that? How do you know Jedediah did it?" she stammered out, her mind swirling with far more questions than she could express.

"I just watched him sign my arrest papers," he spit out, "charging me with rustling and the murder of John Hargrove. He signed them with his flamboyant 'X,' the signature he's been known for. *'Vigilante X.'* It's not that he can't read . . . more like a badge of arrogance and power when he was one of the Montana Vigilantes. They were responsible for stringing up road agents whenever they thought it was necessary. All lawful, I might add," he finished, bitterness filling his voice.

Patience sat stunned with this new information about Jedediah. How she wished he'd told her all this himself. "But why did they hang Russell? Was he guilty? Or — were you the thief?"

Nathan gave a quick nod and finally sat back down on the cot. "Me and Russell stole to add to our small herd so we could make money quick. I thought we'd never be caught. Russell paid for it with his life, but it should've been me. There was another man, Cody. I can't forgive myself, and I doubt God will." Nathan's head was once more in his hands, and he groaned pitifully.

Cody too? Patience tried to absorb all he was telling her, and she found that she believed him. She shifted on the cot, and finally said, "God forgives us no matter what we've done, Nathan, so why shouldn't we forgive ourselves?"

"I doubt He will forgive me," he argued.

"When you are in doubt, see what God says in the Scriptures."

"I bet you've never had *those* kinds of doubts, Patience."

"But I have, Nathan, and I'm not too proud to say so."

He simply stared across the small cell at her.

"The man you mentioned, Cody," she said slowly. "Was his last name Martin?"

"Yes, he just happened to be in the wrong place, and the vigilantes thought he was part of the gang."

Patience licked her lips and tried to still her heartbeat. Things were falling into place now. She felt sorry for Nathan. "Cody's alive and works at the Cross Bar Ranch," she said softly.

"What did you say? *Alive?* He can't be! They strung him up, and Jedediah was the one that gave the word." Nathan was staring wide-eyed now.

"It's a long story." Patience heard Jedediah returning from across the room. "I'll pray for you, Nathan." She wanted to ask if Russell ever had any intention of marrying her, but she couldn't bring herself to do it. Not now.

"I'm as good as convicted," Nathan solemnly said. "We both know that."

"Time's up!" Jedediah called, turning the key and unlocking the cell.

"Goodbye, Nathan," Patience murmured, giving Nathan one last look before she slipped out the cell door.

"Why didn't you tell me?" she said, her lips held tight, as she led Jed over to the corner.

"Tell you *what*?"

"That you were once known as 'Vigilante X' and responsible for *hangings*!" Patience knew her voice was loud and shrill, but she couldn't help herself.

Jedediah's face held a stunned look, as though she'd hit him over the head with one of her prized frying pans. When he didn't answer for a moment, she started for the door. But he finally said, "Because I didn't see how that could matter now."

Patience swung back, trembling. "Matter! *Matter?* When you were responsible for *killing the man I'd hoped to marry?*"

He looked genuinely bewildered. "What man? I didn't know you were intended for someone else . . . you never said."

"It doesn't matter now, does it, because Russell is dead," she said flatly.

"Russell? You're talking about Russell Watkins? You mean you'd have married a *cattle thief?*" he shot back.

She lowered her gaze, crestfallen. "I didn't know that until just now," she said, her voice low.

"I've never hanged an innocent person."

"I need to go. I just —" She picked up her skirts and spun around to leave. Suddenly loud voices were heard outside. Jedediah locked the front door, then looked out the window, a scowl on his face. A crowd was shouting for the prisoner to be released to them.

"They were here earlier with threats to take Nathan," Jedediah muttered. "It seems they believe they can administer justice better than me — like I'm not the peacemaker." He dropped his hand from the window sash. "Monty's with them now. I never thought I'd live to see my best friend turn against me."

Suddenly a shower of rocks hit the window, and Patience jumped. "Step back, Patience. Looks like some very angry people in the street. I don't want you to get hurt. Folks don't agree with me taking Nathan to Helena tomorrow."

"What will you do?"

"I'll go out there, try to talk some sense into Monty and them. But you stay inside here. Some of these guys are just along for the ruckus, and they've been drinking. No telling what they're liable to do." He took her elbow and guided her to a chair away from the window. "Stay here and don't move."

Patience did as she was told, knowing he was right. For her own safety, Jedediah didn't want the crowd to know she was there, she reasoned. She sat down away from the window as she'd been instructed, turning over in her mind all the new information she'd learned today.

Jedediah checked that his badge was in plain sight, lifted his carbine from the wall, added shells, and hoped he wouldn't have to use them. He was not about to let them take the man that his posse had hunted down, and he sure didn't need any more trouble. But it riled him that a handful of renegades wanted to do just that.

It wasn't the first time he'd seen this kind of behavior that turned into hanging mobs. He eased over and peered out the window at the men milling about in the street — Monty at the center of it. He would try to reason with them.

He slid the lock open, stepped out onto the porch, and locked the door behind him. Somebody poked Monty and pointed to Jedediah. Everyone quieted down, their attention riveted on first one, then the other of the two men.

Monty spoke first. "Jedediah, you need to turn that low-down varmint over to us. If you're feelin' squirrely 'bout what needs to be done here, we'll see to it for you. Nobody'll be the wiser."

Jedediah simply stood there for a moment.

The crowd waited, but the tension in the air was intense. "He's not going anywhere until I say so, and where I say." Jedediah's response was both calm and unmistakable. "I think the summer heat must have baked your brain. Since when do any of you want to take the law into your own hands? Those kind are called outlaws."

"Since that man killed John Hargrove, that's when!" Monty shouted, and the crowd joined in with their agreement.

"We have no proof of that," Jedediah told them in a loud voice.

"He's stole John's cattle twice!" a burly man in the crowd yelled.

"I'm not discussing this any further with you. Go home peacefully, and leave this matter to me and the law. I was still the marshal last time I looked at my badge." The setting sun glinted on it when he glanced over at Monty. "That goes for you too." Monty grimaced and threw his cigarette down to grind it into the dust with his heel.

The small group of rabble-rousers was surrounded by a growing crowd of curious onlookers. Monty and his cohorts were grumbling among themselves. Jedediah wasn't sure what they would decide — if they would simply go away and let him handle this or not. He raised his voice again and said, "Everyone go on home now to your suppers. The law will do what it's supposed to do — protect the innocent and prosecute the guilty."

Some in the crowd began moving away, and Jedediah stepped backward, quickly unlocked the door, and slipped inside, securing it behind him. It wouldn't be safe out there for a while, he knew.

He strode over to where Patience sat, back straight, barely looking at him. "Patience, you'll have to stay here until those men are gone. It's not safe for you to leave yet."

"What's going on?" Nathan demanded from his cell. His face was white as he held on to the bars and stared at his jailer.

Jedediah walked over to him. "I'm afraid they're after your hide."

Beads of sweat had formed across Nathan's forehead, and his shirt was drenched. "So what are you gonna do? Turn me out?"

"I'm thinking about it." Jedediah snorted. "Then I could be rid of you."

"Did you tell them that I didn't kill John?" Nathan put in, eyes wide with fear. "Well? Did you?"

Jedediah grunted. "I told them we have no proof and to leave the rest to me. But to tell the truth, there's about ten of them and one of me." Jed turned on his heel and walked back to his desk. It was nearly dark so he struck a match, lit the kerosene lamp, and fixed his gaze on Patience. "I'm afraid you're stuck here with me for a while, just to play it safe."

"I'd rather go home," she muttered.

"Sure you would, but once they know you're in here with me, they may not take so kindly to a virtuous woman who spends time with a vigilante marshal."

Patience harrumphed. "I'm not afraid of them."

Even angry, he thought, *she's awfully attractive with her green eyes snapping like wildfire.* " 'Course you're not, but I am."

"You?"

Jedediah sighed. "Yes, I know when it's the better part of wisdom to be cautious. I don't want a shooting, and you might be harmed, just out of their cussedness. I *am* afraid when a crowd of men takes it into their minds to do the dispensing of justice."

"Yes, I just bet you know all about 'dispensing justice.' " Patience folded her arms and looked away.

"Look, can we just let that go for now?"

She blew out a long breath but didn't answer. He decided to take that as a momentary truce.

"All right," he said. "I'll brew us a pot of coffee. I'm afraid we'll be here a while." He couldn't help but be glad she was here with him, but he sure wished the circumstances were different. Just an hour ago he was pretty sure she did care for him. And now . . . ?

He went over to the stove, stoked the fire, and started the water boiling for coffee. He had a blinding headache anyway. Those things she accused him of had hurt him, but he also realized he had hurt her even worse, though certainly unknowingly at the time. *I gave the order that took the life of her beau.* What kind of forgiveness would that take?

Keeping out of sight of any who might be lingering in the street, Jedediah sidled up to the window while the coffee brewed. Most of the crowd had dispersed, but a few folks were still hanging around. He couldn't see Monty among them and hoped this would be the end of it.

He poured coffee into two blue-and-white spatter mugs and sat down to face Patience. She took the cup from him, her fingers brushing his fingertips. He wanted to hold those fingers against his chest and tell her he was sorry for the sadness reflected in those lovely eyes.

She blew on the coffee to cool it, looked at him over the rim of her mug, then finally took a sip.

To his amazement she said, "You're getting better at coffee making."

"Thank you. Fresh is always better." *So has she decided she can find it in her heart to forgive me?*

He paused a moment before quietly asking, "Patience, could you tell me more about the man you were going to marry?"

She twisted one way, then the other, in the chair, finally putting her mug down on a nearby table. "There's really not much to tell. Russell was beginning to add to his small herd, and he worked hard building a ranch with his brother, Nathan. He was courting me, and I believe he was getting ready to ask me to marry him . . ." She gazed out the window, a faraway look in her eyes, and Jedediah wondered if she had truly loved this man. If so, how deep was that love? And maybe most significant, how were her feelings affected by what she had learned today from Nathan?

"So he hadn't actually asked you yet?"

She sat up straighter. "Well . . . not in so many words." Then she looked down at her coffee. "Now that I think about it, I may have assumed too much. I couldn't bring myself to ask Nathan about it today, but I think he wouldn't want to hurt my feelings if the answer was no."

Jedediah sighed. "Either way, I'm sorry Russell didn't ask you, but hanging him was legal — fair and square." *Though if I had known it was going to hurt you, I would not have done it.* He sighed again. "If it hadn't been for the Montana Vigilantes, we wouldn't have been able to keep up with all the crimes the road agents were responsible for. We were able to rid Montana of some of the worst — Clubfoot George Lane and Jack Gallagher, to name a couple."

Patience cocked her head and looked him straight in the eye. "Then it was fair to hang an innocent man like Cody?"

He almost choked on his coffee. "What are you talking about, Patience? Do you mean Cody who now works at the Cross Bar?"

"One and the same," she answered in a clipped tone.

Jedediah just stared at her for a long time. "Cody is alive and well," he mused, looking away.

"Nathan confirmed to me that Cody is the man you hanged that day."

Jedediah was bewildered and shook his head. "How on earth can that be?" Surely she was confused — he'd watched the man die. Had him cut down and carted away to the medical facility.

"Apparently, Cody's neck didn't snap like it should —" She paused and looked away, her knuckles white as her hands clasped tightly in her lap. She finally said through clenched teeth, "When you told someone to cut the body down, then take it to the local medical teaching lab for research, he wasn't actually dead, but his throat was severely injured. That's why he has a raspy sounding voice — he's fortunate that he can talk at all. Cody explained to me that he wears the blue neckerchief to cover the scar. He said he was innocent, and I believed him when he told me. Now Nathan confirms it. Cody came here to find the one who hanged him, though I didn't know it was you till today." She looked away and gave a long sigh. "It's a lot for me to take in, I don't mind saying, especially knowing you had a hand in Russell's death."

Jedediah leaned back in his chair, his heart as heavy as he'd ever felt it. Now he knew why Cody seemed familiar, but the raspy voice had thrown him off. *I am responsible for the hangings.* He shook his head, bewilderment once more coming over him like a shroud.

"Come to think of it," he finally said, "I didn't ever see Cody's face. It was covered with a muslin sack." He paused, thinking. "Is he looking for revenge?"

"Something like that, but I've been trying to talk to him about moving on in his life and learning to forgive." Patience lifted her coffee mug once more and took a sip. Then she set it down again and looked at him. "But I am wondering if I can forgive you for not telling me who you really are, Jedediah."

"You know now, Patience. Do I seem like the same man Nathan talked about?" When Patience didn't answer, he went on. "I sure hope not. I've been doing a lot of soul searching ever since I became marshal here. Though those hangings were legal, like I said, they have been coming back to haunt me. Whether it was moral is another question — one I can't answer right now." He stared into his cup.

"None of us is perfect, Jed, including me. I'm so glad God loves us, even when we sin and make mistakes." Her voice caught on the last words.

He looked up to see her eyes were full of tears. "I believe that to be truth. Otherwise, He couldn't love me." Jedediah spoke quietly. He stood to his feet. "I'm having another cup of coffee. How about you?" She held out her cup.

Maybe we're making some headway, he thought as he carried their mugs over to the stove. He sure hoped so.

"Is that coffee I smell, Marshal? I could sure use a cup," Jedediah heard Nathan yell. Patience started to get up, but Jedediah motioned for her to stay seated. "I'll get him a cup," he told her. "You stay put. We've got more talking to do." She blinked at him and nodded.

I sure would love to know what's going through her mind, he thought as he brought the coffee to his prisoner. He went back to the stove for the refills and returned to his place for more conversation with Patience.

24

If it weren't for the current tense situation, Jedediah's office would seem almost cozy, the glow of the lamp casting his shadow on the wall while Patience sipped at her second cup. She was very conscious of the danger, though, as Jed frequently made cautious trips to the window to check on things. She watched him now, standing to one side of the panes and peering out.

Nathan was silent, and Patience figured he'd gone to sleep — or maybe he was praying for a miraculous rescue. She assumed Jedediah lived upstairs, and probably in rather bare-bones accommodations. She suddenly felt sorry for him. He was alone most of the time. *Wonder why he never married?* she mused. Maybe no woman wanted to have a vigilante for a husband.

Jedediah returned from his check of the street, then pulled his chair closer. "Still some guys out there," he said as he sat down. Patience rather liked the mixture of leather and soap when he leaned close enough to see her face in the dim light.

"I sure wonder what they're hatching. Hope it's nothing."

"Maybe they'll realize you are right, that the best way for justice to be done is by the law, and eventually go home." Jedediah didn't say anything, simply nodded thoughtfully.

Patience chewed her bottom lip, trying to get up her courage, then said, "Jed, why haven't you ever married?"

His face registered surprise. "This new question gives me a momentary reprieve from the uncomfortable discussion about how I've lived my life?"

She felt herself blush and was glad the light wasn't all that bright. "I just wondered, that's all."

Jedediah leaned forward, both elbows on his knees, cradling his mug. "Truth is, I had found what I thought was a rather nice young woman years ago and wanted to settle down, but the lady jilted me." He stared at his coffee. "Seems she had her eye on bigger and better things. It took me a long time to get over it, and I've never seemed to find a lady to court since —" He looked up at Patience. "And then I met you.

302

I never had much mothering growing up and was raised in Pennsylvania with little education. I think I already told you I've worked as a shoemaker and a brick maker. Then the small farm in Kansas, but couldn't make a go of it. And now . . . well, only you can tell me about now."

"I don't know, Jed. I was beginning to think we had something special, but that was before today — before learning more about your past. And not merely your past, but something that directly impacted me. I'm just not sure . . ."

"I have so many regrets," he finally answered, "things I need to rectify. But some can't be undone. I've made my peace with the Lord, Patience, and now all I want to do is keep the peace in Nevada City. And — if you'll let me — win your heart and your hand."

Patience took a deep breath and put her cup down. "I — I'll think about that, Jed, and I will pray about it to. I suggest you do that also."

He smiled and nodded. "Fair enough. So tell me something about you that I don't know."

"I'm sure you have guessed by now that my mother and I aren't close, never have been. However, when she came here to visit, we were able to close that gap somewhat. I adored my father, but he passed away. I eventually left home because I didn't want my mother to control my adult life as she did my growing-up years. She made it clear to me early on that I was 'Plain Jane.' I've always worried about how I look to others. I'd like to be as pretty and slender as Emily." She tried to chuckle, but it really didn't work.

"I'd say you're awfully brave to start out on your own, restoring and running a boardinghouse. That takes a lot of gumption, like my grandma used to say. You're mighty pretty to me, inside and out. I like your cheerfulness and spunk. You make things — well, interesting — and life has gotten a lot more appealing for me with you around." His eyes crinkled at the corner as he smiled at her. "You don't need to look like or be like anyone else but yourself," he added.

"Well, the boardinghouse was a gift from my grandmother after she passed. That was another thing my mother didn't like. Actually, I think she didn't like that my grandmother and I were close . . . maybe she felt hurt." Patience looked away, thinking about that possibility.

"Seems like your mother was pretty hard

on you," Jedediah said after finishing his coffee.

Patience sighed. "It was just her way, once she began having heart problems, and after Russell was . . . was gone." She took a deep breath before continuing. "I couldn't bear the 'I told you so' look in her eyes, nor my friends' pitying glances." She looked over at him with a rueful expression. "Maybe you were right when you told me I have no humility."

"I really didn't mean that," he said quietly. "Well . . . maybe just a little." He quirked an eyebrow at her, and they both smiled.

She turned serious again. "I think you might be right. I've always expected every-one to live up to my standards and think the way I do, and that's not fair. Actually, come to think of it, that's what I accuse my mother of doing. Maybe we're alike." Patience was lost in thought for a while. "The last couple of months, while writing in my devotional journal, I believe God has been revealing my own inadequacies. Just like He's done now. I need to learn to be more accepting of others, not rushing to judg-ment — like I've done with my mother, with Russell, and with you, too, Jed."

"I'm grateful, Patience." He reached out and took her hand. "Am I forgiven then?"

he asked.

Patience looked over at him with a brief smile. "Forgiven. Can you forgive me for acting so high and mighty?"

Jedediah squeezed both her hands, and leaned over to give her a hug.

A sudden flash of bright light through the window brought them both to their feet, and Patience could see men waving torches high, joining others who had been milling about while she and Jedediah were talking.

"Hey, Marshal! It's time you hand him over," came a shout that sounded like Monty.

Patience stiffened and put a trembling hand on his arm. "What are you going to do?"

"I'm not rightly sure," he said, keeping his voice low. "I could let them have Nathan. It's what he deserves for his thievery, but I don't know if I can live with that. Also, I think he could provide information about what really happened with John's murder, knows who might have been involved." Jedediah drew her toward the dark corner, out of earshot of Nathan. "I'm going to see if I can talk some sense into their thick skulls. Stay here," he said again with a quick hug.

Patience's heart pounded as she watched

him open the door and heard the shouts suddenly louder through the opening. He quickly shut and locked the door behind him.

She didn't want Jedediah to be in harm's way. *Lord, please keep him safe,* she prayed. She went back to her seat and prayed earnestly . . . for Jedediah — for Judith — for Nathan.

Jedediah prayed he was doing the right thing. He stood at the top of the steps, carbine at his side, and waited for the crowd to settle down. He noticed several women standing among them. Monty was front and center.

The torches illuminated the faces of the mob, their anger and determination clearly evident. He didn't want to rile them any further than they already were.

They had momentarily quieted when he came out of the marshal's office, but now they all started talking at once. They wanted vengeance for John's death — why was he so blind, so stubborn, protecting a killer? On and on it went until Jedediah fired off a bullet into the black sky.

In the sudden silence, he said, "Listen here! I don't appreciate threats, and in case you've forgotten, I am the legally appointed

US Marshal and will arrest anyone who ventures near this door tonight. And a reminder — attacking a marshal is a federal offense."

Monty stepped out of the crowd. "Jedediah, my friend," he began, obviously attempting to sound conciliatory, "how can you let that man sit there in your jailhouse after what he's done? Just release him to us, why don't you? We'll take care of —"

"Because it's the law," Jedediah said, cutting him off, "and we don't have any proof he murdered anyone. He has a right to a trial." The carbine was hanging down, but anyone could see he was keeping it in position to fire at a moment's notice.

"You've strung men up before," someone from the back shouted, "and you never minded then. What's got into you?"

"That was a different time, different laws. Now the law is represented by this badge. And this means I will take him to the judge in Virginia City. Step back and stay back. It's my solemn duty to protect the prisoner, and I intend to do it!" Jedediah looked out over the crowd and watched as they muttered among themselves. Out of the corner of his eye, he noticed Joe, Hannah, and Cody — of all people — coming near. *What's Cody doing here?*

"He's nothing but a coward," shouted Walt, a known troublemaker, above the other voices, "and he's lost his guts to hang him, but we haven't. Right, men?"

"There's only one of him and plenty of us," another agreed.

Jedediah raised his carbine. "Don't any of you do anything you'll be sorry for."

Joe came up the steps and stood beside Jedediah. "I'm with you, Jed! They'll have to climb over me to get inside."

"Thanks, Joe."

Another shouted, "I say we get him now, and then we'll all sleep better."

Cody sidled up to where Jedediah and Joe stood side by side, legs spread, ready to protect the prisoner. "Can I say something?"

The crowd, probably as surprised as Jed, settled down again, and he nodded to Cody.

"Folks, the marshal's right. The man deserves a trial, nothing more but nothing less. Why don't you go home and let Jedediah run him over to Virginia City so the judge can decide if he deserves a hearing."

"Why should you give a flying bat's wings if he deserves anything more than a rope and a tall tree?" another onlooker asked.

Cody glanced at Jedediah. "Because our laws say every man accused is given a trial, and that's what Jedediah is aiming to do."

"How do you know?" Walt sneered. "And who the heck are you, anyway?"

"Jedediah used to be a vigilante, but he is a peacemaker now." Cody whipped the kerchief off his neck, exposing the deep scar on his throat. "This is what the Montana Vigilantes did to me, and I was innocent." Cody paused, then added, "You see, when people take the law into their own hands, this is the kind of thing that can happen. The wrong man was punished, and that was me."

There was deep silence over the crowd. Jedediah glanced at the scar, then dropped his gaze, remorse washing over him. *And the man was innocent* whirled through his mind.

Cody continued, "Is that the kind of law you want in this town? Act first, ask questions later? I hope not. I was lucky when the rope didn't snap my neck."

Murmurs and whispers were heard, and Jedediah leaned toward Cody. "Why are you doing this?" he asked.

Cody responded, "Two wrongs don't make a right."

Patience had come out and joined them, slipping one arm through Jedediah's and the other arm through Cody's. Jedediah was honored and humbled. *Why?* he wondered. *I don't deserve this kind of support.*

Slowly the crowd, grumbling and complaining, dispersed to their homes, and Jedediah hoped it was for good. By morning he'd be long gone with the prisoner. Patience, Joe, Cody, and Hannah stepped inside his office, and Hannah hugged Patience while they talked in low voices. The men stayed by the door.

"I want to thank you, Cody. I didn't deserve your help tonight," Jedediah commented. "I thought I had the right outlaw back then, but I sure was mistaken. It's another proof that real laws work a lot better than a vigilante posse."

Cody shifted from one foot to the other. "I'll just say every man deserves a second chance. You can thank Patience here for convincing me of that, or else I would've been in the crowd yelling for revenge too and hoping you'd get in the way of a stray bullet."

Jedediah nodded, not knowing what to say. He held out his hand, and Cody shook it, his face solemn.

Joe said, "Get some shut-eye, Jed. Cody and I will take turns on watch just in case. You need your rest for tomorrow."

"Joe, why don't you walk Patience and Hannah home first?" Cody asked.

"Good idea. I'll be back." He crooked his

elbows out and turned to the women. "Ladies . . . shall we?"

They both smiled, said good night to Jedediah and Cody, then headed down the street — with Joe recounting with as much pride as if he'd done it himself how Jedediah stood up to the lynch mob.

25

At one end of Wallace Street, Jedediah left with his prisoner, and at the other end, Patience watched from her porch as the funeral procession for John Hargrove began to form. She'd been waiting for Judith to come downstairs, and Cody had offered to drive them to the cemetery overlooking a hill where the more "respectable" people were buried. She heard the door behind her open and Judith walked out dressed in full black mourning attire, including a black hat whose veil covered her still-swollen eyes.

Cody stepped down to help the ladies into the carriage. After they were seated, he asked, "Anybody else from here going?"

"No. Emily is going to have a light meal ready for anyone who would like to extend their condolences to Judith after the burial."

"That's a nice thing to do," he said with a nod as he climbed back up in his seat and picked up the reins.

Judith dabbed her eyes underneath the veil. "You and Emily have been just like family to me, Patience. I don't know what I would've done without you."

Patience patted Judith's arm. "You'd do the same for me, I'm sure."

Cody clicked at the horse and steered it in behind the hearse headed to the cemetery just down the dirt road a ways. Patience found herself hoping Jedediah would be back from his delivery of Nathan in time to have a bite to eat with everyone. She was proud of the way he'd responded last night, how he diffused a volatile situation. But she was even more impressed when Cody showed up. The man's forgiveness of Jedediah surprised and delighted her at the same time. She could hardly wait to see Jedediah again, to talk with him about everything that had happened in such a short time.

After they arrived at the cemetery, Monty slowly walked over to Patience, head down and twisting his hat in his hands. "Miz Patience," he began, "I guess — well, I sure got caught up in the moment with the crowd last night. I was enraged about John's death, 'long with everybody else. I reckon I was outta line. I sure hope Jedediah will understand and will — will still be speaking to me." Monty had dark circles under his eyes. Probably hadn't slept much.

Patience wasn't sure what to say, so she simply nodded.

Reverend King from Virginia City had come to preside over the funeral, and the crowd of people who were there to honor John Hargrove watched silently as the casket was lowered into the ground.

"Dust to dust . . ." And the all-too-familiar words hung over them while Judith sobbed quietly, Patience's arm around her.

Though Jedediah failed to get back in time for the luncheon, in Patience's estimation the cemetery service and the meal at the boardinghouse had gone well. Judith held up as reasonably as could be expected.

When the guests had departed, Judith told Patience that she'd decided she was ready to go home. "I think I want to be alone now. I can't thank you enough for all you've done, both you and Emily."

Patience nodded and took the woman's hand in both of hers. "I certainly understand."

Monty, still looking a bit sheepish, stepped forward from the hallway. "I'd be happy to bring you back, Miz Judith." At her nod, he turned to Emily. "How 'bout you ride along with us, and I'll bring you back. With everything going on lately, it'll give us time to catch up. That okay with everybody?"

"Perfectly fine, Monty," Judith said.

Emily glanced at Patience.

"Certainly, she can go," Patience agreed. "Almost everything has been picked up and washed and put away." Patience patted Emily's arm, and Emily shot her a bright smile, hurried to hang up her apron, and grabbed a light wrap.

No sooner had Patience settled in the parlor, removed her shoes, and propped her feet on a footstool, than the doorbell rang. She was sure her guests were out or up in their rooms. In stocking feet she padded to the door and checked through glass panes. Jedediah stood there, a smile greeting her as soon as she opened the door. "Come in, Jed. I was hoping you'd make it back for the luncheon after John's funeral, but everyone has left now. Maybe we can find something for you in the kitchen."

She didn't say anything more when she saw Jedediah looking down at her feet, and she put one behind the other, trying to hide them. She didn't have small feet, and it embarrassed her to have him notice them.

He simply chuckled and held out his hand to her. "I see you're getting comfortable. Shall I come back another time?"

She felt her face warm, but she took his hand. "No, please stay. I left my shoes in the parlor. Follow me."

"Please don't put them on for me. I'm sure you must be tired."

"No more tired than you no doubt are." She noticed shadows under his eyes, and he hadn't had a shave, but he was still handsome to her. "Did you turn Nathan over to the authorities? I hope you had no trouble with him. He does have a good side, believe it or not."

"Yes, he was placed in a cell until a hearing, and more than likely a trial. One for cattle rustling and one for murder." Patience motioned toward the settee, and both took a seat on it. "I won't stay long, Patience, because I'm tired. Where's Judith?" He leaned back, his head resting against the wall, and closed his eyes.

"Judith decided to go back to the ranch," Patience told him. "I couldn't blame her for wanting to get away from all the well-wishers and be alone right now." Patience reached over to pat his arm, and he cocked an eye at her. "Yes, you are weary, I can see," she told him.

"But looking at you is probably just what I need," he answered with a grin and covered her hand on his arm with his.

317

"Monty asked Emily to ride along," she explained as she straightened and pulled her hand back to her lap. "They'll return soon, I imagine. Would you like me to get a plate of food for you?"

"Nah," he drawled. "I don't need food as much as some time to look at you."

She laughed softly, her face coloring. "Looking at me isn't going to —"

But Jedediah had taken her hand back and was looking at the palm. "You have hard-working hands, Patience, but they are beautiful." He placed a kiss in the calloused palm and gently placed her hand back in her lap.

Patience looked at this man who had at first seemed so rough and unpleasant, so utterly opposite the kind of man she'd thought she would find appealing, and she marveled at the change . . . *in him, or in me?* she wondered. She noticed his strong jaw, the care in his eyes — and maybe something more.

He smiled at her, straightened, and said, "I'm going to go get some sleep, my dear. Looks like you'd appreciate some rest yourself."

She smiled in return. "To tell you the truth, I might enjoy a little nap before it's time to fix supper." She thought they both might like to stay right where they were, but she moved to stand.

Jedediah was standing, and he reached to pull her up too. "All right, then. I hope I'll see you tomorrow."

She walked him to the door. "Thanks for stopping by. I was worried about you, alone with Nathan and all, and I'm proud of you for not releasing Nathan to the crowd."

He cocked an eyebrow. "Really?"

She nodded.

"Then I'm a lucky man." He squeezed her hand and walked out to the steps, then turned to tip his hat with another smile. He strolled down the sidewalk, whistling.

She leaned dreamily against the doorjamb and watched until he was lost in the crowd. *He forgot to pay me for the boxed lunches!* she thought with a little grin. *He'll have to come back tomorrow.*

It was proving to be a fine morning, and Patience was in great spirits as she walked up the street to The Star Bakery. She planned to fill her basket with Hannah's baked goods for her boardinghouse guests.

Creekside was doing wonderfully well, and she was proud of the changes she and Emily had been able to accomplish — without much cash, but with ingenuity and hard work. All of it no doubt was helping them keep the rooms full.

Partnering with Emily had turned out to be the best thing that could've happened, but from the looks of her friendship with Monty, the young woman wouldn't be at the boardinghouse much longer. Of course, Patience was happy for Emily but wasn't sure how she would manage without her.

Patience opened the bakery door, and the bell tinkled a welcome. Hannah seemed happy to see her and hurried from behind her counter to give Patience a hug. "Well, my, but aren't you looking well and happy today?"

"Yes, I am, but you seem unusually cheerful yourself, Hannah." Patience leaned back to look into her friend's face. "Now, maybe you and Joe — ?"

"You might say we've become attached," Hannah put in, her face flaming. She placed her hands on her cheeks and chuckled. "I told him as long as he continues to stay away from the bars, there might be a future for us in our old age," she said with another chuckle.

"Old? You're not old, and if Joe can put that glimmer in your eyes, then I say congratulations." Patience hugged her back and placed her basket on the counter.

"Looks like you plan to shop," Hannah said.

"I'm here for your cinnamon rolls for dessert tonight. I thought I'd give my residents a special treat, and it might even be good for your business too," Patience said with a smile.

"Oh, dear, I appreciate that, but how many will you be needin'?"

"A dozen will do," Patience answered.

"I'll go to the kitchen and see what I have." Hannah hurried behind the curtain to her baking area, eventually bringing back a bag of the rolls. "There's only ten, but I could bake another dozen if you want to come back."

Patience furrowed her brow in thought. "Actually, they're so large I believe I could slice them in half."

"That should work. Now tell me, do you know if everything went all right with Jedediah and his prisoner?"

"Yes, Hannah, it did. We still don't know who murdered John, but Jed believes that Nathan probably knows who it was, even if he didn't do it himself. I was proud of the way Jed handled everything, and since I was stuck in the marshal's office for a while, we talked over a lot of things. It turns out Jed used to be a part of a secretive Montana vigilante committee, and he gave the order to hang Russell, the man I might have married. Nathan is Russell's brother, and they both turned to rustling cattle till Russell got caught. Nathan got away, and he's one of those who stole John's cattle."

"You don't say?" Hannah cocked her head, but something about her expression made Patience take a step back.

"Hannah, did you *know*?"

"I — I'm afraid I did, Patience," the woman answered, her voice full of contrition. "But I felt it was best to let you find out your own way. Besides, I wasn't sure you had come to terms with Russell's death. Please don't be angry with me. I was only trying to protect your heart."

From whom, Jedediah or Cody? Patience felt a surge of anger. Hannah had no right —

"I've had my suspicions about Cody," Hannah was saying. "Him being new in town and not a miner. But I don't know anything specific about him. I do know if Jedediah could ever forgive himself — and if you could forgive him — you two might be a good match." Hannah brushed the crumbs away from the counter and into the trash. "I've been praying for him since the day he arrived with that troubled expression on his face."

322

"Your prayers have worked then," Patience said, her ire fading.

"And now there's Judith, and she's gonna need some tender care in the coming months. Such a sad, sad thing. John was a fine man — a temper sometimes, but a fair man to his ranch hands and supported our town financially."

"That's what I've heard, but I didn't know him very well." Patience handed over the money for the rolls and tucked them in her basket. "I must be going, Hannah, but I'm so happy things are working out for you and Joe."

Hannah walked her to the door. "Yes, he helps me fill the lonely hours, and we have lots to talk about. Has Jed asked you yet?"

Patience paused at the door, giving her a sideways look. "Asked me what?"

"To be his bride, of course!" Hannah said, her hands resting on her ample hips.

Patience laughed. "I don't think he's ready for that — at least not yet!" She laughed again and Hannah joined in.

But I might be . . .

26

Summer was beginning to wind down a little each day, and Jedediah was ready for a nice fall. Summer had never been a favorite season of his. But the change in season would mean a lot of miners would be packing up to go home, wherever that might be, if they hadn't been able to strike a rich vein. Winter would be long and slow, but he had plans for his time — and they all had to do with Patience.

Deep down in his heart, he wished that during the long winter nights to come he'd be snuggling in bed with her. He looked in the mirror above his washstand and frowned, seeing the lines around his eyes. He sure wasn't getting any younger. It was time he had a wife. He knew he wanted Patience, but did she want him? He'd been tossing and turning the last few nights, contemplating the possibility of marriage.

But he didn't have a lot to offer such a fine lady.

He had offered to drive her out to the Cross Bar to visit Judith today. He pocketed his watch fob, grabbed his hat, and ran downstairs to check on the two drunks he'd hauled in last night for disturbing the peace. They were sleeping it off in separate cells. They never knew he was there. Just as well, he'd be back in time to let them out at supper time with a stern warning.

He'd rented a buggy from the livery, making sure it was one that had a top for shade against the sun. He stopped the buggy, set the brake, and hopped down. When he rang the bell, Emily greeted him with her usual cheerful smile.

"Hello, Jed. Patience will be right out. Would you like to come inside and wait?"

"No, thanks. I'll just wait here on the porch. It's nice out today."

"Oh, here she comes now." Emily stepped aside, opened the door wider, and slipped away to the kitchen.

Jed's breath caught as he watched Patience descending the wide staircase. *Looks like a bride already,* he thought. She wore a cream-colored lace shirtwaist trimmed with black beads where it met the pretty gray skirt with its black braiding. Her dark hair was pulled back into a chignon, and she sported a bonnet trimmed with gray-colored ribbon and white silk roses.

She seemed to float down the stairs toward him, and he wished he could crush her to his chest and hold her. "You look wonderful," he finally managed to say. "Do you always go calling so dressed up?"

She smiled with eyebrows raised. "Only when I have a handsome driver."

"Then the driver needs to show up more often," he joked in return.

As he offered his arm, Patience called to Emily in the kitchen, "We won't be long."

"Take your time, as long as you're back before supper," she said from the kitchen doorway. "You know I can't cook much."

Jedediah laughed. "Poor Monty." Emily blushed, gave him an embarrassed glance, and with a little giggle disappeared into the kitchen.

"Shall we go, Patience?" She nodded, and they walked arm-in-arm to the buggy.

The ride ended all too soon. The two laughed and talked until Jed brought the carriage to a stop in front of Judith's house. He helped Patience down, and she waited as he drove the carriage over to a large shade tree at the side of the house.

326

Judith seemed glad to have company and immediately made them feel at home in her spacious parlor, serving coffee as they settled in for the visit. She was thinner than she should have been with the baby due so soon, Patience thought, and her eyes looked sad with their dark circles. She watched as Judith poured their cups and talked about trying to run the ranch without John. *Amazing how much she seems to have aged in such a short time.* Patience tried to imagine how difficult it was for her to continue on without her husband.

"If it weren't for Monty and Cody, the ranch would have to be forfeited. John always took care of everything, so I was in no position to see that things were run properly after . . . after he was gone," Judith admitted, dabbing at the corners of her eyes with a handkerchief delicately monogrammed with an *H.* She turned to Jedediah. "Do you have any news of John's killer?"

"I wish I did, Judith, but I can tell you this, the truth will come out somehow, somewhere, and not too far in the future. Nathan will have his day in court."

"That is comforting to know."

At her smile he asked, "Do you feel safe enough out here on the ranch?"

She nodded. "Yes. Yes I do. Along with Monty, all the ranch hands carefully look after me. I don't venture out alone, and I can see the concern in their faces when I do go for a walk. One of them always trails along behind me."

"That's very good," Patience murmured. "And I hope you know you're welcome any time at my place whenever you feel like a change."

"Thank you so much, Patience. I'll have to take you up on that sometime soon. Now, how about some tea cakes with your coffee?"

"Don't go to any trouble," Patience said.

"No trouble at all — I made some just yesterday, and I'm so glad to have you here to share them with me." She sniffled and left them alone.

Patience shook her head. "I wish there was something I could do to help."

Jedediah patted her hand. "You're doing that right now," he said quietly.

"She has a lovely home, doesn't she?" Patience glanced around the parlor, admiring Judith's meticulous detail to create such a beautiful and welcoming room.

Jedediah nodded. "Yes. Would you like a home like this someday?"

Patience lifted her shoulders. "Maybe. But

if I marry, I'll be happy no matter where I am as long as I'm with the one I love. It's not the material things that really matter." She took a quick glance at him, but she couldn't tell what he might be thinking.

Jedediah cleared his throat. "I suppose you're right about that."

Judith returned with a tray of fresh coffee and tea cakes. "This is my mama's recipe."

Jedediah took a bite. "Mmm . . . these are really good."

Judith smiled, but it faded quickly. "They were John's favorite."

"I can surely see why," Patience told her. "You should see if Hannah would sell them at her bakery. I don't believe I've ever seen tea cakes among her goodies, have you, Jed?"

"I have not. These would be a nice addition." He finished his tea cake off with a drink of coffee.

"Oh, I don't know . . . Hannah does her own baking."

"True," Patience said. "However, she's very busy, as well as spending a lot more time with Joe these days. She might just as soon have another treat that's special. You could take a few to her and ask. Might help you with something to do."

"You have a point there, Patience. Maybe

I could —"

A knock at the door interrupted their conversation, and before Judith could answer, the door swung open. In walked Monty. Patience thought it was a bit presumptuous. Maybe they'd allowed him that freedom when John was alive, but it didn't seem appropriate now.

"Oh, sorry. I didn't realize you had guests." He paused, removing his hat and looking surprised. "What are you doing here, Jed?" he inquired.

"We came to visit Judith. Why?" Jedediah said.

"Oh, no reason . . ." Monty directed his gaze toward Judith. Patience thought it was nice she was so well revered by everyone. Most likely she wouldn't want for anything — except John.

"What can I help you with, Monty?" Judith asked.

"It wasn't important. It can wait." He smiled, put his hat on, and began backing out of the room.

"Wait, Monty. I'd like to talk to you for a minute." Jedediah stood up and gestured toward the door.

"About what?" Monty's cheerful smile disappeared.

"About that night John was murdered,"

Patience heard him say, though his voice was low. She took a quick look at Judith, but she didn't seem to have heard as she started to gather up their cups and food items.

Patience saw Monty hesitate. "Sure, I don't know what more I can add. Don't you think the man you caught was the one?"

"That's just it — I think he may be telling me the truth," Jedediah said as he walked out the door, Monty following him.

Patience took the last sip of her coffee and placed it on the tray. "Is there anything at all I can do for you, Judith, or something in town that you need done — an errand, perhaps?"

"Honestly, I can't think of a single thing. This afternoon I'll write again to John's mother back East. I sent a telegram right away to tell her the sad news, and I'm sure she's heartbroken. I haven't heard from her yet, but getting mail way out here takes a long time." Judith stared out the window, lost in her own thoughts.

"Well, if there's anything at all," Patience finally said gently, "you must let me or Jed know."

"That's very kind of you, but Monty has been such a big help, truly."

They continued chatting until Jedediah

returned. "Are you about ready to leave, Patience? I've brought the carriage around." His face held a serious look, and she wondered if something was wrong.

Patience glanced at the watch hanging from a slender gold chain around her neck. "Oh my, look at the time. Yes, we must be going," she said, getting to her feet.

"It is wonderful of you both to be concerned about me," Judith said, her voice shaky. Patience gave her a brief hug, and Judith choked back tears.

"My offer stands if you get too lonely or simply want a change." Patience smiled, hoping Judith would return her smile, but she only looked at her with a bleak gaze.

"That's right," Jedediah said, doffing his hat. "You're surrounded by men out here, and I'm sure you could use friendships of the female kind."

"I'm thinking you're right," Judith said as she walked them out the door. "Who knows, maybe I'll make a batch of tea cakes for Hannah to sample." She gave them a weak smile.

"We'll see you soon," Patience said as Jed helped her into the carriage. He clicked the reins, and she turned in her seat to wave at Judith. When she did she noticed Monty near the barn, waiting.

As soon as they were rumbling over the road back to town, Patience turned to look at Jed directly. "Is something the matter?"

Keeping his eyes on the lane ahead, he said, "Doing some thinking, is all."

"About Judith?" she pressed him.

"Well, maybe indirectly. Ever have a feeling that something isn't quite right?" She nodded, and he continued. "Monty showing up and walking in like he did didn't sit well with me. I know he admired John a lot, and that's why he was with the crowd demanding revenge."

"So what are you thinking?"

Jedediah glanced at her. "I'm not sure. It appears to me he's made himself in charge of the ranch — maybe of Judith too."

Patience thought about that for a moment. "Wouldn't it be normal for the foreman to take over the ranch in these circumstances?"

"I reckon so, but did you see the way he looked at her?"

"I did, but maybe he's just being nice — she's lost her husband not that long ago, Jed." *What is he getting at?*

"Probably so." He shrugged, then asked if

she was pleased with how Creekside was doing.

"It's been coming along nicely. Emily is a hard worker and spreads her cheer to every resident without fail each day. Our partnership is working out great."

"That's good. And I owe you for the last lunches you made. Remind me when I leave you at the boardinghouse. It slipped my mind that night I returned from Helena." He gazed over at her with a grin. "I wonder why?"

She laughed. "I have no idea. So maybe there's someone you'd like to know better?" Patience teased.

He hooted, then recovered. "That's the best idea I've heard in a long time."

Patience's heart was soaring. This rough, tough former vigilante's heart was softening, and it was *she* that he wanted to know better. *Bye bye, Millie,* she thought mischievously.

27

After he'd delivered Patience to Creekside and returned the rig, Jed decided to pay Hannah a visit. This hour of the day the bakery was devoid of customers. "What do you know about Monty?" he asked after the usual pleasantries. "You've known him longer than I have," he added.

Hannah wrinkled her nose. "Let's see. He was John's foreman. And John, we know, was considered a good judge of character."

"Anything else?"

"Monty's worked for John — and now Judith — about three years. He's ambitious, I can tell. He used to drop in when he came to town for something or other and often said he'd own a spread as big as John's someday soon. Always talking about betterin' himself."

Jedediah rubbed his chin thoughtfully. "Is he courting Emily?"

"Now how you expect I know all this

335

about folks?" She gave him a shrewd look.

He had to chuckle. "I know you have plenty of customers, and they say things and you listen — like me. You also keep an eye out for this kind of thing."

Hannah poured them both a cup of coffee, and they sat down at the little round table. "Ah, feels good to get off my feet. Let's see. Last I heard he was courting her. She's a sweet gal, and I hope he does good by her. But to tell you the truth, I always assumed he'd find someone of substance. You know . . ." She didn't finish the thought.

"Like Judith, perhaps?" Jedediah said, looking at her over the rim of his coffee cup.

"Judith Hargrove? Land sakes, no! She's married — I mean widowed . . . What are you getting at, Jed? I know something is running around in that head of yours."

"You always have been able to read me better than anyone. I was just wondering if he knows more than he's saying about John. That's all," Jedediah answered. He swallowed the last of his coffee and shoved his chair back. "Thanks for the coffee."

"I'll ask Joe to keep his ears open, but he's promised me not to go near the saloon, and that seems to be where he hears most everything — gossip, I mean."

"I'm glad you two are getting along so

well. Joe seems like a changed man."

Hannah beamed. "You know he's thinking of coming to work with me in the bakery, giving up his claim?"

Jedediah grinned. "Now that's about the best news I've heard all week. I hope he does it." He left change on the table for the coffee, tipped his hat at her, and left.

Patience sliced apples for the strudel she was planning for tonight's dessert. One of the things she loved to do most was bake. She'd already rolled out the dough very thin — all she had to do was fill it with apple slices and roll it up to bake. She wanted it to be extra special since Jedediah was going to join them for supper. She felt a little giddy at the thought since he'd never actually eaten at the Creekside before.

"Patience! Come!" Emily sailed into the kitchen. "There's a delivery for you."

"What delivery? I haven't ordered anything —"

"I don't know, but hurry and let's find out." Emily tugged on Patience's arm. She dropped the knife into the bowl of sliced apples and followed Emily through the hall and out to the porch.

Four men grinned at them from their perch on a wagon's front seat, and four more young fellows waved at the two women from the back of the wagon. A large object between the men was covered with canvas.

"What's this all about?" Patience asked.

"Come see for yourself," one of the men said, jumping down and motioning for Patience and Emily to follow. He strode to the back of the wagon, and the others helped him peel back the canvas.

"A piano!" Patience gasped. "There must be some mistake. I — I haven't ordered one." The young men in the back laughed, then hopped out of the wagon. Patience looked at Emily, who held her hands palms up and shook her head in bewilderment.

"It ain't no mistake, lady. You're Patience Cavanaugh?" the driver asked.

"Yes, but —"

"Then we're at the right place." He turned to the men and gave them orders. "We'll have four of us on each side." He swung around. "Now, ma'am, if you'll just tell us where to put this." A curious crowd was gathering about them.

"I — I don't know . . ." Patience stammered. "I guess in the parlor."

"All right, men. You heard the lady."

"I'll go open the door," Emily said. "It's a double one, so I think you'll be able to get the piano through there."

Patience watched in utter shock as the men took their places to lift the instrument. After it had been lifted over the side, her hands went to her mouth, and she stumbled back a step. *It's* my *piano! The one I played when I was a little girl!*

Patience found herself stunned but thrilled at the same time. She slowly went over to it, afraid it would disappear into thin air, and traced its fine craftsmanship with her hand. How had Mother ever come to part with it? This said a lot about her new relationship with her mother, and tears filled her eyes and threatened to overflow to her cheeks. Patience would be able to play for her residents and guests. Oh, what a perfect evening it was turning out to be. She forced herself to contain her enthusiasm and not to actually shout "hooray" in the street.

Patience clasped her hands together in nervous delight and watched the men huff and struggle with the weight of the piano up the steps. But somehow they managed to set it in the parlor near the window. A perfect spot where she could look out as she played. *Oh this is too wonderful to be true!*

"There you are, ma'am. Oh, I almost forgot," the driver said, fishing in his pocket and handing her an envelope. She fumbled to get it open.

Dearest Patience,

I thought you should have the instrument of your heart as you continue with your business and possibly a church. The piano, without you, is of no use to me now. I'm sure you will enjoy it and entertain your friends.

Now you know why I seemed to protest when Judith offered to donate one to you for the boardinghouse. You can tell her about this and thank her for her offer.

I enjoyed my visit immensely, and Daddy, I'm sure, would be proud of his little girl, all grown up.

With deep affection,
Mother

Patience folded the letter, brushing new tears from her cheeks. She reached into her apron pocket for a tip for the driver and his workers.

"Thank you kindly." The driver doffed his hat and the delivery crew departed.

When the door had closed behind them, both Emily and Patience hugged and jumped up and down with joy. "I'm in shock," Patience said, catching her breath and holding out the note to Emily.

"This calls for a celebration tonight!" Emily said, still smiling as she looked up from reading the letter.

"Let's shut the parlor doors now and not say a word until after supper. Then we can tell our residents. By then I can get my piano music out of my trunk." Patience looked around in a daze. "I wonder if I still know how to play?" She paused. "Jed will be coming to supper tonight, and I want to make a good impression."

Emily took her elbow. "You will, but go find the music now, and I'll finish peeling the apples. I can do that without causing too serious a calamity, right? We must hurry if we're to have supper ready on time."

Twinkling lights along with fiddle music flowed from the two saloons, burgeoning with miners spending their gold. *Guess they'll never learn,* Jedediah thought, shaking his head as he walked over to Creekside for supper. He'd finally get a home-cooked meal that Patience had prepared, and he was mightily looking forward to it. It'd also be a few hours without worries about John's killer.

Patience opened the door to him, looking fresh as a daisy wearing a green dress with a delicate white collar. Immediately, Jed's palms started to perspire. Not even when he was drawing his gun on a bandit did he ever have sweaty palms. This is what she did to him — and she had no idea.

"I'm glad you're here, Jed," she said. "Please come in. We're gathered in the dining room. May I take your hat?"

He felt like a schoolboy. "Oh, why, yes, of course." He handed his Stetson to her, and she hung it on the hall hat rack.

"Let's join the others." Patience led the way, the vanilla scent she wore compelling him to follow her — anywhere.

He was greeted by several guests who'd already taken their seats. Patience waved a hand toward Jed. "Everyone, I'd like you to meet our marshal, Jedediah Jones." They all nodded, and she introduced each guest. "You already know Emily, Will, and Liza, and this is Mark, Conrad, Michael, and Matthew."

"You're in for a real treat, folks," Emily announced, returning from the kitchen with a platter of fried chicken and placing it in the center of the table.

"This is my favorite part of the day, Marshal," the gentleman named Will said. "I'm always delighted to see what Miss Patience has cooked up for dinner."

"Will, you enjoy *all* of Patience's cooking, not just dinner," Liza pointed out.

"It sure does look tasty to me," Jedediah agreed, taking the seat Patience offered beside her.

Emily sat down and began to pass the bowls around. Small talk around the table was soon going strong, but Jedediah didn't have much to add to the conversation. For some reason he'd never given much thought to the eligible men staying at the boarding-house. Some were only passing through, but Michael and Matthew were brothers who owned one of the largest mines.

While he dined on Patience's delicious fried chicken, Jedediah chided himself for his lack of awareness. The brothers were friendly toward their hostess, but as he observed them, he soon realized they had one focus — their mine and their workers, not Patience. Every chance he got, he glanced at her and decided that she was like a warm, gentle rain to his soul.

"Do you have an opinion, Jedediah?" Will was asking.

"I'm sorry, I guess I was savoring every bite," Jedediah said. "What was the question?"

"There's a rumor that Patience may consider forming a committee to get a church going in the community," Will repeated. "What do you think about a church?"

"Is that so?" Jedediah looked at Patience. "I think it's a fine idea. Better than having to go over to Virginia City, so I would agree." He considered himself less than an authority because he'd attended only a few times. He'd have to do better.

Patience took a deep breath. "It seems others have determined that I should take on this venture. It was all started by my mother when she was visiting, and you know how insistent she can be."

"We'd help in any way we can, wouldn't we?" Emily said, looking around the table.

The topic was thoroughly discussed, including securing a piece of suitable land on which to build a church, the means, and the funds. It made for some lively conversation until Patience said, "We'll have to see what happens with all this. And now it's time for dessert."

After the even more highly praised apple strudel, Patience stood. "We can all retire to the parlor, including you, Emily. We'll take care of the dishes later."

Emily smiled knowingly at her. "I won't mind at all."

Patience motioned toward Jedediah, and they walked together into the parlor.

Liz was the first to notice. "Oh my goodness, Patience — you've bought a *piano*?"

"No, it is a gift from my mother."

"I hope this means you are going to play for us," Jedediah said, lifting a piece of music from the stand, and the others added their encouragement.

"I'll do my best," Patience said, delighted at their enthusiasm, "but, Emily, you must sing."

"Only if you do with me." Emily stood next to the piano as Patience took a seat in front of the keyboard and began to play.

The two voices filled the room with the sweetness of song, holding everyone's attention through several patriotic songs, a love ballad, and two hymns. *This is really a special treat,* Jedediah thought, *especially in this town.* Here was a side of Patience that he didn't know. He was enjoying discovering new things about her, her interests and talents. *And that strudel was awfully good,* he told himself with a little grin.

"That's enough of the two of us tonight. Would anyone else like to play or sing?" Patience asked, rising from the piano bench. She sat down by Jedediah on the settee. There were no takers for more piano and singing, and soon the group was relaxing — some reading the paper, others talking business or town doings.

Jed saw nobody was looking and reached

over to squeeze her hand, soft against his weathered one. She didn't seem to mind, and gave a little squeeze back before putting her hand demurely back in her lap. "I really liked the singing and piano playing," he leaned over to tell her, his voice low.

"Thank you. I was truly amazed that Mother would send it to me, but maybe it's her way of saying she's sorry for the past and wants to make it up to me."

Jed nodded and told her he thought that might be the case. They talked quietly together until the boarders began taking their leave to go to their rooms. All of them agreed they'd had a lovely evening.

Jedediah decided it was time to excuse himself too, and Patience walked him to the door.

"This is the best night I remember since arriving in Nevada City. Thank you for inviting me."

"I'm glad you enjoyed yourself. We'll do it again — when I cook something special."

"Everything you cook is special," he said. "We'll have to have that picnic soon under the ponderosa pine." Her lips turned up in a gentle smile. He sure did want to kiss her — but not here in the hallway.

"And we will, soon. I promise." She handed him his hat. "By the way, let me know if you hear anything at all about Nathan."

"I certainly will. Well . . . good night." He caught her hand, then quickly donned his hat and left. As he walked home, he realized more than ever, he didn't want to part with her. *It seems as if she likes me,* he thought, *but is she ready to spend the rest of her life with me?*

28

It was late by the time Patience and Emily had gotten the supper dishes washed and put away. Patience was tired, but a good kind of tired, she decided. From all appearances Jedediah liked the food and the entertainment, and it seemed to her that he'd had something further than his stomach or enjoyment on his mind when she walked him to the door. *Wouldn't I love to be a mind reader,* she thought, but then decided that could be dangerous.

"Emily," she said over her shoulder as she reached a serving bowl up to a high shelf, "you should've asked Monty to supper tonight. It's only a short ride to town from the ranch, you know."

Emily removed her apron and hung it on a peg by the pantry door with a sigh. "I saw him at the post office, and he hurried right out with little more than a 'hello.' I got the feeling he wasn't keen on spending time in town . . . at least not with me."

"Hmm, I thought he was courting you."

"Maybe it was all a misunderstanding on my part. At any rate, he was in a hurry and wanted to get back to the ranch. Said he didn't want 'to leave Judith alone, just in case, you know . . .' It sounded kind of, well, mysterious to me."

"I see. I do understand about Judith, but he seemed a little uneasy to me when Jed and I drove out to the Cross Bar for a visit. He considers himself in charge of the ranch now, and I'm sure Judith is glad to have his experience and all."

Patience noticed the downcast look on Emily's face. Why hadn't she realized that Emily was troubled? Patience walked over to her and put her arm about Emily's shoulders. "I'm truly sorry, Emily, if he's hurt your feelings. I shouldn't have brought up the subject of Monty."

Emily looked at Patience. "It's not like he ever said we were a couple. I assumed too much," she said with a little shrug as they both started up the stairs to bed.

"I know exactly how that feels, Emily. Remember the man I hoped to marry that I told you about?" Emily nodded. "Well, once I got over my anger at Jed, and finding out Russell was guilty of theft, I realized that

I'd assumed too much. I had it in my mind that Russell was going to marry me . . . and he'd never said so. I was being a little too optimistic." Patience stopped as they reached the top of the stairs. "But think of where I'd be if I *had* married Russell the Rustler." She stopped to chuckle with Emily joining in, and they quickly covered their mouths to stifle the sound for any sleeping guests before continuing down the hall to their rooms.

Patience stopped Emily at her door with a hand on her arm. "You see," she finished in a whisper, "it hurts your heart, but one thing I can tell you, it's not the end of the world. Russell certainly wasn't part of God's plan for me."

Now Emily had tears in her eyes. "I'm sorry about all you went through. Thank you for your very good advice," she whispered back. "You're such a blessing to me — a sister I never had." They said good night and slipped into their rooms.

As Patience prepared for bed, she stopped and thanked God for all the good things that had happened, even though there had been bad things too. Nathan had been found — and had told her important information, her mother had given her the piano and their relationship seemed to have started fresh, her partnership with Emily was fruitful. *Lord, heal Emily's tender heart, and thank You for healing mine,* she whispered as she slipped under the covers. *Please don't let me make the kind of mistake I could have made with Russell. Guide my mind and my thoughts as I get to know Jed.*

As soon as she closed her eyes, Jedediah's image seemed to look back at her. Did he think of her at different times of the day, the way she did of him — wondering what he was doing or where he was? And did this mean she was falling in love with him?

She yawned and decided she would leave her future to God's guidance. *That means I need to be alert to hearing what He is saying to me,* she thought as she turned over for sleep.

Jedediah had just saddled Charlie when he saw Joe approaching. "What's up, my friend?" he called.

"I was in Helena yesterday an' thought I'd stop by and tell you that Nathan didn't confess to murderin' John. He's sticking by that. 'Course he could hang for cattle thievin'." Joe scratched his beard. "You know, Jed, something about this whole thing about John don't make sense to me."

"I know what you mean," Jed said as he

cinched the belt tight underneath Charlie's belly.

"So where are ya headin'?"

"Thought I'd do a little ridin' this morning."

"Mind if I come along? Wouldn't take but a few minutes to get my horse."

"I don't see why not. I'll wait for you right here. But be quick about it." Jedediah looped the reins over the hitching post in front of his office and leaned against the porch, arms crossed, as he watched Joe move down the sidewalk like a younger man. Jed sure was tickled to see how things were working out for Joe and Hannah.

Jedediah gazed down the street, observing folks go about their daily duties. He stepped forward when he thought he caught a glimpse of Monty but couldn't be sure. A moment later, he was able to make out Monty coming out of the bank, then leaving on his horse. Strange. In the past, Monty had always stopped by the office to say hello. *Probably still peeved at me. Well, he's just gonna have to get over it.*

Joe came back, and the two set out. Jedediah had already decided he would go in the direction where he'd found John, see if there was anything he might have missed. It felt awfully good to be outside with the scent of evergreen and the slight breeze at his back, with the mountains to the west. He loved nature and lately had been giving some thought to buying a piece of land for a homestead. He'd been saving his money — what else did he have to spend it on?

They rode in silence until they were deep into the Hargrove property.

"Did Hannah tell you I'm gonna be helpin' her at the bakery?" Joe asked, breaking the silence.

"She did. I think it's a great idea. You definitely won't be lonely anymore. Hannah will see to that." He looked over at Joe and grinned. "You know you're going to have to wash up a lot when you're working around food."

They both laughed, Joe bobbing his head. "Yep! It'll take everything inside of me to stay clean, body and soul, but I've made a vow that I won't touch a drop. 'Cept water." Another shared chuckle.

"I'll send up a few prayers," Jedediah said, turning serious. "You're gonna need them, for sure." He slowed Charlie to a walk. "Yes, this looks like the place John was found." They dismounted, and Jed said they should keep an eye open for any clues that might have been missed.

"You know," he mused as they searched,

"I just don't understand what would motivate someone to kill John when they already had his cattle."

Joe's mouth pulled down at the corners as his eyebrows drew up. "Mebbe that no-good varmint wants more'n jes cattle — mebbe he wants the whole ball o' wax."

"You mean the whole ranch?" Jedediah thought about that for a moment. "I hardly think that's the case, Joe, but I've heard crazier things in my life."

"Somethin' ta think about," Joe said. "John have any enemies ya know of?"

"I've done a lot of asking around, and I've heard nothing but good things about him." Jed turned toward their horses. "I see nothing here, so we may as well go check on Judith, since we're near the Cross Bar."

As they headed that direction, Jedediah turned over the list of ranch hands in his mind, wondering if one of them had a motive. He couldn't think of any. John always said Monty was a good foreman, and he trusted him with his life.

The Cross Bar looked strangely deserted as they neared the sprawling ranch buildings. Jedediah guessed the hands were out somewhere on the range. As he and Joe left their horses at the hitching post a few yards from the house, he thought he heard arguing. Jedediah put his finger to his mouth, signaling to Joe to be quiet as they crept to a side window.

"Now see here, Judith," they heard through the opening, "all you have to do is sign on this line right here. The document I got from the bank is all legal, giving me the power to run the ranch. Which I'm already doing for you." Jedediah recognized the voice. What was Monty trying to do?

"I don't know, Monty," Judith was saying, sounding upset. "John never mentioned I'd have to do this if something happened to him . . . of course I never dreamed —"

"That's right — you couldn't possibly know that it would come to this," Monty interrupted, obviously trying to sound conciliatory.

"I think I should go to the bank and talk to them," Judith replied. But her voice was a bit shaky. "To get a better understanding of what this document means for me."

Jedediah peered through the window of the parlor. Judith and Monty were standing next to her writing desk, and Monty held a pen in his hand. *That's why Monty was coming out of the bank earlier. Probably made up some cockamamie reason.* Could this be the same Monty he knew?

"Aww, there's no need for that, Judith.

You know John wouldn't have suggested it if he didn't trust me to run things for you."

"That's just it — John never mentioned anything like this to me."

Jed watched Monty take a step closer to her. "That's because he didn't want to worry you about details. He wanted you to concentrate on having children to fill this house."

"How — how could you know that?" Judith's hand went to her mouth, and she seemed to sway slightly.

"He told me."

Jedediah had no doubt Judith would be signing her rights away if she believed this lie. He and Joe stiffened and looked at each other with a nod of mutual understanding.

"That's very odd, Monty." Judith had recovered her equilibrium and stood straight, her voice firm. "We were very private about our life together." She looked away sadly as if Monty weren't even in the room.

Monty dropped his voice provocatively, no doubt attempting to sound tender. "You must know I have always had feelings for you since the day I came to work here. Now that John is out of the way, so to speak, it's me and you running the largest ranch this side of Alder Creek. I know John wouldn't have wanted you to be alone at a time like this . . ."

Judith gasped and stepped back, but Monty grabbed her and pulled her to his chest as she struggled to get away. "Now won't that be sweet," he was saying in a tone that made Jed's blood run cold. "A foreman coming to the rescue of a wealthy widow." Monty chuckled and stared into her white face.

Jedediah wanted to rush in and knock him out cold, but he signaled to Joe that they should wait. If Jed gave him enough rope, Monty — his friend? — would surely hang himself.

"What are you talking about?" Judith tried to break free, but Monty held her tight. "Did you — it sounds like *you* had something to do with John's death." A sob escaped her throat.

Monty kept her against him. "John was in the wrong place that night."

"Please, let me go! You're hurting me," Judith shouted.

That was all Jedediah needed. Motioning for Joe to stay put for now, he drew his gun and raced up the steps.

He flung the door open, and Monty spun around, drawing his gun at the same time. Judith screamed. The man pointed the gun at her head, his other arm around her neck.

"Now, what do we have here?" Monty sneered. "My friend *Vigilante X* coming to the rescue! Keep your nose outta what's none of your business, Jed."

"Monty, put down that gun and release Judith."

"I can't do that. She's my partner now, see?" Monty's wild stare looked more alarming to Jed than the gun.

"You and I both know that's not true, Monty." Jedediah held his tone steady, matter-of-fact, hoping he could talk some sense into this — this common criminal gone mad. "Now, step to the side and let go of Judith. Slowly put your gun on the floor," he said in a controlled, even tone.

Monty shoved her aside and she fell against the desk. Her hand flew to her cheek, and blood flowed between her fingers. He growled, "Jed, just go away and let me work this out with Judith. No harm will come to her."

"This is the way you intend to treat Judith?" Jedediah tried reasoning, keeping his plea even and calm though he felt like shooting the man in the chest. "Come on now, Monty — you know better than this."

Monty fired, knocking Jedediah's Colt .45

from his hand. "We'll see about that, won't we?"

Jed looked over at Judith. "Leave, Judith. While we talk this over."

"Stay, Judith!" Monty shouted. "You know we were meant to be together." But she slid away with her back to the wall and fled down the hallway.

"I can get rid of you right now. There's no witnesses, and Judith won't open her mouth when I get through with her," he said through clenched teeth.

"No, you won't, Monty!" came a voice from behind Monty. "Drop the gun, and I'll spare your life," Joe ordered, his gun held in a two-handed grip that filled Monty's face with surprise and fear.

"Ha! I'm not afraid of an aging miner," Monty spit out, but his voice belied the words.

"I may be a miner but I'm far from aging." Joe had moved around to face the man, his gun level with Monty's chest. "Funny thing," he barked, "I'm so old I don't have to answer to anyone. So if you value your life, you put down your gun now! Or I promise I'll shoot you six ways from heaven before I see any harm come to Miss Judith or Jed. Your choice."

Monty, his face full of rage, looked back

and forth between the two men. If the man moved even a muscle, Jedediah knew Joe would shoot Monty point-blank. And if that didn't stop him, Jedediah would already have his gun back in hand and finish him off.

Monty took a minute to decide, but in the end he dropped his gun. Jedediah kicked it aside while Joe kept his gun pointed at the man's heart.

Jedediah walked over and snapped handcuffs on his wrists. "You're under arrest for the murder of John Hargrove."

29

By the time Jedediah and Joe had gotten
Monty's horse ready, Judith walked timidly
into the yard, her hair coming loose from its
pins and fluttering around her battered face.
She had fastened a cloth on her cheek, and
the wound oozed red around the edges of
the bandage and was already bruising. She
was holding her stomach, and her hands
were trembling.

Jedediah hurried over. "He can't harm you
now, Judith." He patted her shoulder, feeling awfully sorry for her with this new turn
of events on the heels of losing John. "Are
you and the baby all right?"

She nodded through her tears. "I think . . .
I think Monty must have lost his mind, Jed."

"He surely must have — or something like
it." He patted her arm again. "I don't like
to require this, but we will need for you to
come back into town with us. I'll write a
note and post it on the door for your men."

She nodded, folding her arms across her body.

"Joe, go hitch my horse to Judith's wagon — she's coming with us." Jed held the horse and shoved Monty upward, hands still cuffed, onto the mount. Jedediah noticed something blue in Monty's vest pocket. "Hold there a minute." He reached over and pulled out a blue kerchief, exactly like the one Cody wore and that he'd found when he searched the boardinghouse.

"How do you like that, Joe?" he called as the man led Judith's horse over to her. "Here's one of the clues I've been looking for." Jed looked up at Monty astride the horse. "Bob told one of the drovers about seeing something blue that night the cattle were stolen. No doubt you were wearing this at the time — hoping to incriminate Cody for your crimes. Sounds like you and Nathan were in cahoots to me."

Monty's voice was full of venom. "Cody came swinging into the Cross Bar like he was the new foreman and had John wrapped around his finger. We couldn't let that happen." He swung his head to stare at Judith. "Take care of that baby, darlin' . . . I'll be back."

Jedediah saw Joe give Judith a look of sympathy, then help her into the wagon that he'd hitched Charlie to. As he took a seat next to Judith, he ordered Monty to sit behind them. "Let's let Judith stay in front so she doesn't have to see her attacker," Jedediah said to Joe, keeping his voice low. "And by the way, thanks for saving my life." Jedediah reached over to clap Joe on his back.

Joe beamed at him, his smile splitting his beard. "Anything for a friend."

"You're the hero today." Jedediah glanced back at the silent and stone-faced prisoner. He never said another word. Jedediah didn't know what to think about Monty's mental state. At least now the townsfolk could rest easy, having the likely killer caught. The judge in Helena would take care of the rest.

As soon as Jedediah returned to the jail-house and locked Monty up, he took down an official statement from Judith.

Word had gotten around quickly, and Patience wasn't surprised when Jedediah arrived with the distraught Judith. Patience quickly came down the steps to bring the woman into the parlor. "I'm so sorry, Judith, and with you barely recovering from your loss," she murmured as they made their way up the steps and into Creekside.

Emily, her face still blanched white with

363

shock at the news about Monty, told them she'd make some tea and get proper dressings for Judith's wound. The abrasion wasn't deep, but Patience cleaned it and covered it with a fresh bandage. "I believe you'll have a black eye tomorrow, but I'm not certain of that."

"Patience," Judith said, her lips trembling, "it was like Monty suddenly had these grandiose ideas that he and I were meant to be together. Nothing could be further from the truth!" Judith glanced over at Emily. "Oh, dear girl, I'm so sorry you had to hear this."

Emily's hands shook as she poured the tea. "I'm so shocked — that's all. I suppose we never really know someone, do we?"

"Well, not always, I'm afraid," Judith replied, shaking her head. "I fear if John were alive today, he would have done some serious damage to his foreman — if he'd gotten to him before the law did."

"Well, thank the Lord you didn't miscarry and you still have a part of John to love and nurture when your baby comes," Patience said. "But you've had a most dreadful experience, so after you finish your tea, I want you to go up to my room and lie down for a while," Patience said.

They helped Judith upstairs and got her

settled. "Judith, may I pray with you?" Patience asked. At her nod, Patience laid a hand on Judith's head and asked for the Lord's healing and protection — body, soul, and spirit — as she recovered from her ordeal.

Not long after supper, Jedediah returned to Creekside and asked Patience if she'd like to take a walk with him.

"I certainly would," Patience said as she stepped outside. "Have you had anything to eat?"

"Yes, Joe asked Hannah to bring over something for both —" He stopped abruptly, then sighed and finished, "for both the prisoner and me."

She slipped her arm through his. "Jed, I'm so sorry you've lost a friend, and in this horrible way."

He patted her hand on his arm. "I think I found a true friend today — Joe." He told Patience the story of the day's confrontation and ordeal, then about Joe saving his life.

"Then I'm deeply grateful to Joe as well, Jed." She turned her head and smiled at him.

"And Monty's cooked his own goose with his threats to Judith, then all but admitting in front of Joe and me that he is responsible for John's death. That if he had to, he'd let Cody take the fall for it."

"Could there be another mob demanding revenge?" she wondered aloud.

"I don't think so, but I deputized Joe earlier. He's on the job so I could pay you a visit." They continued to stroll in the evening light. "He'll stand trial. I'll take him over to Helena, and he and Nathan can share a cell."

"Judith certainly is relieved," Patience said, "and she told Emily and me that she can feel safe at the Cross Bar again." She paused. "But I get a distinct feeling that she may sell and go back East where John's family is."

"Wouldn't surprise me," he said.

After his recounting of events, Jedediah fell silent. Patience wondered if he was still mourning his lost friendship. They strolled until the boardwalk ended, greeting folks as they passed. Patience enjoyed being on his arm and was proud to be seen with one of the heroes of the day. He squeezed her arm against his side, and they headed back to Creekside in companionable silence.

"Patience, after I get things settled with all this, I hope we'll get the chance to have that picnic we've talked about." Jedediah had paused at her front door, taking hold of her hands. "And now with Cody at the ranch, let me know if there's anything you need repaired or done around the boarding-house. I did make that promise to you . . . you know, back when . . ." They looked at each other, then started laughing at the memories of their early sparring.

"You have enough to take care of right now," she told him when she had caught her breath, "but later I have a few cabinet doors in the kitchen that need tightening at the hinges. I could probably fix some of them myself, but I don't have the proper tools."

He smiled. "I don't doubt you could, Patience, but I'm your man. I've got the tools, and that won't take any time at all." He squeezed her hands, still in his.

"That . . . would be great," she managed to say. "I'd better go now, and you need to make sure Joe is fine on his own. I'll be praying that there's no trouble tonight before you leave." She turned the doorknob to go in, but he stopped her.

"Thank you for believing that I'm a changed man now," he said, his voice low. "I'll be going now, but very soon we need to have ourselves a good, long talk." He let her hands go, slowly backed away, then strode up the boardwalk.

A good, long talk sounded more than good to her. And she had a good, long talk with God before finally falling asleep that night.

Half the morning was spent turning Monty over to the sheriff in Helena. Since Sheriff Thompson knew Jedediah from earlier days, Jedediah decided to sign his name one last time as "Vigilante X."

It gave him a feeling of a job well done seeing those two men, Nathan and Monty, in jail cells. Two men likely to be hanged for their crimes, but this time the court would decide.

He tapped Charlie on the flanks and took off in the direction of the Cross Bar. He had one last piece of business there.

Judith answered the door. "Jedediah, I was not expecting to see you today," she said with a surprised look. Her fair skin was discolored near her eye, turning several shades of the rainbow.

"Sorry to bother you again, Judith. I hope you're feeling better."

"Please, won't you come in?" She stepped aside, and he removed his hat and followed her to the parlor. "Can I get you something to drink?"

"No, ma'am. I wanted to see how you are doing, but also I wondered if I might speak with Cody."

"Of course. A moment ago he was in the barn. He may still be there." She looked anxious. "Is anything the matter?"

"No, no, nothing at all. I merely need to return something." He turned back to the door. "Patience tells me you might be going back East. Are you planning on selling the ranch?"

"It's a possibility. I'm going to stay with John's mother until after I have the baby, but I'll be leaving the Cross Bar in Cody's capable hands until I decide. Why?"

"I'd like you to keep me in mind, if you decide to sell. I've been saving for a place of my own."

Judith smiled. "Rest assured you will be the first one to be informed. Thank you again, Marshal, and to Joe for what you did. I probably wouldn't be here . . ."

"Just doing my job, ma'am," he said quietly when she didn't finish.

"Still, I'm very grateful to you and to Patience for taking care of me. She's a jewel, you know."

Jedediah felt pleasure at simply the sound of Patience's name. "Yes, I do know that." He tapped two fingers against his hat brim.

"Let me go catch Cody before he takes off. You take care now." He turned, walked out the door, and strode over to the barn.

Cody was in the tack room and looked over his shoulder when Jedediah walked in. "Hi there, Jed. What brings you out here?"

"Unfinished business, you might say. I didn't thank you properly, Cody, for forgiving me for the hanging, for your damaged voice and scarred neck. I wish I could take that night back." Jedediah shook his head. "I have to tell you I did have suspicions that you might be the cattle thief. I was wrong about that too." He paused and took out two blue neckerchiefs and handed them to him. "I believe these are yours."

"I don't understand. How did you come to have these? I thought I'd misplaced a couple of them." Cody stared down at the blue squares in his hands.

"One I found at the boardinghouse after you left, and the other was on Monty. He'd been wearing it while committing his crimes, hoping you'd be accused of the cattle rustling — and John's murder."

Cody stuffed the scarves in his pocket and shook his head. "I knew he didn't like me. John told me so. But I didn't know he hated me enough to try and pin a murder on me. According to Judith, he's got some real problems."

"He does. And another thing, Cody. I need to tell you I was even more suspicious of you because I thought you were attracted to Patience, so it fueled jealousy and distrust. But I was wrong *again.*"

Cody chuckled. "Anyone could see that Patience had eyes only for you, Jed. I liked her a lot, but more as a friend, because she was so nice to me. Me being new here, no one trusted me. But she did. And as angry as I was that it turned out you were the man I was looking for, she made me think about it. Had I killed you, what purpose would it have served? Satisfaction for a day, maybe. And then my second hanging, for real this time. But thanks to her — and God — I'm still alive."

"Think we could shake on it and be friends? I could use a few more myself," Jedediah said with a little grin.

Cody reached out and they clasped in a firm handshake.

"I'm going now," Jed told Cody, "but if you need me for anything at all, just let me know."

Cody grinned. "I'll do that, thanks, . . . and be good to Patience, or I'll come after you."

"I don't doubt you would!" Jedediah

smiled. "Be seeing you around then."

On the ride back into town, Jedediah had never felt as clean and free as he did at that moment. Patience would say it was God at work — and he believed she just might be right.

30

Patience walked back from the post office, thumbing through the mail and pretending to herself that she wasn't searching for a response from the publisher. As she walked up the steps to Creekside, she hid her disappointment behind a cheerful smile for the residents and Emily.

She sat down at her desk and thought of her new plans for fall. She and Emily could decorate with pumpkins and twigs with golden leaves, and make delicious pumpkin soup. Christmas was Patience's favorite holiday, and she could hardly wait to decorate a tree in the parlor, make Christmas cookies, and sing Christmas carols.

The doorbell rang, and Patience rose to answer it. There in the doorway stood Judith, her pregnancy showing. The scar on her cheek was hardly visible.

"Good morning, Judith." Patience was truly happy to see her.

Judith stepped into the foyer, carrying a covered plate. "I brought you some of my tea cakes. I dropped off some for Hannah as well, along with the recipe if she likes them," she said with a little smile.

Patience took the plate and lifted the linen napkin. "Oh my! They look and smell wonderful. Let me put these in the kitchen." Judith followed her.

"Why don't we have some with tea or coffee?" Patience suggested. "Do you have time?"

"I'd love to," Judith assured her, "but I'm leaving on this afternoon's stage in a half hour. I'm going to visit with John's mother. I wanted to go before autumn and the snow comes."

"You're going to be missed."

"I'll decide while I'm gone if I will come back to stay or sell the place," Judith explained. "I know Cody will do a good job of managing it, getting the steers to the cattle yards this fall. So I'll still be in touch."

"Is there anything I can do for you?"

"No, but thank you for offering. Please tell Emily goodbye for me, and let her know that true love will soon be hers and it'll be the right one this time."

Patience walked her back to the door. "I surely will. Write me when you're settled. I love receiving letters. Would you like me to walk with you to the depot to see you off?"

"I love getting letters too, but it's better if I go to the depot alone. I hate goodbyes, and Cody delivered my bags there for me earlier today." Judith gave Patience a quick hug. "I must get going now. Let me know when wedding bells ring for you."

Patience felt her cheeks getting warm, and she didn't know what to say other than goodbye. After Judith left, Patience felt sad. They were becoming good friends, and she cared for Judith, even more so after John's death. She couldn't be sad for long, though. She had the picnic with Jed to look forward to on Saturday. *Now, what shall I wear?*

Jedediah wanted the picnic to be something special. Although Patience had offered to pack their lunch, he'd decided to give her a gift that day — a leather-bound notebook he'd found at the general store. It was the kind journalists carried when they traveled across the country for writing their news reports and articles. He hoped she wouldn't mind that it wasn't very feminine looking, but it was all he could find on short notice. He wanted her to know that he supported her writing.

It felt like a great load was lifted off his

375

mind now that the murder was solved, Cody was in charge of the Cross Bar, and Judith had left with a promise to give him first chance to make an offer if she decided to sell. He didn't want to get his hopes high, but he couldn't help but dream of a real home and a wife and perhaps children one day. If not at the Cross Bar, he'd look elsewhere.

Jed was on his way to Patience's to see what was needed for her kitchen cabinet doors. He was pretty much a jack-of-all-trades when it came to handyman stuff, so it shouldn't take too long. Besides, he'd get to watch her working on the evening meal.

Delicious scents were already making their way out to the sidewalk when he arrived. Emily opened the door for him, but her smile was fleeting. "Come in. Patience is in the kitchen, so just go on in," she said, then returned to her chores, her shoulders drooping.

Jedediah wondered what was troubling the usually cheerful Emily. He went to the kitchen and found Patience at the stove in a day dress and her usual starched, white apron — face flushed and tendrils of damp hair curling around her forehead.

She must have felt his presence in the room because she turned while still stirring a pot of beans. "Oh, it's you, Jed. I didn't hear you come in." Spoon in hand, she walked over to him with a smile. "I see you've got your tools with you," she added as he placed several canvas bags on the table.

"I could smell good cooking all the way outside. I guess you know you're a fine cook!" he told her with a return smile and a pat on her arm.

"I've had years of practice, but I enjoy hearing it from you. I'm happy to see you," she said.

His heart skipped a beat. "I love hearing you say that, Patience. All right, show me which cabinet doors need fixing."

She laughed and it sounded like music to his ears. "Well, that'd be most of them," she told him, waving the spoon toward the array of cupboards. "But I'll be happy if you can keep even half the doors from falling off their hinges. You probably don't know this, but the boardinghouse is not that old. It's just that it was built in a hurry and shortcuts were taken to get it completed fast because of the gold strike at Alder Creek." She stepped over to the cabinets and pointed out the worst ones.

He examined the doors. She was right. They were thrown together without enough screws to support their weight. "I can fix this without a problem." He walked over to the table and opened the first bag.

"Oh, that's wonderful! I'll be right here if you have questions for me. Can you stay for supper?"

"Thought you'd never ask. I'd like that just fine." He paused, screwdriver in hand, and took a moment to watch her bustle around the kitchen. A vision of loveliness — yep! She'd make a very good wife. *Lord, I hope and pray she's mine.*

Patience too had noticed Emily wasn't her usual self. She seemed distracted most of the time, quiet, and talking only when she had to. A perfunctory smile to the residents was all she seemed to be able to manage.

Later that evening, Patience doused the lights and went upstairs to see if Emily wanted to talk about whatever was on her mind.

Tapping softly on the door so she wouldn't disturb other residents, she asked softly, "Emily, can I come in?"

A moment later, Emily opened the door. "Did I forget to do something?"

"Of course not — you never forget. May I come in?"

"Yes, please do." Emily stepped back and

motioned her to the single chair in the room, but she wouldn't look directly at her. Patience could tell she'd been crying. Emily went to the bed, sank down onto it, and tucked her bare feet under her, staring at her clasped hands.

"What's bothering you, Emily?" Patience asked from her seat nearby. "You don't seem yourself. Is it Monty?"

Emily lifted her head, looking at her with red-rimmed eyes. "I don't know . . . It's everything. Trying to make a new start out here in the West, falling for Monty way too quickly . . . Sometimes I feel invisible, even to the residents."

"Would you rather not keep working here?"

"It's nothing like that. I enjoy my work, but none of the boarders stay here long enough for me to get to know any of them — even the eligible men. And since most are miners, they're always on the move. How am I ever to meet someone like . . . well, like Jedediah? Is there something wrong with me?" She looked away, clasping and unclasping her hands in her lap.

Patience's heart twisted as she heard the pain in Emily's voice. "Dear Emily, there's nothing wrong with you. Nothing at all, and I'm so sorry you have even wondered that for a minute. Maybe you did fall for Monty too soon, but remember, he was Jedediah's good friend too. So even our marshal, who's supposed to recognize this kind of shiftiness, didn't know the real Monty." She reached over and gave Emily's hand a squeeze. "You're so attractive and good-natured — a truly wonderful young woman. At first I found myself envying you."

"Me? Really?" She looked quite astonished.

Patience nodded. "Yes, you. I even talked with Jedediah about it. My confidence suffers because I compare myself to you and other women who are tall, slender, and pretty. Heaven knows I've tried every corset or contraption to give me a smaller waist. Do you remember the night I nearly passed out and made a fool of myself with Jedediah?"

Emily covered a giggle. "I remember."

"Do you know what Jedediah said?" She didn't wait for Emily's answer. "I shouldn't compare myself to anyone or try to be like someone else. Simply be the person the good Lord wants me to be."

"I like you just as you are, Patience, and you're very pretty."

"I don't know about that, but thank you. What he said made me stop and think. God gave each one of us a unique ability and fashioned us in His image. Who am I to tell Him He's wrong? I'll never be any taller, and most likely never truly slender because that's not the way I'm made — that and the fact I have a sweet tooth, though I'm not going to blame that on our Creator. I'm learning to accept the things I can't change, work on the things I can change, and do what I know how to do even better."

"I know you're right, Patience. But maybe I should leave Nevada City —"

"What? You mean run away again? Never! You must face your battles or you will continue to struggle with the same things you did in the past."

"I suppose you are right."

"Oh, and I forgot — Judith said to tell you goodbye, and that true love will be yours soon."

"She's a good person to remember me even in a time of grief. You're right. I need to be patient . . . but it's hard because I want to be loved like Jedediah loves you."

Patience's heart leaped at the words, though she didn't feel quite as sure as Emily was. She said, "Then we'll just pray for God to guide you to just the right one, Emily. I'll let you get to bed, but I want you to know that you are valuable to me and valued in God's eyes. Don't *ever* think differently." Patience stood and kissed the top of her head. "Good night and sweet dreams."

Patience quietly slipped across to her room. She knew her statements to Emily were true, but she also understood the trials the young woman faced, the questions about the future.

She needed sleep, but her mind kept drifting to Jedediah in the kitchen today. She could feel his eyes on her as she cooked supper, and every now and then, she would glance over and see the muscles bunched beneath his chambray shirt while he worked. She imagined his arms around her. *Does he love me as Emily believes he does? Do I love him?*

Tomorrow, they would have their long-planned afternoon picnic, and she could hardly wait. *Maybe that tells me something.*

31

"Jed's here," Emily announced at the kitchen door. Patience was hurriedly searching a cupboard for something.

"Do you know where the honey is, Emily?" she asked, sounding a bit frantic. "I'm making up a fresh batch of switchel for our picnic — I've got the vinegar and ginger, but where's the honey? Molasses will do if we're out of honey."

Emily chuckled, walked over to the adjoining cupboard, and reached in to pull out the pot of honey with its wooden dispenser. "Here it is, my friend," she said with a smile as she placed it on the table.

"What would I do without you?" Patience exclaimed. "Could you put those sandwiches, the pound cake, and huckleberries in that basket while I finish up the switchel?"

Emily quickly did so, and Patience soon said, "I'm ready now." She put a jar of the cold drink in the basket and laid a blue-

and-white checkered dishtowel over the picnic lunch. "I hope he likes what I packed." She lifted the towel. "Yes, I already have cups."

"I hope you have a really good time," Emily said with a twinkle in her eyes. "I'll take care of things here, if anything is needed. You owe me for that!" she teased. "And since you've got the supper items ready and all I have to do is heat them, I'll even serve supper to our residents."

Patience smiled and nodded her head. Her wide straw hat went askew, and she retied the ribbons. "I know I owe you, and I will return the favor, I promise. How do I look?"

"Like the sweet angel you are."

"Oh, thank you. You always say such encouraging things. Let's hope Jed agrees with you. Be back in a couple of hours." She gave her a little wave and hurried out to Jedediah waiting next to the buggy.

"I hope there's some good vittles in your basket," he said with a grin as she came down the steps.

"I think you'll like them. It does look like a fine day for a picnic, doesn't it?"

"Sure does. I can't wait to get away from the noise and the bustle of all the miners in town on Saturday. But I won't have to worry about anything. Joe's in charge for the next few hours."

He took the basket and placed it in the buggy, then took her hand to assist her up. After running around to the other side, he climbed in next to her. Flicking the reins over Charlie's back, they took off at a trot, Patience with one hand on her hat and another holding on to the side of the seat. *What's his hurry?* she wondered.

Once Jedediah was outside the city, he slowed Charlie's pace, and Patience relaxed and took in the beautiful countryside against the backdrop of the mountains. She was grateful it wasn't as hot as it had been the last few weeks. The fragrance of the juniper and wildflowers heightened her senses, making her appreciate once again the beauty of God's creation. There wasn't a cloud in the cerulean sky.

A couple of miles from town, he turned off to a spot near a stand of magnificent ponderosa pine trees on a slope. He tied Charlie to a branch, helped Patience down, and handed her the basket.

"I've brought a large blanket for us to sit on," he said, reaching for it in the back of the buggy. "Your skirt won't get soiled," he told her, snapping the blanket open and spreading it on the grass.

Patience placed the basket on the blanket,

adjusted her skirt beneath her, and sat down, Jedediah next to her.

"Aren't these magnificent trees?" He waved his hand above his head in admiration. "Their strength and size never cease to amaze me."

Patience leaned her head back, hand on her hat. "I'm glad I wore this hat since the trees really don't provide much shade."

"Most of these trees are mature," he explained, "and some stand around one hundred sixty-five feet tall. So the branches and needles are far above where they'd be able to provide shade."

"How long, I wonder, does it take them to grow so tall?"

"I read somewhere that it takes three hundred to four hundred years to reach maturity."

Patience's eyes widened. "That's truly remarkable!"

"It really is."

She looked over at him to find him leaning back on an elbow, watching her.

He said, "But only remarkable if you're with me . . ." Then he looked away sheepishly.

"That's a very sweet thing to say." Her heart was thumping against her rib cage.

"Shall we eat now?" she suggested. Her

throat felt dry. "I have fresh switchel for us." She began unpacking the roast beef sandwiches and napkins. Patience handed him the jar while she held out the two cups for him to fill.

"This is a treat. I don't get switchel very often. It's a nice change from coffee, especially on a warm day like this."

"I'm happy you like it, Jed." Patience smiled.

"I'm feeling like you're spoiling me. Delicious biscuits, apple strudel, complete suppers at your place, now switchel . . . But I'm not complaining. Spoiling feels kind of nice." He set the cup aside while Patience handed him a sandwich. "Mmm . . . ," he said around a bite. "Delicious — add roast beef sandwich to the list."

"Why, thank you. I'm glad to know I can do something right."

He gave her a long gaze. "Oh, you're doing many things right, Patience. You've been so kind to Cody, then Judith, when they both really needed a friend. Cody could've still been after me. I don't know how you did that — changed his mind, I mean."

"Perhaps it wasn't me. I was simply God's instrument to help Cody see that revenge never works the way we want it to."

Jedediah polished off his sandwich, leaned

back against the trunk of the pine towering above them, and lifted his cup of switchel again. "Ah . . . that was good. Just the right amount of sweetness. Like you." He looked at her for a long moment, and she felt her cheeks grow warm.

He finally said, "Did Judith tell you before she left that I asked her to give me first chance if she decides to sell the ranch?"

"No, I don't believe she did. That would be a big ranch to run, I should think." Patience wrapped what was left of her lunch in the basket and pulled out the sliced pound cake. She put a slice of cake on a small plate and added huckleberries.

"It could be, but I've been saving up because I've always wanted to buy a spread of my own someday — get married and have a family, if it's not too late for me."

Patience wasn't sure how to respond so she took a bite of her dessert and waited for him to speak again.

He finally broke the silence. "That was a delicious lunch, Patience," he said, wiping his mouth.

"Thank you." She leaned on the tree trunk next to him, curling her legs underneath her skirt. They sat without saying anything further for a few minutes, then Jedediah suddenly shot straight up.

"I nearly forgot. Be right back." She watched as he loped over to the buggy and lifted a parcel out from under the seat. Returning and seating himself closer to her, he handed her the brown-paper-covered package. "I found this at the store, and I thought maybe you could use it."

"Goodness . . . a present?"

"Go ahead and open it," he urged.

Patience removed the paper wrapping to discover a journal. She ran her hand across the smooth brown leather. "Jed," she turned to look at him, "this is the best gift I've ever received — well, other than the piano from Mother," she added with a smile.

He grinned back at her, then turned serious. "I want you to know that I support you in your writing, wherever it takes you."

She could hear the sincerity in his voice. "Thank you so much. I sent my writings off to a publisher, hoping at the very least that someone would actually read them, but I don't really expect to hear back."

She leaned over to give him a quick hug, her hat slipping off the back of her head, and then he put his arms around her and held her for what seemed like a long minute. When she drew back, he looked into her face, then tipped her chin up and leaned over to give her a kiss that jarred her senses.

389

When he released her, she wondered if she could catch her breath again.

Jedediah took her hand in both of his. "Patience, I've waited for just this very moment . . . to ask you, will you marry me?"

She blinked, thinking she must be dreaming. With her heart racing, she took a deep breath. "Are you sure, Jed? Do you really want — ?"

"I've never been more sure than I am at this moment." He drew a ragged breath. "I didn't mean to catch you off guard, but I couldn't hold my feelings in any longer. I've been thinking of nothing else but us for weeks now. Since the first day you marched into my office, I couldn't help but be attracted to your spritely courage to dare question my authority. And your solid faith drew me to you, even though at first I tried to deny it. My heart is hoping you feel the same way about me . . ." He looked away, as though afraid of what he might see in her face.

"Oh, Jed," she exclaimed, taking his face in her hands, "I do, I do! Since we've spent time together lately, walking and talking, I've been certain I love you too! But I couldn't let myself believe you might feel that way about me." He pulled her hands from his face and held them tightly.

"Is that a 'yes' then?" His dark eyes seemed even darker as they searched hers.

"Yes . . . I mean 'yes' to your question!" Patience felt tears in her eyes as he brought one of her hands to his lips and kissed it as though it were some fine object, holding her other hand to his heart.

"I'm sorry I have no engagement ring for you today, but we'll pick out wedding bands together," Jedediah told her. "I promise to do all that is within my power to make you happy . . . to give you a home with children if you want them like I do."

Patience brushed at the tears sliding down her cheeks. No one had ever talked with her about love, about her happiness before. "I do want to have children, and there's nothing I'd rather do than spend my life making *you* happy."

Jed pulled her into the crook of his arm. "Let's set a date — not too far away — and plan our future together," he said in a husky voice.

She made herself comfortable, her head on his shoulder, and they talked and laughed and planned until the waning sun began to dip along the horizon.

Patience and Jedediah suddenly found themselves the center of attention after telling first Emily, then Hannah and Joe, about their engagement. Before long it seemed like the whole town knew.

The boarders were gathered in the parlor after dinner, and congratulations came from each of them when Patience joined Jed on the settee.

"This is so exciting! Have you set a date yet?" Emily asked from the kitchen doorway.

"We want to get married a week from next Saturday," Jedediah announced.

"We have a lot to do before then!" exclaimed Emily. "Oh my, and —"

"Slow down, Emily. We'll make a list of things we must do," Patience assured her.

"Then you'd better be on your way now, Jedediah."

There were good-natured laughs, but folks decided Emily was serious when she took Jedediah's arm and pulled him to the door. Patience followed, laughing.

"Guess that means I'm leaving," Jed chuckled ruefully, turning to wave good night to the residents.

"I hope you have a good night, Jed," Patience said as they walked out to the porch. "Emily's right, we've plenty to do."

Jedediah leaned over to steal a quick kiss. "Good night, my dear. I'm a very happy man, you know."

Patience felt like she'd been walking on air ever since their picnic. She was surprised she could keep her mind on her duties at all.

She went to find Emily so they could start making the plans for a small wedding celebration. When she entered the kitchen, Emily was there, ready with a pad and pencil.

She started right in before Patience even got herself seated. "Since the town doesn't have a church building, we can have the wedding here at Creekside or maybe out-doors. What do you think about that?"

Patience chuckled. "I love having your help with this, Emily. But first things first: would you be my maid of honor please?"

Emily jumped up, clapped her hands, and hugged Patience. "By all means! I would be *very* honored." The two hugged again, then Emily asked, "Who will be Jed's best man?"

"He's going to ask Joe. This will be a small wedding, but let's start a list since it's less than two weeks away. I wonder if Hannah has ever baked a wedding cake?"

"Oh, this is going to be so much fun!" Emily exclaimed. "Where will you find a wedding dress on such short notice?"

"I'll be wearing my mother's gown that's in my trunk. We'll have to get it out right

393

away, air it out, and look for anything that needs mending or altering. It's very beautiful," Patience said, "but it probably will need to be let out a bit —"

"Ooh — I can't wait to see it," Emily put in with more clapping.

"I've already sent a telegram to Mother. I do hope she can come."

The two of them made wedding plans until they were both yawning. "We must get to bed, Emily, or I'm afraid I'll fall over."

"Me, too." Emily closed the notepad. "But this is a nice kind of tired, don't you think?"

Patience nodded in agreement as they climbed the stairs. "I'm hoping I sleep better than I did last night," she said. "I was so full of thankfulness and love and hopes and dreams . . ."

". . . that you couldn't sleep," Emily finished for her, and they held their hands over their mouths to silence their chuckles.

32

Sunlight played over Jedediah's face, and for a moment he thought Patience was blowing kisses to him. He jerked awake, looked at the clock, and realized he'd slept much longer than usual. As he dressed and prepared for the day, Patience's face and her "Yes!" response that would make him a husband played across his mind. He smiled into the mirror. "See, there is someone who cares, who loves this face," he said aloud. *Thank you, Lord, for bringing Patience here.* He couldn't help but grin as he shaved around his mustache.

He had no family to inform about the wedding and had happily left most of the details to Patience. He decided he'd wander over to the bakery and have some of Hannah's biscuits. He had no inmates in cells presently, and hopefully his presence of authority around town was making any lawbreaker types think twice.

He was soon headed toward Hannah's, and she was waiting for him with a cheery "Mornin', Almost-a-Bridegroom!" She walked over to him, and Jedediah grabbed her hands, began humming a tune, and waltzed her around the small shop while she laughed breathlessly. Folks having their morning coffee clapped in time to the beat, laughing along with them.

When they had finished, Jedediah and Hannah moved to the counter while she poured him a cup of coffee. He was surprised to see tears. "Oh, no — don't you dare cry," he ordered.

"I'm so happy for you both that I could bust!" She handed him the coffee, then dabbed her eyes with the corner of her apron. "You couldn't have chosen a better woman to marry than Patience."

"How right you are, Hannah. Now, how 'bout a biscuit or two to go along with my java," he said with a wink.

He took his breakfast over to the only remaining table. As other customers were leaving, most of them offered, "Congratulations, Marshal," as they passed.

When he was finished, he called over to Hannah, "Joe around?"

She nodded, went through the curtain into the kitchen, and soon had Joe seated across from Jed with his own cup of coffee and a refill for Jed.

Joe, in his white starched apron and flour-streaked face, leaned across to murmur he was "learnin' how to make those biscuits you like." Jed grinned but didn't say anything. *As if nobody would know just looking at you.*

"Since you're my deputy," Jed told him, "I'll need you to keep the law for me for a few days. Think you can do that along with your baking?"

"You know I can." Joe grinned, patting his shiny new deputy badge showing above the apron.

"I have one more duty to ask of you, Joe. Would you be my best man?"

"Jumpin' Jehoshaphat! *Me?* Well, I'd be downright honored to, Jed." He turned his head and sniffed. "Uh-oh . . . I think my biscuits are burning," he said, and rushed back to the kitchen.

Hannah walked over to the table, once more wiping her eyes with her apron. "Now I'm going to cry again," she said. "Thank you for asking Joe. He's trying so hard to get folks to think of him as an ordinary citizen rather than the town drunk. But that's in his past now, and seeing him up in front with you and Patience will be a big help."

"I pray it stays that way, Hannah." He stood up, placed some coins on the table, and thanked her for the breakfast.

As he started out the door, he saw Patience and Emily across the street, their heads together, looking over what seemed like a list. They were really out early. The two then separated, Emily going into the general store and Patience heading toward the bakery.

Jed opened the door for her and took her arm. "Good morning, my dearest," he said, keeping his voice low. "A very nice way to begin the day, looking into your lovely face." He wanted to kiss her, but he could imagine the buzz *that* would start across the town. "I'm surprised you are already out and about this morning so soon after breakfast. Hope you slept as well as I did."

"Well, Emily and I worked too late last night — with wedding plans running through my head, I didn't have such a good night."

"Here, have a seat." Jedediah pulled out a chair and helped her into it.

"I'm really here to see if Hannah could bake us a wedding cake," she said as Jed sat down one more time.

"Did I hear someone speak my name?" Hannah called over as she and Joe walked out of the kitchen carrying a pan of fresh biscuits. She hurried over to give Patience a kiss on the top of her head. "I've already said my congratulations, but you can't imagine how happy I am that you found each other."

Patience blushed prettily and murmured her thanks. Jedediah was surprised at this unusually shy side of Patience.

"Help yerself," Joe said, bringing over a plate of biscuits. "Made 'em myself this morning — with a little help from Hannah."

Hannah laughed. "We had to throw out the first batch, Jed — it got burned while you and Joe were jawin', but I guarantee these are good."

"Hannah, have you ever baked a wedding cake before?" Patience asked.

"Only once or twice. Why? Are you asking me to bake yours? You know I will —"

"Oh, that would be wonderful!"

"You let me know what kind and how big, and I'll make you a cake that'll knock that straw hat off your pretty head."

They all laughed. It felt awfully good to Jedediah that he had managed to find some really nice folks as friends . . . and even nicer, a woman to be his wife.

■ ■ ■ ■

By the time Patience and Emily met up again that morning, they were pleased to discover they'd completed quite a few things on their list. The cake was ordered and Emily had found decorative paper for the handwritten invitations to be given to the small group of friends the couple wanted to invite. Patience's mother's wedding gown and veil were airing out in her room. *Hopefully most of the wrinkles will fall out,* she thought once again.

"I'm so glad your mother's dress needed only a little alteration," Emily was saying. "It won't take me long to finish it up, with you telling me exactly what to do."

"I don't know what I'd do without your help, Emily. I knew the dress would be tight." She sighed. "I'd better not have any sweets from now till the wedding."

Emily said, "By the way, will Reverend King from Virginia City marry you and Jed?"

"Oh my goodness — I never thought about that!" Patience exclaimed. "I'll talk to Jed this very afternoon and see who he knows. On second thought, I'll do that now. I won't be long. I'll see you back at the boardinghouse."

She didn't have to go very far to find Jedediah standing outside the mercantile talking to the store's owner, Benny Foster. Jedediah saw her coming and greeted her with a welcoming smile. "I thought you were busy with wedding plans," he said, holding out a hand toward her.

"Hello, Benny," she said as she joined the two men.

"Congratulations, Patience. I hope you'll both be very happy."

"Thank you." She looked up at Jedediah. "May I speak with you, Jed — privately?"

Benny picked up his broom. "I'll leave you two alone. I've got plenty of work to do. Patience, if you need anything at all to help with your wedding, let me know."

"That's very kind of you, Benny."

After the man had disappeared inside, Jedediah asked what was on her mind.

"We need someone to marry us, Jed, and Nevada City doesn't have a preacher. Do you think Reverend King will marry us here?" Her voice sounded as worried as she felt.

"Mmm . . . I guess I'm the only one in town that's licensed to do the marrying." Patience felt her heart drop till she saw the twinkle in Jed's eyes. "We'll figure out something, Patience," he said with a pat on her arm. "In our excitement we seem to have forgotten that small detail. But I'm sure Reverend King will perform the ceremony." He thought a moment, then snapped his fingers. "I'll ride over to Virginia City and ask him right now."

"Thank you. That would be one less thing to worry about. I do hope he's free next Saturday."

"Don't worry. If not him, I'll think of someone else. I'll stop in later and let you know what he says."

Jed's going to take care of this! She wanted to hug him, but didn't dare in public. "I'm sure you're right." She gave his arm a firm squeeze, then whirled around, picked up her skirts, and hurried back to Creekside, Jedediah's chuckles following her down the boardwalk.

"That didn't take long," Emily said. "I need you to slip on your gown. I baste-stitched it together like you showed me, and I want you to see if it's right before I do the final stitching."

"All right. Let's go do that right now before I write the invitations. Hannah said Joe's going to hand them out for me. What a sweetheart he's turned out to be."

Emily laughed. "He surely is, though I don't know if he'd like being called that to his face. On second thought, maybe Hannah does when nobody's listening." They both laughed at the thought.

"See? That's what I keep trying to tell you, Emily. Those two found each other — patience *is* a virtue." Emily giggled. "I wasn't trying to be amusing," Patience said, but she smiled.

"I know what you mean," Emily said, turning serious. "I think it's only a matter of time before Joe will ask Hannah to marry him."

They climbed the stairs to Patience's room, Buttercup at their heels. Moments later, Patience had slipped on her mother's wedding gown and veil, and she felt transformed once again. "It fits perfectly now, thanks to you, Emily," she said, looking down at herself and smoothing the gathers around the waistline.

"I wish we had a full-length mirror — you're going to be a *very* beautiful bride." Emily had tears in her eyes. "Here, let me hold the mirror so you can see more of the dress." She soon had it positioned, and Patience gazed at the stranger in the lovely gown looking back at her.

"With the gown, somehow I can see myself as pretty," she mused. "I don't think I've ever felt that way. It almost seems like a spiritual experience. Does that make any sense?"

"It does to me. You'll be the bride of Jedediah, and marriage is a sacred ceremony."

Patience almost didn't want to take the gown off, but eventually with Emily's help she had removed it and was back in her regular clothing. "I so appreciate you doing this altering for me. And I'm sure you'll make the stitches tight and close together. I don't want to burst out the sides during the ceremony."

Emily shook her head. "You talk as though you're the size of a horse — which of course you are not. So please quit saying those kinds of things about yourself."

She shook her head in chagrin. "You're so right. I have a man who believes I'm beautiful, and good friends, and the love of God. That's all that matters."

The doorbell from downstairs caught their attention. Emily laid the gown across the bed and offered to answer it.

"I'll come down too," Patience told her. "I have many things to do before fixing supper."

As they started down the stairs, she said, "We soon must get the house cleaned for the wedding and the reception, so I'm not all worn out that day."

"I know what that means — shaking the rugs, cleaning the floors, dusting, washing windows. Maybe I can find a couple of girls to help us," Emily said. "By the way, where will you live once you're married? Surely not the room above the jailhouse."

They shared a chuckle, and Patience said, "No, we'll live here for a while." They were at the door by then, and opened it to find Hannah carrying several flowers.

"Please come in, Hannah dear!" Patience greeted her, pulling the woman inside the foyer. "We've just had a fitting with my mother's wedding gown. Emily is going to make it work for me."

"I wanted to see if you might like something like this to carry as your bouquet, Patience. They bloom till summer's end." Hannah held out lavender flowers framed with two darker purple ones.

"Oh, Hannah, they are lovely. I know the lavender ones are bitterroot, but what is the other one?" Patience asked, examining the delicate blooms. With only a week to prepare, it would be very difficult to find fresh flowers in a mining town. These would do nicely.

"They're lupine. We could mix the two, making a pretty nosegay. Joe and I went out searching for what we could find in the woods this morning."

"I think they will be beautiful, Hannah. Don't you, Emily?"

"Oh, yes. Hannah, you're a genius," Emily exclaimed.

"Good, then leave that to me. It's one less thing you have to worry about — along with the cake." Hannah turned to leave. "I'll get out of your way — I know you have plenty on your minds."

"What an endearing woman," Emily commented as Hannah walked away.

"She surely has been good to me," Patience said, "and gave me good advice when I really needed it." She took a deep breath. "What next, Emily? Oh, yes, I must write the invitations."

"And I'm going to go finish your dress alterations," Emily said, already on her way back upstairs. "I'll leave your gown hanging up," she added over her shoulder, "then later, before the wedding, I'll press whatever wrinkles remain."

With a bubble of excitement filling her chest, Patience went to her desk, pulling paper and pen out, anxious to get the invitations to the guests.

Patience wrote, *Please come to witness the marriage of Jedediah Jones and Patience Cavanaugh.* She stopped and smiled softly to herself as she picked up her pen once again.

33

Patience liked to think God had painted the sky a sapphire blue and added a few puffy clouds just for her wedding. She leaned out her bedroom window, feeling like she would burst with joy. *Thank You, Lord,* she whispered as she drew back. *It's our wedding day — mine and Jed's. Thank You, thank You for bringing Jed and me to Nevada City, for letting us find each other.*

She couldn't help but wish her father could be here to enjoy it all with her. However, she was grateful that God had seen her through all the difficult times in her life without him.

Her mother had arrived, and Patience had lovingly welcomed her and taken time from her wedding preparations to help get her settled into the only vacant room in the boardinghouse. It took both of them to carry the two large bags up to her room. Patience hoisted the case onto the bed and unlatched the straps.

"Mother, do you think you brought enough to get you through the weekend?" she teased with a smile.

Charity opened the other bag and glanced over at her. "I like to be prepared in case I change my mind and don't return that soon. I'm happy you're going to wear my gown. It'll take me back . . ." Her eyes misted, and she stared into space.

"I miss Father too, especially at this time. I like to think he knows, don't you? And I'm so glad to be able to wear your wedding gown."

"I hope so." She reached over to take Patience's hand. "I'm very happy about your wedding. You have my blessing, and I'm praying that you and Jedediah have a bright future. Soon, I hope, you'll give me some grandchildren. I'm getting old, you know."

Patience patted her mother's hand, noticing the veins visible through the pale skin. "I'm glad you like Jedediah, Mother. We both want children, and I hope you'll be able to visit our family often."

They both began unpacking the two large cases, and Patience said, "I can't thank you enough for sending the piano. I was so surprised and delighted. We've had some wonderful times singing in the parlor here since it arrived."

Her mother's smile crinkled the lines around her eyes. "You're so very welcome, dear. I know you'll get more use out of the piano than I will — I have no one to listen to me play."

"You certainly should play it while you're here," Patience urged. "I love to play the piano. Sometimes playing it on my own is just enough for me. If I'm having a difficult day, it relaxes me." Patience went to place her mother's hairbrush and comb on the dressing table.

"You often played when you were angry with me. I feel like we've finally bridged that gap, don't you?"

Patience looked at her mother. "Yes, I do. So we have even more than a wedding to celebrate, don't we?" She moved over to give her mother a hug, and the pressure of her mother's arms around her brought a lump to her throat.

Charity stepped back and briskly asked, "What's for supper? I hope it's not that tough beef again with the salty gravy."

Patience took a deep breath. "It's roasted chicken, Mother. I think you'll like it. These days I'm going easy on the salt and putting a salt cellar on the table for guests to add to their own liking." Some things would never change, but Patience could live with that.

It seems like everything is falling into place, she mused as she added some of her mother's underthings to a dresser drawer. *Now, if only Emily could find someone.*

Supper had come and gone with few complaints from her mother, and though Patience had gotten little sleep with all the emotions filling her mind, the big day had finally arrived. Hannah and Emily carefully slipped the wedding gown over her head before helping Patience with her toilette. Emily fixed her hair in an intricate style, assuring Patience that this was the latest fashion in the East, according to the newspapers she'd seen lately. A few tendrils framed her face and the edge of her neckline in back.

"Let's get this hoop in place," Hannah said. "I think you can just step into it, and I'll pull it up underneath the skirt." She tugged it into place at Patience's waist, tied it, and smoothed the skirt down over the hoop. She took a step back. "I must say, it's very beautiful. Never had one myself —"

"Oh, I'm so sorry, Hannah." Patience looked into Hannah's face, each line reflecting her character and compassion. "You can

411

always borrow mine, when you and Joe marry."

Hannah laughed. "He hasn't asked me yet. Besides, dear, there's no way I'd fit into your gown!"

Charity appeared in the bedroom door, and the three women circled around the bride to take in the lovely vision before them.

The gown was ivory *peau de soie* satin, fitted at the waist and falling in folds to a deep alencon lace that Emily had added to the border, and ended with a short train. The hoop held the skirt wide and full. The scooped neckline with the same wide lace trim flattered Patience's face.

"It's nearly time, Patience. Let's attach your veil." Emily placed it over Patience's hair, pinned it in place with a few instructions from Charity, then stood back to admire it. "You look truly radiant, Patience."

"I think you're biased, Emily," Patience laughed. "Oh, my shoes. I must not forget them! They're rather tight, but I can manage for an hour or so."

"I took the liberty of placing your own cream-colored shoes in the pantry, if you should decide you want to change into them for the reception," Emily said.

"Thank you, Emily. You think of everything."

"Who's playing the piano?" Emily wanted to know as she adjusted the gown's train.

"Mary Finney graciously agreed when she stopped by this week to find if we had a room for someone coming to visit. I was so happy to find out she can play too."

"So everything's ready, dear," Charity said, leaning over to place a kiss on Patience's cheek. "I think Hannah and I had better get ourselves downstairs," she added, motioning with her hand, and the two ladies departed.

"Are you ready?" Emily asked, patting an errant strand of Patience's hair into place. "Make sure you take your time on the stairs — you don't want to get yourself tangled up and land in Jedediah's arms too quickly." Their shared laugh was just what they both needed.

She took a deep breath and expelled it. "Yes, I will be careful, but my hands are shaking. Where's my bouquet?"

"Right here." Emily lifted it from the dressing table and handed the freshly picked flowers, arranged in a perfect little nosegay, to Patience.

"Oh, and look how nicely it enhances the colors in your gown," Patience noted, holding it near the lavender and purple silk Emily had made with Patience's help.

Emily reached over for a careful hug, her eyes misting. "Patience, I want to say I'm so happy for you, and will pray that you and Jed find every happiness your hearts desire."

"I can't thank you enough for all your help. But mostly for your friendship. Now, you'd better start down before we're both crying." They smiled at each other, and Emily disappeared through the door and down the staircase.

Patience took one last glance in the mirror. She did look pretty, much to her surprise. Emily was right — she even looked radiant. She hoped that Jed would think so too. But remembering what he'd said about her recently, she felt confident that he would.

Time to become Mrs. Jedediah Jones. And she could hardly wait. With her pulse beating rapidly, Patience slowly descended the wide staircase, eyes fastened on Jedediah smiling at her from the foyer.

The double doors of the parlor were opened wide, and the guests had taken their seats in Creekside's large parlor, rearranged to make ample room for a small ceremony. Yesterday Jedediah had helped move most of the furniture to one wall. The chairs were borrowed from The Star Bakery, which was closed for the day. He wondered where the potted ferns had come from, but knowing Hannah, she'd probably talked the folks at the bank into making a loan that wasn't of the financial kind.

Will and Liza were sitting there, as well as Charity, Benny from the mercantile along with his wife, Cody, and Jedediah's posse — James, Brady, and Kit. Several other Creekside residents were in attendance — Mark, Conrad, and Michael. Buttercup was sitting on her haunches next to Hannah's chair, watching and cleaning her paws. A meadowlark sitting on the open windowsill tweeted its approval.

Jedediah stood in the foyer in a dark suit that Judith Hargrove had given him before she left. "John would want you to have it, and you just might be needing it soon," she finished with a twinkle in her eye.

Joe was beside him, wearing his suit, his normally unruly hair combed flat with the use of a double dose of pomade.

First, Emily walked slowly down the stairs as Mary played the piano. She took her place next to the reverend.

Jedediah's palms felt damp, as well as his shirt underneath the coat. And then Patience was there at the top of the staircase. He moved over to the last step, his hand on the bannister as he watched his bride slowly descending. Patience never took her eyes off of him until she was there beside him, slipping her arm through his. He covered her hand with his and gave it a squeeze, smiling into her lovely face behind its veil. *This is really happening!* The thought whirled over and over through Jedediah's incredulous mind.

The little wedding party positioned themselves between the double doors, Reverend King facing Jedediah and Patience, their witnesses on either side. And the service began with the reverend reading familiar words from Genesis about the first wedding.

Jedediah was very glad to have found two matching gold bands in Virginia City. His and Patience's eyes locked with mutual commitment as they exchanged their vows and wedding rings. *Mrs. Jedediah Jones!* His heart felt like it would burst with love and pride as he looked into Patience's lovely green eyes.

Patience had handed Emily her bouquet with shaking hands before she'd placed the gold band on Jed's finger. She looked up into his face, amazed and overjoyed that this good, decent, honest, handsome man was now her husband.

She heard someone sniffle behind her. Could it be that Mother was crying? She didn't dare look for fear she would start crying too.

Reverend King blessed the couple with a prayer, then said, "I now pronounce you man and wife. Jedediah, you may kiss your bride."

Patience's heart was racing as Jedediah lifted her veil to give her a very solemn, tender kiss. Immediately the guests clapped, and the couple turned to face them as man and wife.

All the guests filed into the dining room to watch the joyful couple cut the cake. It was a little crowded, but no one seemed to mind.

"Before I forget to tell you, Hannah," Patience said, accepting the knife from her, "your cake looks so pretty and absolutely delicious. I can hardly wait to taste it. Thank you for all your hard work on it and for your help in getting us ready for this day."

"Go on with you, my dear — I enjoyed every minute. You and Jed go ahead and share that first piece." Hannah nodded to them both, her face beaming.

Together they sliced into the cake and

took their first bites. "Wonderful!" they exclaimed in unison, and everyone laughed.

"Let me cut the rest, and Emily can serve the guests," Hannah suggested.

The crowd began moving out of the dining room, and Charity Cavanaugh pushed through to put an arm around each of them. "I'm so proud of you, daughter, and so glad I was here to celebrate this day with you. You look lovely in every way, my dear Patience, and you wear the gown with honor." She stopped to blink her eyes quickly, then turned to Jedediah. "And welcome to the family, Jedediah. You will be a son to me, I'm sure, and my sincere thanks to you for loving my daughter as I can see you do."

Patience could feel tears welling up, and she finally was able to whisper, "Thank you, Mother, for everything."

Some guests had found their way to the parlor, others had spilled out onto the front porch, everyone finding places to chat, eat cake, and admire the newly married couple. Patience noticed that Judge Clint Chandler from Virginia City had found a seat next to Emily, and quietly whispered to Jed that they seemed to be enjoying their chat. The judge never took his eyes from Emily. *Maybe this will be the man for her.*

Cody walked over to add his congratulations, leaning over Patience's hand to give her a little kiss. "You know I have a fond spot in my heart for Patience, so you'd do well to be a good husband to her, Jed," he warned with a lift of an eyebrow.

Jedediah's arm went around her shoulder. "Rest assured, I'll have years of practice doing just that."

"And what of you, Cody? Anyone sparking an interest?" Patience asked to tease him a bit.

"Not yet, but I'm in no hurry. I like taking care of the Cross Bar for Judith. I've really come to admire and respect her."

Patience would have liked to tease him further, but instead she took Jedediah's hand. "Come, let's ask Mary to play something for our wedding dance." She pulled him to the front of the room and soon Mary was at the keyboard. The guests looked on with expressions of surprise and awe as the bride and groom waltzed in the space left in the parlor.

"We've not danced since the Hargrove doings, have we? Not too bad," Jed whispered as he swung Patience around. She laughed gaily, remembering the confusion of that night, with both of them having partners they would just have soon traded.

"I'm sure glad," he said in her ear, "we finally got it all figured out."

EPILOGUE

Patience was playing with baby Emily on a blanket under a sprawling cottonwood tree on her ranch, the Cross Bar, while her toddler son, Cody, yanked at her skirts. She turned the baby over on her tummy, then pulled Cody onto her lap. "Needing a little special attention, I see." She hugged the toddler tightly.

Cody grinned up at her with dark, innocent eyes, and her heart melted. She was glad Jedediah had wanted to name his son "Cody," and it pleased Cody to no end to be their ranch foreman. Patience had maintained the partnership with Emily at Creekside, but as more of a silent partner — especially since Jedediah had turned in his marshal's badge. Emily had married Judge Clint Chandler and was expecting their first child, but they remained close friends.

Shielding her eyes from the sun, she watched Jedediah walking over with a package in his hand. He knelt on the blanket, kissed Patience, then little Cody, and patted Emily's head.

He handed her the parcel. "This was sitting on the porch for you," he said, reaching to take Cody from her so she could open it. "One of the hands must've brought it back from town."

When she had removed the wrapping, Patience's heart lurched. "It's the first copy of my book!" She ran her hand across the title, *Daily Devotions,* and her name, "Patience Cavanaugh Jones." Her heart swelled and hot tears stung her eyes. "It's been a while," she whispered as she hugged it to her chest.

"This is wonderful — my wife, a published author. I'm very proud of you!" Jed circled her shoulders with his arm for a hug. "I probably won't even have to read it since you've been preaching all these good things to me already." Patience gave him a playful punch, then hugged him back.

Apparently sensing the spirit of celebration, Cody threw his hands in the air, jumped off his papa's lap, and danced around the blanket. They both laughed as their son jabbered away.

Patience opened her book, staring at the dedication, then at Jedediah. "I wonder what my mother will say when she finds out the book is dedicated to her."

"I believe she'll be surprised but quite pleased," Jed said with a warm smile that still made her heart flutter.

Patience smiled back at her husband, then gazed down at their children with pride and wonder at how God had continued to bless them.

AUTHOR'S NOTE

In the spring of 1863, the discovery of placer gold by Bill Fairweather and Henry Edgar in Alder Gulch began one of Montana's greatest placer gold rushes in history. Between the years of 1863 and 1866, $30 million in gold bullion was mined from Alder Gulch, a lode that would eventually yield $100 million. By late spring of '63, ten thousand miners crowded the surrounding hillside near the Tobacco Root Mountains. There were so many settlements that the area was touted as the "Fourteen Mile City."

But along with the bustling population of 30,000 by late fall, nefarious characters moved in. And without any established law in Montana Territory, *road agents,* as they were called, went about robbing and pilfering and causing havoc until the citizens of Virginia City and Bannock formed the Montana Vigilantes — a highly secretive vigilance committee that systematically hunted down and hanged road agents based on the testimony of other men facing execution. My story is loosely based on John Beidler, Vigilante X, who participated in numerous hangings, though people sometimes did actually survive hangings. One of Jedediah's guns, the Winchester, is on display at the Montana Homeland Gallery in Helena.

Frank Finney and his wife, Mary, were real historical characters and the last holdouts to keep buildings in Nevada City. He hauled wood from Granite and freighted merchandise. They kept horses and cows, which provided dairy goods, a commodity much in demand.

The Criterion Saloon, which I write about in my story, is a real structure and is still standing today. An interesting fact I found — the movies *Lonesome Dove, The Missouri Breaks,* and *Thousand Pieces of Gold* filmed scenes in the Criterion Saloon.

The Star Bakery, another original structure, was purchased in 1864 by Patrick McGovern, who lived in Nevada City with his family, but when the bakery closed in 1865, it became their home. I took the liberty to base his daughter, Hannah, as the character who owned the bakery. Wallace Street is still the main street of Nevada City.

My boardinghouse is purely fictional. I named the Creekside Inn after Shirley and Lloyd Reed's Creekside B&B in Nebraska, which recently closed its doors.

Switchel was a real drink and a thirst quencher. Ladies would take this drink out to the field workers. It's made of water, apple cider vinegar, molasses or honey, and ginger if available.

The ponderosa pine in the story has a lot of meaning for me. Montana's state tree, where Jedediah and Patience had their picnic, is a beautiful, grand tree as noted by its massive size. Its strong, tall trunk has a nice fragrant vanilla scent from the bark. These pines can grow up to 165 feet, a process that can take 300 to 400 years. I wanted to mention the ponderosa since a grove of them was planted in my brother's memory in Glacier National Park after his untimely death while a deputy superintendent there. It was my honor to go to Glacier Park with park ranger officials and with my brother's widow and daughter to collect the tiny seeds needed from the pine cones for them to plant. I hope to go back soon and see how tall they've grown. The ponderosa pine plays an important role in Montana's ecology and wildlife habitat, providing valuable grazing for wildlife and livestock, as the forests are usually open, park-like areas. Native Americans ate the pine seed, and the Cheyenne Indians used the pine pitch inside whistles and flutes to improve the instruments' sound.

The meadowlark singing at the wedding is Montana's state bird.

ACKNOWLEDGMENTS

No author takes their writing journey alone, without a team. Many thanks go to my wonderful editors, Andrea Doering and Carol Johnson, and the Revell editorial team for their valuable insight.

My gratitude to the Revell marketing team — too many to name — who patiently answers all my countless questions. Thanks to Revell's wonderful design team that creates the best eye-catching covers!

Much appreciation to Natasha Kern, my agent. I know I can rely on her knowledge and her prayers.

I'm so grateful for my critique partner and best friend, Kelly Long. We share much laughter during our brainstorming sessions, and so much more.

To my family, Bruce, Sheri, Bobby, Jared, and Amy, for your constant support and love, but most of all for believing in me.

Last, but definitely not least, to the One

who formed my most inward parts, and in your Book are written all the days that were ordained for me when there was not yet one.

ABOUT THE AUTHOR

Maggie Brendan is a CBA bestselling author and won the 2013 Laurel Wreath Award and the 2014 Book Buyers Best Award in the Inspirational Romance category. She has been a finalist for the 2014 and 2013 Heart of Excellence Readers' Choice Award, the 2013 Published Maggie Award of Excellence, and the 2012 Inspirational Reader's Choice Award. She is married, lives in Georgia, and loves all things Western. She has two grown children and four grandchildren. When she's not writing, she enjoys reading, researching her next novel, and being with her family.

Maggie invites you to connect with her at www.MaggieBrendan.com or www.south ernbellewriter.blogspot.com, on Facebook at www.facebook.com/maggiebrendan, or on Twitter @MaggieBrendan.